GÜNTER GRASS

Local Anaesthetic

FAWCETT CREST • NEW YORK

LOCAL ANAESTHETIC

THIS BOOK CONTAINS THE COMPLETE TEXT OF THE
ORIGINAL HARDCOVER EDITION.

Published by Fawcett Crest Books, a unit of CBS Publications,
the Consumer Publishing Division of CBS Inc., by arrangement
with Harcourt Brace Jovanovich, Inc.

ISBN: 0-449-24257-9

Originally published in Germany under the title *Örtlich Betäubt*

Printed in the United States of America

Original Fawcett Crest printing: March 1971
New edition: November 1979

10   9   8   7   6   5   4

Local Anaesthetic

Part One

I told my dentist all this. Mouth blocked and face to face with the television screen which, soundless like myself, told a story of publicity: Hairspray Vesuvius Life Whiterthanwhite . . . ah yes, and the deep freezer in which my fiancée, lodged between veal kidneys and milk, sent up balloons: "You keep out of this. You keep out of this. . . ."

(St. Apollonia, pray for me!) To the boys and girls in my class I said: "Try to show forbearance. I've got to see the tooth plumber. That can drag out. Be good in the meantime."

Mild laughter. Moderate impudences. Scherbaum made a display of esoteric information: "My dear Herr Starusch. Your decision, tested in suffering, prompts us, your sympathetic students, to remind you of the martyrdom of St. Apollonia. In the year 250, during the reign of Emperor Decius, the poor thing was burned in Alexandria. Because the mob had previously pulled all her teeth with blacksmith's tongs, she became the patron saint of all those who suffer in their teeth and, unjustly so, of dentists as well. She is to be seen with tongs and molar on frescoes in Milan and Spoleto, on the ceilings of Swedish churches, but also in Sterzing, Gmünd, and Lübeck. We wish you pleasure and pious devotion. We, your junior class, shall pray to St. Apollonia to intercede for you."

The class mumbled blessings. I thanked them for the middlingly amusing nonsense. Instantly Vero Lewand asked me for a favor in return: my vote for the smokers' corner beside the bicycle shed, which the students had been demanding for months. "Surely you wouldn't want us to smoke unsupervised in the john."

I promised the class to come out for limited smoking rights at the next parents' and teachers' meeting provided that Scherbaum agreed to become editor-in-chief of the students' newspaper if the Students' Co-operation Organization should offer him the post. "Forgive the comparison. My teeth and your rag are in need of treatment."

But Scherbaum declined. "Until Student Co-operation is combined with student participation in policy making, I'm not doing anything. You can't reform an absurdity. Or do you by any chance believe in reformed absurdity?—You see?—Incidentally, the business about the saint is true. You can check in the Church calendar."

(St. Apollonia, pray for me!) For a single plea gets nowhere with a martyr. I set out late in the afternoon and postponed my third plea. It was only on Hohenzollerndamm, a few steps from the number plate which promised me a dentist's office on the third floor of a middle-class apartment house, no, only in the stairwell, amid vaginal art-nouveau ornaments ordered into a frieze that climbed the stairs alongside me, that I made up my mind to the third plea: "St. Apollonia, pray for me. . . ."

Irmgard Seifert had recommended him. She called him reserved, considerate, and yet firm. "And just imagine: he has TV in his office. At first I didn't want it on during the treatment, but now I've got to admit it's a wonderful distraction. You're far away. And even the empty screen is stimulating, somehow stimulating. . . ."

Has a dentist the right to ask a patient where he comes from?

"I lost my milk teeth in the waterfront suburb of Neufahrwasser. The people there, longshoremen and shipyard workers, were addicted to chewing tobacco; their teeth looked it. And wherever they went, they deposited their marks: tar-stained oysters that no frost could freeze."

"I see," said the man in tennis shoes, "but today we are seldom called upon to treat teeth impaired by chewing tobacco." And he was off on another subject: faulty articulation and my profile which since the age of puberty a protruding lower jaw has endowed with more strength of will than early dental treatment could have prevented. (My former fiancée likened my chin to a wheelbarrow; and in the margin of a carica-ture circulated by Vero Lewand still another function was attributed to my chin: that of a power shovel.) Oh well. I'd always known it: I have a chopper bite. I can't grind. A dog tears. A cow grinds. Man chews with both movements. I lack this normal articulation.

"You chop," said my dentist. And by that time I was glad he didn't say that I tore like a dog. "So we'll make a set of X-rays. Just close your eyes. But if you prefer we can turn on the . . ."

"No, thank you, Doctor."—Or did I slip even then into the familiar "Doc"? Later, in a state of dependence, I cried out: "Help, Doc! What should I do, Doc? You know everything, Doc. . . .")

While with his eleven-times buzzing X-ray machine he seized upon my teeth, meanwhile chatting—"I could tell you stories about the dawn of dentistry . . ."—I saw many things on curved frosted glass, Neufahrwasser, for instance, where, across from the Island, I lowered a milk tooth into the Mottlau.

His film began differently: "We must start with Hippocrates. He recommends mashed lentils for abscesses in the oral cavity."

And my ma shook her head on the screen. "No, we won't lower it, we'll keep it in the jewel box on blue cotton." Slightly curved, kindness spread out before me. While my dentist spoke in historical maxims— "Gargling with pepper solution, according to Hippocrates, is helpful for gum boils"—my ma spoke in our kitchen-living room: "And I'll put the garnet brooch in with the amber and Grampa's decorations. And we'll keep all your milk teeth carefully so later on you can tell your wife and children: This is what they looked like."

But his concern was with my premolars and molars. For of all my molars the wisdom teeth—or third molars—were most secure: they should become abutments and with the help of a corrective bridge attenuate my chopper bite. "Work," he said. "We may as well face it. There's quite a bit of work to be done. And now, while my assistant develops the X-rays and I remove your calculus, or tartar, may I offer you some sound and motion?"

Still: "No, thank you."

He renounced principles: "The East German program, for instance?" I was satisfied with the all-suffering screen on which I slowly and repeatedly saw myself across from the Island, lowering a milk tooth into the harbor sludge. I still enjoyed my family history because it had begun with my milk teeth: "Oh yes, Ma, I lowered a front tooth into the river—there's one missing, you see. And a fish swallowed it, not a pike, a sheatfish that lived through all the hard times. He's still on the lookout—because sheatfish live to be very old—for more milk teeth. But the rest of my baby teeth are sparkling milky-white and tartarless on red cotton, though the garnet brooch and Grampa's decorations were lost. . . ."

My dentist was meanwhile in the eleventh century, talking about Albucasis, the Arab doctor of Córdoba who had been first to speak of tartar. "It has to be chipped off." I also remember sentences like this: "When the acid residue becomes alkaline, in other words, when the pH is over seven, tartar forms because the submaxillary glands eject saliva on the incisors and the parotid on the first upper molars, especially when mouth movements are made, as in yawning. Let's see you yawn. Fine, that will do. . . ."

I went along, I yawned, squirting tartar-producing saliva, but I failed to arouse my dentist's interest: "Well, Doctor, what shall we call my little production?—The rescued milk teeth. Because in January 1945 when my ma was obliged to pack up—my father's job at the pilot office enabled him to make arrangements—she was taken aboard the last troop transport leaving Neufahrwasser. But before taking off, she packed the most indispensable articles, including of course my milk teeth, in Father's big sea bag which, as tends to happen in cases of precipitate flight, was by mistake put aboard the *Paul Beneke,* a sidewheeler ordinarily used for excursions, which did not hit a mine but reached Travenmünde safe, sound, and overloaded, whereas my dear ma was never to see Lübeck or Travemünde, because that troop transport, which I claim to have been the very last, struck a mine south of Bornholm, and went—if you'd kindly look behind you and forget about my tartar for a moment—straight to the bottom with my ma, then amidst snow and sleet as now on that gray screen of yours. Only a few of the gentlemen from district party headquarters managed to transfer to a torpedo boat. . . ."

My dentist said: "And now rinse please." ("Again," he requested, insisted, shouted in the course of a protracted treatment, so permitting me to avert my eyes.) Only rarely did the little images of my production manage to follow and to fade in with the waste matter, the chipped-off accretions of tartar for example, in the cuspidor: the interval between screen and cuspidor, the images flickering out on my retina while saliva pressed for release, was rich in stumble-wires and yielded bracketed sentences: classroom heckling from my student Scherbaum, private quarrels between Irmgard Seifert and myself, the daily trivia of school life, questions asked at the second teachers' examination, and metaphysical problems wrapped in quotations. But hard as it was to find the way from TV screen to cuspidor and to fade in again after rinsing, I almost always managed to avoid transmitting interference.

"You know how it is, Doc: for years my milk teeth lay in storage; because what once is rescued isn't so quickly lost again. . . ."

"But let's not delude ourselves: there's no way of preventing tartar. . . ."

"When the son went looking for his parents, he was given a sea bag. . . ."

"So today we shall attack your tartar, your Enemy Number One."

"And every girl who took me for her future fiancé was shown my rescued milk teeth. . . ."

"Because in principle every dental treatment should include removal of tartar. . . ."

"But not every girl thought Eberhard's milk teeth attractive or interesting. . . ."

"Recently an ultrasonic scaling technique has been devised. And now rinse please."

An, as I at first thought, annoying intercut, for with the help of my rescued milk teeth I had almost succeeded in luring my former fiancée onto the screen and in beginning (as now at long last I am again trying to begin) my lament, but my dentist was against it: Too soon.

While I copiously rinsed, he entertained me with anecdotes. He told me about a certain Scribonius Largus who invented a tooth powder for Messalina, first wife to the Emperor Claudius: burned hartshorn plus Chiot resin and sal ammoniac. When he admitted that Pliny already mentions a popular good fortune powder made of crushed milk teeth, my mother's words once again knocked on my ear: "Here, my boy, I'm putting them in green cotton. One day they'll bring you good fortune. . . ."

What do you mean, superstition? After all, I come of a seafaring family. My Uncle Max was lost at Dogger Bank. My father survived the *Königsberg* and was on active pilot duty until the end of the Free State period. And the boys called me Störtebeker from the very start. I was the ringleader to the end. Moorkähne played second fiddle. That's why he wanted to break up the gang. But I wouldn't stand for it. "Listen to me, boys."—And that's how it was until the gang was nabbed because that skinny stinker had sung. One of these days I ought to cough up and let the whole thing flicker past in proper order as it really happened. But now with the usual suspense effects—rise and fall of the Dusters Gang—more along analytic, scientific lines: teenage gangs in the Third Reich. For to this day no one has disinterred the dossier of the Edelweiss Pirates that lies in the cellar of Cologne police headquarters. ("What do you think, Scherbaum? That ought to interest your generation. We were seventeen at the time, as you are now. And certain other traits in common—no personal property, a girl shared by the whole group, and absolute hostility to all grownups—cannot be overlooked; even the jargon prevailing in this junior class reminds me of our private lingo. . . .") True, that was in wartime. We didn't go in for smokers' corners or any such kid stuff. . . . Think of the left side altar of the Church of the Sacred Heart, when we . . . When no Winterfeldplatz we . . . Our resistance was real. Nobody could get us down. Until Moorkähne ratted on us. Or that string bean with her incisor teeth. Should have turned them both over to the cops. Or made a strict rule: no dames. At that time, incidentally, I kept my milk teeth in a little pouch slung from my neck. Anybody admitted to the gang had to swear by my milk teeth: "The nothing nihilates unremittingly." Ought to have brought them with me. "You see, Doc? How times passes. Only yesterday I was head of a gang feared throughout the district of Danzig–West Prussia; and today I teach German and history and try to persuade my student Scherbaum to give up his juvenile anarchism: 'You ought to take over the school paper. Your critical gift demands a field of activity!' Because a teacher is a reoriented teen-age gang leader who—if you don't mind taking me as an example—has felt no other pain than toothache, toothache, for weeks. . . ."

My dentist attributed my bearable but persistent toothache to bone and gum recession which exposed the sensitive necks of my teeth. When another anecdote failed to go over with me—"Pliny's recommendation for toothache: sprinkle the ashes of a mad dog's skull in your ear"—he pointed his scraper over his shoulder: "Perhaps we ought to turn on . . ."—But I insisted on the pain: A cry. A lament that is never adjourned. ("Forgiven me if my mind seems to be wandering.")

My student rode his bicycle through the picture. "You and your toothache. But what's going on in the Mekong Delta? Have you read?"

"Yes, Scherbaum, I've read. Bad. Veryvery bad. But I must admit that this ache, this draft that always hits the same nerve, this pain, which isn't even so bad, but which I can localize and which never stirs from the spot, affects me, shakes me and lays me bare more than the photographed pain of this world, which for all its enormity is abstract because it doesn't hit my nerve."

"Doesn't it make you angry or at least sad?"

"I often try to be sad."

"Doesn't it make you indignant, the injustice of it?"

"I do my best to be indignant."

Scherbaum dissolved. (He lodged his bicycle in the bicycle shed.) My dentist was there in normal listening volume: "If it hurts, make a sign please."

"It hurts all right. It aches here in front."

"That's the tartar on your exposed necks."

"Christ, it hurts."

"We'll take some Arantil later."

"May I rinse, Doc, just a little rinse?"

(And apologize. Never again will I . . .) Already I could hear my fiancée's voice: "You with your little aches and pains! None of this nonsense now about a sorrowful parting. Tell me where you bank and I'll send a salve. An annuity. You've got it coming. Start something new. Cultivate your hobby: Celtic mortuary ornaments."

(The scene shifts from the cuspidor to the basalt pit on Mayener Feld. No, there she flickers in the cemetery at Kruft. Or is it the cement depot and she in the midst of cored cement blocks. . . .)

"Make yourself useful. I bet you'll be a first-class screw."

(No cement: Andernach. The windy Rhine Promenade. Between the bastion and the car ferry, counting clipped plane trees . . . Back and forth with words that tot up accounts.)

"Think of all the educational principles you've spooned into me. Don't chew your nails. Read slowly and systematically. Recapitulate before disgressing. Fed me Hegel and your Marxengels. . . ."

A rigid goatface with balloons rising from it, full to bursting with tartarsludge memorygravel hateslag. (Ah Lois Lane!)

"I'm grown up. I'm through with you. Through at last. You coward failure superwashout!"

(And behind the talking machine, movement upstream and down: Puff! Puff!)

"You were a good, rather plaintive teacher."

(On the right bank Leuterdorf with its twice-humped, brown-black rain-drenched Rosengarten vineyard. Sigh! Sigh!)

"Do something with your talents. Get away from

pumice and cement before it's too late. How do you want the fifteen thousand?"

(At the foot of the vineyard: freight trains and motor traffic. Motion exerts itself in the background. Words passing me to left and right, spat onto the empty terrace of the Hotel Traube: Blah! Blah!)

"In installments or a lump sum?"

(There I stand in my billowing trenchcoat: Superman's advance fee.)

"Out with it. Where do you bank?"

(Once upon a time the Andernach bastion was the customs barrier of the archbishop-electors of Cologne. . . .)

"Take it as a war-damage indemnity and stop sniveling."

(. . . later it became a First World War soldiers memorial. The camera shifts. An assistant director had persuaded my fiancée to feed seagulls: Squawk! Squawk!)

She paid me off. And I, conscious of my goal, invested the money. A late student changes his majors. The University of Bonn—I wanted to stay near her— transformed the industrial engineer and specialist in centrifugal dust removers into a substitute, then a regular teacher, who since last fall has held a permanent post teaching German and history. "In view of your specialized knowledge," it was suggested to the reconverting student, "wouldn't you do better to major in math?"—And looking up from my tartar the man in the tennis shoes also said: "What gave you that idea? When you had an engineering degree? That takes forever."

I rinsed thoroughly: If I was to change, then radically. So she wouldn't have thrown away her money for nothing. There was even three thousand or so left over (which I had to transfer to his account later on because the health insurance was unwilling to pay more than half the bill). Surely my chopper bite was worth that much to me. For that sum I sat down in his semiautomatic installation, bearing the name of Ritter, which played the multiple instruments into his skillful little hand in order that he, while I, no, both of us, in my little head which welcomes visitors, might . . . "What do you think, Doc, should I have had my pockets sewed up?"

My fianceé broke off the televised program from Andernach: "We have just seen the devastating effect of green cryptonite on Superman's dental enamel. But how will Superman's teeth react to red cryptonite?—That we shall see in our next Superman program. Meanwhile suppose we take a look at the cryptonite man's workshop. . . ."

She showed me my environment: "This beautifully shaped aspirator with retrievable tubing is operated by means of a jet pump. Thanks to its high-volume suction it has been a leading attraction at all dental fairs."—With the wispy voice of one lauding Christmas tree decorations she lauded the flow of water in the cuspidor and the Ritter's two-jointed cuspidor arm: "It enables us to move the basin vertically as well."—And she on the screen and his assistant with the clammy fingers both transmitted instructions by means of a push button on the front of the floating bracket table. How they waited on me. How they lured the aspirator from its niche. It amused me the way it lapped blubbered thirsted before it was plunged into my saliva.

"And kindly let your tongue lie flat and relaxed."

My dentist bent down over my offering, covered four-fifths of the screen, sought support for his right elbow between hip and ribs, and poked about between the tartar-encrusted necks of my upper incisors: "Don't swallow, the aspirator takes care of that. Breathe deeply, like this.—But don't you want me to . . ." Nonono. (Today it's still no.) I wanted to hear him chipping the lime from my incisors. . . .

You see, Scherbaum, that too demands to be described: I collect saliva foam and blood mingled with gritty grinding chips. After letting my tongue grow curious and shrink back, I eject this wealth into the cuspidor, seize the handy, purposely small glass— it mustn't beguile the patient into rinsing more than once—rinse, contemplate my expectoration, see more than is there, take leave of my frazzled tartar, put the glass back and look on with amusement as it automatically fills with lukewarm water. The Ritter and I cooperate methodically.

Yes, Scherbaum, the simultaneity of multiple activities demands to be described: while I sit openmouthed, inwardly quoting the Lamentations of Jeremiah, the Ritter balances the bracket table with its left hand and the man in tennis shoes summons forth the mobile cabinet on which tools await his call, for instance, the portable low-voltage electronic pulp tester with its self-charging battery; he can carry it about with him in his pocket while strolling on the wooded paths around the Grunewaldsee or by the Teltow Canal, or while attending the Agricultural Show, wherever, a dentist goes stalking his game: "Just a moment. Do you mind? My card. Frankly, you have a chopper bite. With that protruding lower jaw of yours it gives you an unduly striking profile. Brutality comes to mind. Inhibitions demand compensation. Bridgework is in order. A phone call will do it. We'll work out a mutually convenient schedule. Six or seven appointments at most, barring major complications. Leave it to me and my discreet assistant. What's more, TV will provide distraction. And even the empty screen can fade in the flow of your thoughts; I must only ask you to share my faith in my high-speed drill and in the three hundred fifty thousand r.p.m. provided, with a minimum of noise, by the turbine head of my air drive!"

"Really?"

"I change drills and polishing disks without the slightest effort."

"And all my pain?"

"Local anaesthesia."

"But is it necessary?"

"When we've finished and done the final polishing, you'll see that you fiancée didn't indemnify you for nothing."

"All the same we were engaged for two and a half years."

"Unburden yourself, my friend, unburden yourself."

"It was in the year 1954. . . ."

"A good beginning. . . ."

I told my dentist all this: "But I'm warning you, Doc, I shall be speaking of trass, pumice, limestone, marl, and clay, of slate and cement clinker, of villages called Plaidt, Kretz, and Kruft, of Ettring tuff and articles manufactured from Kottenheim basaltic lava, of the pumice beds on Korrelsberg and the tertiary volcanic basalt deposits on Mayener Feld, but first—before anything is said of myself, Linde and Schlottau, of Mathilde and Ferdinand Krings—there will, I warn you, be talk of cement."

My dentist said: "My working materials include not only plaster but also certain special cements; we shall be dealing with them."

And so I began: "Cement is a commercially produced dusty powder. It is made by milling a slurry of limestone or marl, and clay, by crushing and grinding calcined cement clinker, by flotation and spray-drying in a rotary kiln. . . ."

(I still had it down pat. Even then the idea of surprising my students with this technical knowledge was ringing at my doorbell. Scherbaum certainly regarded me as an unworldly nut; and to my dentist I recommended the centrifugal removal of his dental work dust. He pointed out that since he irrigated while grinding the dust production remained within tolerable limits.) "That may be. But our goal is complete dust removal. The dust is removed from cement works by dust chambers in the kilns, by centrifuge, filtration, crushers, classifiers, and by the transportation and distribution of cement dust across the Rhine between Koblenz and Andernach. . . ."

"I know the Lower Eifel. A moon landscape."

"Still, as you see, it lends itself to outdoor shots."

"Once when attending a dentists' congress in Koblenz some colleagues and I took a little trip to Maria Laach."

"That was still in our dust-precipitation zone; because before my time the two stacks of the Krings Cement, Trass, and Cinderblock Works were only 125 feet high. At that time the discharge was deposited only in the immediate vicinity of the plant, whereas now that the stacks have been extended, and especially since the switch to crush-driers, dust precipitators, and a cooling tower by-pass, Krings Cement can boast that dust pollution has been reduced by 0.9 percent and the dust is wafted across the Rhine, to be evenly distributed over the entire Neuwied basin. . . ."

"What splendid public spirit on the part of the factory management."

"It might be preferable to speak of a sound profit motive; the dust reclaimed by the electrofilter system comes to as much as 15 percent of the total cement clinker production. . . ."

"And I, an obscure dentist dependent on the daily papers for my information, thought industrial dust control was motivated exclusively by concern for the public welfare. . . ."

(Later I acquainted my junior class with the problems of increasing air pollution. Even Scherbaum was impressed: "I don't see why you took up teaching when you could have done a lot more in dust control. . . .")

"I believe, Doc, that we can speak of a twofold development. By the mid-fifties, thanks to my prompt action, we were able on the one hand to rationalize our production by utilizing the high-grade dust and on the other hand to check the wave of justified complaints from the local authorities, which were giving our management no end of trouble. At first Krings rejected my proposals: 'What volcanic eruptions, erosion, and dust storms were to antiquity, the smoke and dust of our industrial concentrations are to us today. Since we live by pumice, trass, and cement, why shouldn't we live with the dust?' "

"A modern Stoic."

"Krings knew his Seneca."

"A philosopher from whom we can still learn a thing or two."

"To make my arguments more striking—it took practical examples to convince Krings—I concluded a paper on the anti-air-pollution policy of the Federal Republic with the following image: 'If industry continues to employ the atmosphere chiefly as a carrier of suspended solids and gases, and if furthermore the interaction with the air continues to take place in the low-lying stratum which is the breathing space not only of men and animals, but also of plants, then it is high time for us to subpoena nature as a witness for the prosecution.'—Here, Doc, you see a simple snapshot of the old beech tree in the park of the Villa Krings, popularly known as 'the Gray Park.' This wide-branching tree had a leaf surface of fifteen hundred square feet. Since an acre of beech woods under continuous exposure is subjected in the course of a year to roughly six tons of fine dust, it is not difficult, on the basis of this one beech tree, to form a devastating picture of the state of the entire park, which measures 2.4 acres, all the more so as half its trees are conifers and an acre of fir woods is encumbered with as much as seventeen or eighteen tons of fine dust in the course of a year. . . . I admit that my paper may have impelled Krings to consent to the installation of electric kiln-dust removers."

"All in all, you were successful."

"Nevertheless Krings Park, because of its proximity to the factory, will always be 'the Gray Park,' although, thanks to my persistence, there is now greater hope of beech green."

My dentist made me doubt his interest when he remarked: "Nature will be grateful to you." (This fear of not being taken seriously also sits in on my classes: the smiles of a few students—or when Scherbaum tilts his head as though worried about me—makes me falter or digress, and often enough one of the students, Scherbaum for instance, has to call me back with an indolent "We were talking about Stresemann"; just as my dentist brought me back to my subject with the encouraging question: "And what became of your Krings?") "If you'll kindly rinse again first . . ."

There wasn't much left to come. Tartar muck. A rustling of notes. Nausea from too much reading. Then an attempt to recall an early summer landscape on the surface of the accessory table between the ampoule warmer and the Bunsen burner. The accumulated misgivings of a high-school teacher. Vain attempts to be sad, angry, dismayed. A draft between the necks of my teeth, Scherbaum's dimples that came out when he smiled.

"Anyway, Doc, that's how it began. . . ."

Long shot of the Lower Eifel landscape, focusing from Plaidt in the direction of Kruft. The title "Lost Battles" backed up by summer cloud formations. A slow ride through the eroded, ravined, and heavily scarred pumice-mining region toward the Krings Works with their two stacks. More titles. Now I speak as though addressing a guided tour of the plant:

"For the benefit of the newly developed West German construction industry the Krings Works are converting the rich and varied mineral wealth of the volcanic Eifel into materials for underground and surface engineering, and for road building. The expansion of the cement industry before and during the last war—permit me to recall the Autobahn, the fortification of our western border, the development of concrete air-raid shelters, and last but not least the imposing concrete structures along the Atlantic coast—has had gratifying repercussions for the peacetime development of trass cements and pre-stressed-concrete construction. Investment is the order of the day, and investment implies modernization.—Our Krings Works will also have to adapt themselves to this trend. Today tons and tons of high-grade cement dust escape through the stacks and are lost to the productive process; tomorrow, however, electric dust removers . . ."

The voice of the industrial engineer is slowly faded out. The camera follows the chimney smoke. Long shot of waste gases, and their dynamizing cloud effects. Followed by smoke-screened bird's-eye shot of the Lower Eifel between Mayen and Andernach and across the Rhine, closing in in a nose-dive on Krings Park and the slate-roofed, basalt-gray Villa Krings: close-up of cement dust on beech leaves. Knobs and craters. Porous islets washed by the last rainfall. Purling dust settles. Jagged cement structures on convulsed leaves. Slipping sliding avalanches of dust above unmotivated girlish laughter. Overloaded leaves sag. Laughter dust-streamers laughter. And only now the group of girls in deck chairs under the dust-bearing beech tree. Camera rigid, then gliding.

Inge and Hilda have covered their faces with newspaper. Sieglinde Krings, generally known as Linde, sits upright in her deck chair. Her oval, uncommunicative face, to which goatlike rigidity lends expression, ignores the laughter duet under the newspaper. Inge lifts the paper from her face: she is smooth unmarked pretty. Hilda does likewise: soft and healthily sleepy, she is given to blinking. On the sewing table, between the Coca-Cola glasses protected by notebooks, lies a third sheet of newspaper with a cup-sized pile of dust on it. The camera concentrates on the still life. Partly obliterated headlines truncate the names of Ollenhauer and Adenauer and the word "rearmament," Linde's girl-friends giggle while the cement dust from their newspapers trickles down onto the little pile.

Hilda: "It won't be long before we've saved a whole pound of Krings cement."

Inge: "We'll give it to Hardy for his birthday."

Now they chat about vacation plans. Inge and Hilda are undecided: Positano or the Adriatic?

Hilda: "And where is our little Hardy planning to go?"

Inge: "Is it true that he's getting interested in cave paintings?" Laughter.

Hilda: "And you?" Pause.

Linde: "I'm staying here." Pause and trickling cement dust.

Inge: "Because of your father coming home?" Pause. Cement dust.

Linde: "Yes."

Inge: "How long has he been out there?"

Linde: "Exactly ten years. First in Krasnogorsk, then in solitary in the Lubyanka and Butyrki, then at the end in Camp Vladimir east of Moscow."

"Do you think it's broken him?" Pause and cement dust.

Linde: "I don't know him." She rises and heads undeviatingly for the villa. The camera looks on as she grows smaller.

A monument. It was in my dentist's office that I first succeeded in dissecting my statuesque fiancée: between sequence and sequence she changed skirts, rarely her sweater; alone or with her Hardy she demanded to be faded in, sometimes amid gorse in an abandoned basalt pit, sometimes at the Wild Man Inn just behind the Neuwied dike, sometimes on the Rhine Promenade in Andernach, but also in the pumice mines of the Nette Valley, and over and over and over again in the cement depot; whereas Hardy demanded fade-ins that placed him, a decipherer of art-historical vestiges, amid Roman and early Christian basalt fragments; or else, with the help of a model he himself had improvised, he was explaining his pet project, an electrical kiln dust remover. Cut: the two of them in the distance on the far shore of the Laacher See. Cut: rain has driven them into an abandoned stonemason's shack on the Bellfeld. (Quarrel leading to coitus on the wobbly wooden table.) Cut: she in half-rebuilt Mainz after a lecture. Cut: Hardy photographing the Gerold Cross. . . .

"Who is this Hardy?" my dentist asked. His assistant also betrayed curiosity by the pressure of cold moist fingers "The quadragenarian schoolteacher whose students with good-natured condescension call him 'Old Hardy,' the selfsame Old Hardy whose tartar you, seconded by your assistant's clammy three-finger grip, are dismantling layer by layer, the Hardy who . . ."

I: with my studies of German philology and art history abandoned before it was too late, with my made-in-Aachen engineering degree, with my then twenty-eight years, with my discontinued love affairs and my virtually untroubled engagement: a successful young man amid successful young postwar men. In August 1945 after half-digested war experience, the eighteen-year-old Hardy is discharged from an American PW camp in Bad Aibling at the foot of perpetually rain-drenched mountains—the nickname "Hardy" has stuck to him ever since; Hardy, the refugee from the East, bearer of an "A" refugee card, moves in with an aunt in Cologne-Nippes and hastens to catch up on his high-school diploma; in his first term, while working his way through the university, he remembers a maxim of his father's: "The future of mankind lies in bridge building!" And so, guided by his father's maxim, he plugs away at statics in Aachen and cultivates casually changing acquaintances. Shortly before his examination he joins a fraternity and is introduced to the so-called Old Gentlemen: at the very first try the graduate mechanical engineer Eberhard Starusch, made parentless by the war and hence doubly efficient, finds a foothold with Dyckerhoff-Lengerich, a plant producing cement clinker by the wet process; thus Hardy, who has not abjured his art-historical leanings, visits the archaeological sites of Teutoburg Forest, and thus becomes acquainted with the Lepol gridiron process; for at Dyckerhoff conversion from the wet to the dry process had been planned at an early date: Hardy gains advancement; Hardy writes a study on the practical application of auger and trass cements in the construction of the Brest submarine pens; Hardy is encouraged to expand his study and give it wider publicity, that is, submit it in person to the top management of the West German cement industry. In Düsseldorf, on the occasion of a cement producers' congress that has since then become historical, a nice-looking and for his age knowledgeable and successful Hardy makes the acquaintance of Sieglinde Krings, aged twenty-two, and on the following day— at tea, during a recess of the congress—that of Aunt Mathilde Krings, the monosyllabic lady in black who rules over the Krings Works. As though by chance, Hardy strikes up a conversation with the two ladies. One of the Old Gentlemen of his Aachen fraternity speaks of Hardy in flattering terms to the lady in black. The congress winds up with a ball at the Hotel Rheinischer Hof. Seizing the opportunity, Hardy dances with Sieglinde Krings several times, but not too often. Hardy manages to chat, not only about centrifugal dust removers but also about the beauties of Romanesque basalt architecture between Mayen and Andernach. After midnight, while cement men wax merry-moist-festive roundabout, Hardy confines himself to one little kiss. (Sieglinde Krings utters the momentous words: "See here, if I've fallen for you, it'll cost you plenty. . . .") In any case Hardy makes an impression and soon leaves Dyckerhoff-Lengerich with the best of references: he enters the Krings Works with both feet and succeeds; for he quickly and circumspectly makes himself at home among Europe's largest exclusive group of cement consumers and in the spring of 1954, pressing his advantage with the same sure instinct, makes an engagement celebration fall due; in deference to his future father-in-law, still a prisoner of war, it is held in an out-of-the-way inn in the Ahr Valley: Sieglinde in a slate-gray suit and Hardy in single-breasted basalt gray present themselves on the gray-graduated screen; an up-and-coming couple, a little too slick, capable of alert, watchful glances out of the corners of their eyes, classified as members of the skeptical generation and increasingly suspected of favoring stepped-up efficiency; for under my influence Sieglinde began to be serious: she took up the study of medicine systematically and with utter detachment, while I, with fanatical thoroughness but also with detachment, familiarized myself with the trass of the Nette Valley, with the production of trass cement at the Krings Works, and especially with our obsolete wet process, in other words with pumice.

When my dentist asked me once again to rinse—"And then we'll polish so the tartar won't get a new hold too quickly"—I took the pause as an invitation to deliver a succinct lecture first about Roman trass quarrying between 100 and 50 B.C.—"There are underground galleries between Plaidt and Kretz where you can still run across the Latin scribblings of Roman miners"—and then, while he was polishing, about pumice: "Geologically speaking, pumice is one of the Laach trachytic tuffs. . . ."

He said: "Thorough polishing protects the enamel membrane. . . ."

I spoke of the mid-alluvial epoch, of white trachytic tuffs and their interbedded layers of loess; he referred back to the disencumbered necks of my teeth and said: "There. Isn't that a relief? Shall we take a look in the . . ."

To my dentist's question: "Now what do you say?" I could only answer: "Marvelous, simply marvelous!"

He took refuge in the meanwhile developed X-rays, which his assistant illuminated one by one as though entertaining the family with a slide projector. The pictures revealed a jumble of transparent ghost teeth. Only the gaps in the rows of molars, left right—upper lower—proved to me that my teeth were here revealed to view. I spoke up in self-assertion: "Pumice is found under only three feet of humus . . ."—but my dentist stuck to his subject: "Our X-rays show, to be sure, that the teeth to be bridged over are alive, but I must say that you have an authentic, and authentic means congenital, prognathism, in other words, a protruding lower jaw." (I asked my dentist for the regular TV program.)

A commercial was on; it captured an eighth of my gaze. He painted my bruised gums and went on with his appraisal: "In a normal bite the lower incisors are one and one-half millimeters behind the upper ones. But in your case . . ."

(Since then I have found out that my faulty bite, which he termed congenital and therefore authentic, can be recognized by a horizontal jaw displacement of two and one-half millimeters: my striking profile.)

I wonder if this tooth plumber realizes that his grinding and polishing powders contain pumice? And does this publicity bitch, who looks familiar to me, damn familiar, realize that her cleansers contain pumice, our Lower Eifel pumice?

My dentist stuck to my prognathic jaw: "It leads, as our X-rays clearly show, to a recession of the bone or of the alveolar ridge. . . ."

She was trying to sell me a deep freezer. While my dentist suggested surgical solutions—"By simply sawing through the ascending branch of the maxillary and moving it back, we can correct your prognathism . . ."—Linde sang her refrain: "Always fresh and chock-full of vitamins . . ." and suggested purchase in easy installments. Then she opened the freezer, where in the midst of snap beans, veal kidneys, and California strawberries, clouded with hoarfrost, there lay my milk teeth and school exercises, my "A" refugee card and my study on trass and auger cements, my condensed desires and my bottled defeats; and at the very bottom, between red perch fillets and iron-rich spinach, rested, naked and frost-coated, she who a moment before in sweater and skirt had been spouting publicity: Oh lindelindelindelinde . . . (Good subject for a theme, I'll give it to my class tomorrow: Meaning and implication of a deep freezer.) Ah, how long-lasting she is in the cold smoke. Ah, how pain keeps fresh in the deep freezer. Ah, how is the gold become dim. . . .

My dentist offered to turn off the TV. (Irmgard Seifert had recommended him as a sensitive man.)

I nodded. And when he came back to my prognathism—"But I should advise against a surgical intervention . . ."—I nodded again. (And his moist-cold assistant also nodded.)

"May I go now?"

"Consequently I suggest that we cap your molars."

"Right now?"

"We've had enough to do with your tartar."

"Then the day after tomorrow shortly before the evening program?"

"And now take two Arantil tablets to see you home."

"It didn't hurt much, Doc. . . ."

(His assistant—not my fiancée—handed me the tablets and the glass.)

When I came home, my tongue groped for lost roughness behind my teeth. On my desk, side by side with the ash tray, the corrected notebooks of my junior class, and a few half-read volumes I found the article I had begun to write on student co-operation, including a paragraph on the controversial question: "Where and when is a student permitted to smoke?" And nearby, between pamphlets on secondary-school reform and an empty picture frame buried under newspaper clippings and Xerox copies, lay the exasperatingly thin portfolio inscribed in capitals with a working title. Under chunks of Roman basalt—mostly mortar fragments—which I used for letter weights, I found paper....

Woe, my tooth. Woe, the hair in my comb. Woe, my idea as short as my finger is long. Ah, and the many lost battles. It's always what's closest that hurts loudest. Or what backs up on you and reminds you: This is last year's carp, New Year's Eve. . . . Woe, shadows, woe. Pebbles, woe. Woe, toothache, woe. . . .

Actually I only wanted to have my tartar removed, though I had my suspicions: He's sure to find something. They always find something. Seen it before.

When shortly after my homecoming Irmgard Seifert called up—"Well, how did you make out? Not so bad, was it?"—I could only confirm. Not a sadist. Entertaining and yet discreet. Not without education.

(Knows his Seneca.) Stops at once when it hurts. A rather naïve faith in progress—had hopes of a curative toothpaste—but bearable within limits. And the television is really marvelous, though funny.

To Irmgard Seifert, with whom I have shared the dentist ever since, I praised him over the telephone: "His voice is gentle, becomes didactically forceful only when he starts lecturing. . . ."

What was it he said? "Enemy Number One is tartar. While we walk, hesitate, yawn, tie our tie, digest and pray, our saliva never ceases to produce it. It forms a deposit that ensnares the tongue. Always looking for incrustations, the tongue is drawn to rough surfaces and provides nourishment that reinforces our enemy, tartar. It chokes our tooth necks with its crust. It is consumed with blind hatred for enamel. Because you can't fool me. One look is enough: Your tartar is your calcified hate. Not only the microflora in your oral cavity, but also your muddled thoughts, your obstinate squinting backward, the way you regress when you mean to progress, in other words, the tendency of your diseased gums to form germ-catching pockets, all that—the sum of dental picture and psyche—betrays you: stored-up violence, murderous designs.—Rinse, rinse, don't mind me! There will still be plenty of tartar. . . ."

I deny all that. As a teacher of German and history, I have a deep-seated horror of violence. And to my student Vero Lewand, who a year ago went in for picking so-called star flowers, I said, when she exhibited her collection of sawed-off Mercedes stars in the classroom: "To you vandalism is an end in itself."

Scherbaum enlightened me: his girl-friend had been looking for relevant Christmas tree decorations: "For our school festivities in the auditorium."

Even before Christmas Vero Lewand's metal saw had gone out of fashion. (Later Scherbaum wrote a song which he accompanied on the guitar: "As we went picking star flowers, as we went picking, picking, picking . . .")

Though I did not invoke the patron saint of all those who suffer in their teeth, I went to my next visit well prepared with ready-made sentences to put in his mouth. If he was going to correct my teeth, he would have to put up with a few corrections from me: "You are interested in pumice, aren't you, Doc?"—"About as much as you are in the increase of caries in school-age children. . . ."

In the morning I had had to answer questions from my junior class. (Vero Lewand: "How many did he pull?") I replied: "What would you people think about if you had to sit gagged at the dentist's face to face with a TV set, with a commercial on and some-one offering you a deep freezer, for instance. . . ."

Floundering, sterile answers. I abandoned the thought of a theme on the subject, although Scherbaum's idea that certain immature plans and projects might be put into the deep freezer, to be thawed, thought through, and translated into action at some future date, might have given them something to work on.

"What sort of plan have you in mind, Scherbaum?"

"I've been trying to tell you. Can't talk about it yet."

When I asked him whether his still deep-frozen plan had to do with his taking over the editorship-in-chief of the school paper, he replied in the negative: "That's your beer. You can leave it on ice."

When toward the end of the period I expatiated on caries—"Dental caries means the irreparable destruction of the hard dental tissues . . ."—the class, as promised, listened with forbearance; Scherbaum gave an ironic tilt to his head.

My dentist was less considerate: "We'll settle this once and for all, the four lower molars, the first and third on both sides. . . ."

(This busy jangling of sterile instruments as though he hadn't doubted for so much as a twinkling that I would be back. "Go right ahead, Doc, I'll hold still.") His assistant had already loaded the syringe: "There. And now the nasty little pinprick. Didn't hurt much, did it?"

(Should I, rigged with aspirator, stuffed with cotton rolls, and immobilized by that three-finger grip, have attempted patter: "Not worth mentioning, your pinprick. But those fellows in Bonn. Have you read that: Rock bottom, tighten your belts, for better or worse . . . And the students again, at a mass meeting they've . . .")

His allusion to the pinprick I could expect begat a second stereotype: "And now a follow-up injection. You'll hardly notice . . ."

(Go on go ahead. And leave the picture on, but without the sound.)

"We'll have to wait two three minutes until your gums feel numb and your tongue fuzzy."

"It's swelling up!"

"Illusion."

(A bloated pork kidney. Where do we put it?)

The soundless picture showed a clerical-looking gentleman who, it being Saturday, wished to say a word about Sunday, although this program is televised after 10 P.M. and never before the Berlin evening news: "Yes, yes, my son, I know, it hurts. But all the pain in the world is powerless to . . ."

(His finely articulated fingers. When he raised an eyebrow in mockery. Or his delayed head-shaking: Scherbaum calls him Silvertongue.)

Then the bells rang in Sunday: Bim!—And the pigeons rose up in fright. Boom!—Ah, and the little tin satellites in my head that knows it all tinkled: Bim! Poom! Pumice!

While the puckered goatface announced the documentary: Pumice—the gold of the Lower Eifel —my dentist began to grind down my third right lower molar: "Relax now. We start with the masticating surface and then we taper down around it. . . ."

My pumice film showed how the raw material was brought from the pits into the wash mill, freed from its heavy ingredients, piled, mixed with Standard Binding Material, S.B.M., transformed in concrete mixers into pumice-concrete mix and then, in automatic machines, made into pumice-concrete construction units.

My dentist said: "Well, that does it. Your third right lower molar is ready." (Before he asked me to rinse, I managed, though only for a moment, to show the inventory of pumice-concrete construction units, first in warehouses, then on skids in the open.)

"And here, Doc, amid our standard-size cored blocks, pre-stressed construction beams, spun and molded pipes, steel-reinforced floor slabs and coffer slabs, which in addition to their light weight offer the following advantages: high compressive strength, tensile walls, freedom from dry rot, fire-resistance, nail-penetration property, and rough surface offering firm adhesion to roughcast and joint-sealing mortar; amid these modern construction materials which provide assurance that the housing consumer of the future will meet with no difficulty in integrating himself with the pluralistic society, or more precisely, amid our closely piled standard concrete sizes, also called four-inchers, Linde Krings and Schlottau, the plant electrician, met . . ."

My dentist said: "I see . . .," and I had made thorough preparations: Seen in bird's-eye perspective the cement depot extends between the plant and Villa Krings plus Park. At the dividing line between plant and park a group of visitors in street clothes forms a loose semicircle. Engineer Eberhard Starusch, in white smock and construction helmet, is explaining the production of pumice-concrete construction units. From the Gray Park Sieglinde Krings approaches. Her summer dress, a small-flower print, shows that a wind is blowing outside the park. Coming from the plant, electrician Heinz Schlottau enters the cement depot. While Sieglinde strolls aimlessly along the conveyor paths, Schlottau approaches resolutely, as though looking for her.

Over this slow approach, delayed by accidents, hovers the engineer's text distended by the wind: "When more than six thousand years ago the Eifel volcanoes erupted, the storms must have blown prevailingly from the west and northwest, for otherwise pumice deposits would not have developed to the east and southeast of the points of eruption. Whereas formerly the peasants of the Lower Eifel were also pumice producers, today the firm of Krings has leased the pits roundabout. We are now at the edge of our extensive concrete depot . . ."

Now the long shot closes up to the point of intersection between Sieglinde and Schlottau amid the densely piled standard sizes. They are keeping their distance. They appraise each other by looking past each other. Schlottau's embarrassment grins. Behind her back Sieglinde's hands grope for the surface of the concrete blocks. Feeble and increasingly distant, the voice of Engineer Starusch who likes to and often does introduce guided tours with an impromptu lecture; an echo of his teen-age days, when he was called Störtebeker and sounded off a good deal, an early harbinger of his future activity as a teacher of German and history. . . .

"And what topic are you discussing now with your students?"

"We are trying to lay bare the social background of Schiller's play, *The Bandits.* . . ."

"More echoes of your days as a gang leader?"

"I own that early imprinting has left its mark."

"And your students?"

"Scherbaum wants to do a comic strip of *The Bandits* in collaboration with his girl-friend. The story centers on the nationwide sawing off of Mercedes stars. Mary Lane is to play the role of Amalie, and Superman . . ."

"An interesting experiment. . . ."

"But Scherbaum has no patience. Only ideas. Only ideas . . ."—(which he wants to put in deep freeze, so that someday he can thaw them out, think them through, and convert them into action . . .)—"like this Schlottau in the cement depot. . . ."

Linde: "Do you work for us?"

Schlottau: "Plant electrician since fifty-one. Had a kind of employee relationship with your father."

Linde: "Couldn't you express yourself more clearly?"

Schlottau: "Certainly, Miss. Center Sector in forty-five. Your daddy said: Breslau must be held. Ever hear about Operation Herosnatcher, Miss?"

Linde: "What do you want?"

Schlottau: "Well, take you to the movies, for instance. And find out in two three words when the Field Marshal General is finally coming home."

Linde: "Save your movie money. The convoy is ex-

pected in Camp Friedland at the end of the week.—
What are you planning to do?"

Schlottau: "Oh, nothing special. Just a couple of
buddies and me, we're looking forward to a reunion."

Linde: "I want to know what you're planning."

Schlottau: "Maybe we should go to the movies in
Andernach at that."

Linde: "I see no reason . . ."

Schlottau: "Do you know your father?"

Linde: "He had his last leave in forty-four."

Schlottau: "That's when he was commanding in
Kurland."

Linde: "He only stayed three days and slept most
of the time. . . ."

Schlottau: "At that time I was with the Elk's
Heads, Eleventh Infantry Division. All East Prussians.
—I can tell you, Miss, your daddy is quite a guy."

Linde: "I'll probably get to know him now."

Schlottau: "I could tell you a lot of stories. Funny
ones, too. . . ."

Linde walks away from Schlottau: "Another time,
in case I feel like going to the movies."

("What do you think, Doc: should or can the plant
electrician, left alone amid concrete blocks, end the
scene with the words: 'She takes after the old man'?")

My dentist said: "You've been very patient. That
takes care of the lower left."

"Now what? How do you like the end of my
scene?"

"Now we'll anaesthetize the lower right. You'll

hardly feel it, because the first injections fan out.—See?"

"Or should the dialogue be in the grand style? Accusations. Coarse-grained hatred demanding vengeance . . ."

"This Schlottau you take such a suspicious interest in seems to have the makings of a revolutionary. . . ."

"By German standards. . . ."

"Well, then, of a short-winded insurrectionist. . . ."

"He existed only because Krings existed."

(While the injections were beginning to take effect and the pumice picture was starting up again on the First Program, my dentist asked me for a succinct double portrait of my two interdependent heroes: "Meanwhile I'll be taking copper-band impressions of the teeth we've just ground down; they will enable us to check the accuracy of our preparation."

I rinsed in anticipation and had trouble with the water glass; the swollen feeling and numbness of my lower lip made me misjudge the distance between glass and mouth: water was spilled. My dentist's assistant had to mop me up with a paper towel. Embarrassing.)

"Heinz Schlottau was born in 1920 in Ermland, a Catholic enclave in Protestant East Prussia; the future Field Marshal Ferdinand Krings first saw the light of the Lower Eifel in 1892; his father was a master mason, owner of several basalt pits in Bellfeld. Both grew up without attracting any particular attention. Our interest will also have to wait—unless we wish to speak of Schlottau's apprenticeship in Frauenburg, Krings' interrupted study of philosophy, Schlottau's activity as an electrician and foxtrotter in Allenstein, or Reserve Lieutenant Krings' achievements in the First World War, during the twelfth battle of the Isonzo, for example. But since little time is available before the grinding of my two lower-right molars, we shall skip a rung or two of Krings' Reichswehr and Schlottau's electrical career, and say: In peacetime the famous Eleventh Infantry Division, also known as Elk's Head Division, was stationed in the East Prussian cities of Allenstein, Ortelsburg, Bischofsburg, Rastenburg, Lötzen, and Bartenstein. In the autumn of 1938 the recruit Heinz Schlottau was assigned to the Forty-Fourth Infantry Regiment then stationed in Bartenstein, while the Lieutenant-Colonel in command of an Alpine Regiment, which had participated without loss in the annexation of Austria and the occupation of the Protectorate of Bohemia and Moravia, was stationed in Memmingen.

"Both Schlottau and Krings prepared for things to come. The one on the sandy Stablak drill ground, the other, as ordered, over plane-table section maps intended to impart knowledge of the roads and fortifications of the Carpathian passes.

"Both Schlottau and Krings set out on September 1, in mild summer weather. While the infantryman participated in the breach of the Mlawa border fortifications, in the battle for the Narew crossings, and in the pursuit of the Polish armies through East Poland, culminating in the surrender of Modlin, the other prepared to storm Lemberg: while repulsing Polish

Uhlan regiments on the heights before Lemberg, he had his first opportunity to document his future as a 'fight-to-the-finish' General. In the fighting for the fortress of Modlin, Schlottau, a moderately cautious daredevil, came by a slight wound—his upper arm was grazed—and the Iron Cross Second Class; the hero of Lemberg was cited in the Wehrmacht Report, remained unwounded, and was permitted to give support to another Iron Cross First Class on his spacious chest along with his First World War decorations.

"Both Schlottau and Krings wrote letters and field post cards home. So far there is no discernible reason why the infantryman and future electrician Heinz Schlottau should have been eager in June 1955 to prepare a reception for the Colonel and future Field Marshal General Ferdinand Krings at the Koblenz railroad station."

My dentist seemed satisfied with my double portrait; but his work had to forgo his approval: "The impressions show that our grinding has produced a few grooves. Trifles. We shall have to correct them with a little more grinding: nothing to it. . . ."

"What do you think, Doc? Should we fade the Koblenz station and the mob scenes into the cement film while it's still running . . .?"

"Relax now. And let your tongue lie flat. . . ."

Long shot of the façade of the Koblenz Central Station. Blackened sandstone. Above the granite base, truncated masonry. Railroad station sculpture. War damage, at this late date. (Background too close: the Charterhouse, part of the Koblenz Fortress, crowds the tarpaper roofs.) The unrest on the square commands the camera to rest. It records: unorganized group formation, overlapping simultaneous movements, banners, here held aloft, there being unrolled, elsewhere being rolled up again. (Pigeons who see that their square is occupied and tilt their heads on the cornices.) Sounds: Unintelligible chanting, shouts ("Go on over, George . . ."), group laughter, the glug-glug of bottled beer being passed around. (Cooing of pigeons.) Policemen in readiness outside the Municipal Savings Bank. Only two police cars. Women after shopping. Teen-agers walking their bicycles. (The vender of lottery tickets with the twenty-mark notes in the ribbon of his hat.) Press. On a platform of crates the newsreel camera is set up. Commandlike shouts. Self-generating movement: now the banners are legibly displayed. "There is no Arctic!"—"Strength through Terror!" "Kurland sends greetings!"—"Fight-to-the-finish Krings!" The chanting finds its rhythm: "No more Herosnatching! No more Herosnatching!"—"Count us out! Count us out!" (Some are disappointed because the newsreel camera isn't shooting. Insults: "Go on home, you jerks!"—Pigeons landing and taking off.) The medium shot captures a group led by Electrician Schlottau: "Go home to Siberia, Krings; Go home to Siberia, Krings!"

On the corner of Marienbildchenweg, surrounded by housewives, stands Sieglinde Krings. She is wearing sunglasses. Slowly she pushes through the crowd of men, for the most part war invalids. (Crutches, glass eyes, empty sleeves, disfigured faces.) Unrest and shouts at the main entrance. The crowd presses into the station. Whirlpools form. Cursing. Pushing. The makings of a fight: platform tickets are bought and distributed. (High-power salesmanship: "Get 'em while they're hot.")

The police do not intervene but follow the crowd through the ticket gate. More pushing and shoving. A policeman regulates the flow: "Easy does it, gentlemen, your Krings won't run away. . . ." Running, also rapid limping, through the underground passage, from which the stairs to the platforms, except for Platform Four, branch off. During the movement from the square to the station jumbled fragments of sentences: "Ivan letting him go!"—"Soldier killer!"—"Man, he'd send his own mother into a minefield."—"In East Germany they wanted him to . . ."—"They say he was on the same train with Nuschke . . ."—"Because of rearmament . . ."—"I'm telling you, in a parlor car."—"They got an army over there if our generals start . . ."—"Count me out!"—"There'll be plenty of damn fools to . . ."—"I know the skunk from the Arctic Front . . ."—"Rear guard in Nikopol . . ."—"That swine in Kurland . . ."—"But when's he . . ."—"Brain him with your wooden leg . . ."—"Know what he did to us in Prague . . ."—"Pulling in!"—"Watch out, pal!"—"Train's pulling in . . ."

Silence while the train pulls in. Glances are wrenched forward, snap back, then forward again. Only a few passengers get off. Eye slits search for resemblance. A few men look through the coaches. As the train pulls out again, the conductor calls from the steps: "Don't get excited, friends. Your Krings with his cardboard suitcase got out in Andernach."

Railroad noises overlay scattered shouts of protest. (They drowned out the high register of the air drive that was grinding down the masticating surface of my lower third molar. Reason enough to rinse. My dentist was opposed to my exploiting the disappointment, which was as long as a station platform.)

"To make a long story short, the demonstration disbanded, just as the demonstration against Kiesinger last week disbanded: in an orderly fashion. I was there with a few students and Irmgard Seifert. What a flop! Because he didn't lay his wreath at the memorial on Steinplatz as announced, but surreptitiously in Plözensee. Irmgard Seifert was satisfied all the same: 'Our protest won't fade away.' Scherbaum took a dim view: 'We're only letting off steam.' And next day in class when I tried to defend protest as a moral gesture even when it is seemingly unsuccessful, Vero Lewand stopped me with a quotation from Marxengels (she always has little slips of paper on her): 'Petit bourgeois revolutionaries mistake the stages in the revolutionary process for the final goal which is their reason for participating in the revolution. . . .'—Petit bourgeois, that's me. And that's how you too would be classified, Doc, if it should ever occur to you to face my class with your Seneca."

"You should have answered your quotation-fed student with Nietzsche: 'A transvaluation of values is achieved only under pressure of new needs and of human beings newly aware of their needs. . . .' "

"Whatever may have brought those people out on the streets, a week ago against Kiesinger or in the summer of 1954 against Krings, it was all hot air. . . ."

"All the same, we've succeeded in tapering down your third lower left molar."

"And the newspaper headlines: 'Field Marshal General Krings sidesteps Veterans' Protest Demonstration!'—The ironic touch: 'Count me out!' says Krings.—Or wry: 'Lead absent from Koblenz Melodrama.'—The *Generalanzeiger* reported matter-of-factly: 'The train pulled in on schedule, but without the Field Marshal General; one more protest demonstration has fizzled. . . .' "

"What about your buddy Schlottau?"

While the masticating surface of my lower left molar is being ground down, I introduce an intercut: the veterans evacuate Platform Four. In the crush at the head of the stairs leading down to the main underground passage Linde and Schlottau collide.

Linde: "Can I give you a lift?"

Schlottau: "Damn shit!"

Linde: "My car's parked behind the Hotel Höhmann."

Schlottau: "Who wants to ride with you stinkers!"

Linde: "I thought you wanted to take me to the movies."

Schlottau: "Just like him to chicken out."

Cut, as the two disappear down the stairs to the underground passage.

Because naturally they ride off together. In a

Borgward, now virtually extinct. True, he had dropped her abruptly on the square, or rather, he had revved off (amid pigeons), leaving her to pursue her undeviating course alone, but there's no need to show that. And the short sentences exchanged by Schlottau and his old buddies—"The old man sure took us"—"Never mind, we'll show the bastard"—can be thrown out. (Come to think of it, he bought a lottery ticket on the square: it laid an egg.)

This is the highway from Andernach to Mayen, the car is the Borgward with Sieglinde Krings at the wheel and Heinz Schlottau beside her. Behind the motorists the rigid camera rides with them.

Linde: "I might have known he wouldn't wait for me in Andernach."—Pause for speculations about the detour to Andernach and the failure of the Borgward Corporation, I don't remember exactly when.

Schlottau: "Maybe he stayed in East Germany. The Russkis must have hired him. They're looking for men with experience. Paulus is out there too."—Pause, in which the counterrevolutionary thesis of Teng T'o might be sent up in a balloon: "We salute the motley intellectuals . . .," plus pictures: Krings is welcomed at the Berlin East Station by high functionaries of the German Democratic Republic.

Linde: "I'm waiting for that invitation to the movies."

Schlottau: "Suppose Krings builds them up an army. . . ."

Linde: "I'm waiting for that invitation to the movies. I'm nuts about movies."

Pause, taken up with wondering what pictures were being played in the mid-fifties. *Sissi, The Rangers of the Silver Forest* . . .

Schlottau: "What about your fiancé, Miss? Wouldn't he . . ."

Linde: "He's grateful for any relief."—Pause in which Schlottau is free to read significance into Linde's remark. I rinse because my dentist asks me to. Chalky foam, no blood, but more heckling from my student Scherbaum: "I know all about your NSKK, BDM, RAD, and HKL*—but what about the Mekong Delta . . ." "Yes, Scherbaum, of course. But only when we understand why an attempt was made on the Führer's life . . ."

Schlottau: "By the way, Miss, do you know the joke about the East Prussian peasant who took his cow to the bull? So when his wife asked him . . ."

Linde: "Besides, my fiancé has lost interest in everything but the use of basalt and tuff under the Romans. . . ." Pause that leaves no room for reflections on the highly developed millstone industry of the Romans, especially after the unsuccessful uprising of the Treveri, because the Borgward overtakes a bicyclist. Schlottau looks behind him. His face reflects: astonishment embarrassment hatred.—After a pause of some length devoted to reflections on the end of the

* Initials current in the National Socialist period.
NSKK: Nationalsozialistisches Kraftfahrerkorps, National Socialist Motorist Corps.
BDM: Bund deutscher Mädchen, League of German Girls.
RAD: Reichsarbeitsdienst, Reich Labor Service.
HKL: Hauptkampflinie, main line of battle.

joke about the cow, Schlottau speaks without particular emphasis: "That was him.—Stop, will you? I'm getting out." Linde steps on the brakes: "You can introduce me to my father."

Schlottau. "Scared shitless of the old man, eh?"

Linde: "Yes.—I'm afraid.—So are you.—Okay, beat it."

Schlottau takes his time about getting out: "If you come around to the cement depot again. I finish my rounds at two, then I've got an hour to . . ."—He strides off in the direction of Plaidt with the rest of the sentence.

While Schlottau went off, while I refused to follow him and my dentist withdrew the Airstar because a patient was calling him on the phone, Linde turned on the windshield wiper as though to wipe away Schlottau. Her eyes fixed on the rear-view mirror; and in the rear-view mirror the camera catches the bicyclist pedaling around a slight curve. He has the wind against him. The wind, Linde's breath, and my dentist on the phone—trouble fitting his patient in—are three sounds that get on nicely together.

Reckoning back from today, exactly twenty-two years ago, and from then, more than ten years ago—on May 8, 1945, only a few hours before the capitulation of the Greater German Armed Forces—Field Marshal General Krings in gray civilian clothes left his still embattled armies and his headquarters in the Erzgebirge and flew the last available Fieseler Storch to Mittensill in the Tyrol in order—as he later testi-

fied in court—to take command, as per Führer's orders, of the Alpine Redoubt, where, however, as other
witnesses confirmed, he found neither redoubt nor
combat-worthy divisions, for which reason he exchanged his gray civilian suit for the local costume,
leather shorts and so on, and fled to a chalet in the
mountains, where he waited for a miracle or for a
friendship pact—the natural development, as he de-
clared in court—between the American armed forces
and what was left of the German armed forces. Finally, on May 15, when no such alliance against the
Soviet armies had come into being either by natural or
miraculous means, he requisitioned a peasant's bicycle
and rode, in Tyrolese peasant garb without insignia or
decorations, straight to the American prisoner-of-war
camp in Sankt-Johann, just as ten years later he is
peddling homeward to Mayen against the wind on a
bicycle that he had no difficulty in borrowing in
Andernach. We see him, massive and evenly pedaling,
growing larger and larger in the rear-view mirror of
the Borgward. . . .

("What do you think, could should Linde, left
alone in the Borgward with no one to help her but the
rear-view mirror, mumble something or other: 'Must I
throw myself into his arms? Or just burst into
tears . . .' ")

Meanwhile my dentist with the help of the telephone had made an appointment. The pumice film
luxuriated in Lower Eifel landscapes: a late homecomer on a bicycle and I celebrated reunion with the
Korrelsberg. When Linde got out of the car, my den-

tist's Airstar was once again reducing the crown of my first lower left molar. She opened the luggage compartment. She moved the spare tire. She turned around in the direction of the steadily expanding bicycle rider. History was enacted: Hegel's world-spirit rode across country over fields beneath which pumice waited to be exploited.

("Now, Doc! Now!")

The bicycle rider brakes. Linde stands frozen. He alights ponderously and allows himself and her two paces' distance. (Wind, blinking, pause, and flights of thought back to the dentist's office and from there to my junior class, for only recently we were speaking of the homecomer archetype: "My generation was shaped by Borchert's Beckmann. How do you feel about Beckmann, Scherbaum? Does Beckmann still mean anything to you. . . .") This homecomer also wears glasses. In a gray, too tight-fitting business suit he stands hatless in clumsy high laced shoes. He must have borrowed the bicycle clips in Andernach. His tie, new and too fashionable, stands out. His cardboard suitcase is attached with fuzzy string to the baggage carrier. His muscular face says nothing.

Linde: "We can put your bike in the luggage compartment. I'm your daughter Sieglinde."

Krings: "Thoughtful of you to meet me."

Linde: "We must have missed each other in Andernach. I'd been to . . ."

Krings: "I didn't want to appear without a tie."—His chin motions toward the tie.

Linde: "Nice."—But she does not smile.

Krings: "My sister wrote you had long hair and wore it in a braid."

Linde: "I had it cut before my engagement. Let me . . ."

Krings: "Thank you." With businesslike movements Linde stows the bicycle and suitcase in the luggage compartment. The top won't close. Krings looks toward the Korrelsberg. Something, probably the fact that the mountain is still there, amuses him. Meanwhile the viewer can be wondering about the contents of the suitcase: he is also free to worry about the gaping luggage compartment, the top of which Linde attaches to the rear bumper with the fuzzy string. (Incidentally, Linde had a pigtail when I first met her. Because I wished it, she cut it off.)

Linde: "It'll hold for the few miles."

Krings: "The cement dust on the potato plants is still the same."

Linde: "Even that may change soon."

Krings: "Your fiancé—used to be with Dyckerhoff, didn't he—wants to introduce dust control."

Linde: "First we convert to the dry process and then . . ."

Krings: "First we get there. And look things over. Don't you agree?—My daughter should call me Papa. Is it so hard?"

Linde: "I'll try."

Krings: "Just do it."

Linde: "Yes, Father."—Both get in.

But mightn't this scene, without bicycle, landscape, and car, be moved into the Gray Park?

"What do you think, Doc? Krings turns up with his suitcase—maybe he's pushing the bike. Under the cement-bearing beech tree he runs into Linde and instantly finds his first speech: 'How thoughtful of you not to meet me.' To which Linde: 'I was in Koblenz. There was a big crowd. Looked as if there was going to be a riot.'

"Krings: 'The police of this strange country asked me to get off in Andernach.'

"Linde: 'I was glad when the train pulled in without you, because some of those men . . .'

"Krings: 'My sister wrote me you had long hair and wore it in a braid. . . .' "

My dentist was against the Gray Park, because in reality Linde had picked him up on the road.

They drive off in the direction of Plaidt. The camera looks after them until the Korrelsberg and the Krings Works with their two busy stacks dominate a long shot of the Lower Eifel landscape.

"That does it, my friend. Now the impressions for verification. Then we'll make a plaster model that will give us an exact picture of our preparations."

I tried to be pleased. Krings had arrived. I had no pain. Rinsing was almost fun. Outside, I knew, Hohenzollerndamm was running from Roseneck to Bundesallee. And one of my student Scherbaum's usual heckling remarks: "Exactly why do you teach?," which Vero Lewand seconded with a "How should he know?," did not tempt me to look for helpless answers.

Then one tooth after another was isolated with a non-irritating protective varnish. While he protected all four prepared teeth against outside influence with aluminum shells—"It will feel strange at first when the anaesthesia wears off and your tongue discovers the metal"—she commercialized without overstepping the minutes allotted by law. She began with shampoos, appeared later with pine needle bath salts, and finally anointed herself with night cream. I saw her in profile under the shower, with foaming head. On bare skin the spray pearled, prickled, and thrilled. Exception! Why only toiletries? "Why, Doc, can't everything be advertised with bare flesh? For instance: 'A nude dentist treating a thirty-nine-year-old-high-school teacher—colleague Seifert—grinding down four molars, two on the left, two on the right, which will later be protected against outside influences by aluminum shells.—Or here I advertise your favorite mortician: pall-bearers clad in nothing but a carrier-strap, bearing the still-open coffin in which a highly decorated field marshal general at last lies motionless.—And here I'm making my plea for the reform of the upper class of the Berlin secondary schools: a nude and excessively hairy high-school teacher is lecturing a class of diversely dressed students of both sexes on German history: his student Vero Lewand jumps up in bright-colored wool: 'Your list of the characteristics of totalitarianism applies exactly to the authoritarian school system in which we . . .'—Or Mazda light bulbs: the nude electrician Schlottau is standing on a chair screwing in a 60-watt bulb, while a young lady in sports clothes—Lindelindelinde—looks on. Or Arantil: the

nude lovers are sitting on the couch looking at a television screen on which clothed persons are acting out
the story of a crime: the notorious fiancée-murderer
has escaped, he enters a barn, he writhes fully dressed
in the straw, groans because he has a toothache and
no Arantil, while outside—he sees her through a
knothole—the naked farm girl resolutely crosses the
yard to milk the black-and-white cows.—Animals,
sure, why not? I ask you, Doc, why doesn't the zoo
advertise? Nude families crowding around the cage of
monkeys, baboons, and marmosets . . ."

"There, it fits. The aluminum shells were cut to
size. . . ." (My dressed tooth stumps.)
"And now bite hard. Again. Thank you." His assistant (in her white smock) had removed her carrot
fingers on time.
"But isn't my face crooked swollen bumpy?"
"Illusion. A fiction we can explode with a mirror."
As I was leaving, my dentist (in tennis shoes) advised
me not to wait too long before taking Arantil: "Or
you'll have an unpleasant weekend, no carefree Sunday."

(As his assistant helped me on with my coat in the
vestibule, and in a businesslike tone, not too loud,
bade me avoid food that was too hot and drinks that
were too cold because the metal was a heat conductor—I liked her better, yes, a little better.)

When I returned home with my four foreign bodies,
I shaved, changed, tied up a present (vegetative art-

nouveau glass) with a silk ribbon, reacted—by taking a No. 19 bus to Lehniner Platz—to an invitation to a birthday party, started out by entertaining a group of colleagues (suggestions for a cultural policy), said something witty to the hostess (the birthday child) about her aquarium and its morosely voracious contents—but Irmgard Seifert declined to laugh—, stuck it out until midnight with the help of Arantil, found my desk lurking in wait, wrote on a slip of paper: Let's see what keeps silent in the suitcase . . . fell asleep at once, woke up early with the effect wearing off, but refrained from taking two tablets until after breakfast (tea, yoghurt with corn-flakes), and while still reading the Sunday papers resumed my lament: Oh, Sunday . . . oh, the wallpaper . . . oh, my morning beer . . .

I read it in the *Welt am Sonntag:* They've caught him. No. He gave himself up. For never, not even with warrants on coated stock, would they have caught him, the strangler of his vivacious and only when the west wind was blowing moody fiancée. He strangled her—the corpus delicti was shown in a photograph—with a bicycle chain. His almost father-in-law had, as he testified, borrowed the bicycle in Andernach when after ten years in Soviet captivity he returned home at last and found no other means of transportation for the final stretch. The bicycle chain, many-linked as a rosary, was found twelve years ago at the scene of the crime (a depot for cored blocks): for twelve years he had supported himself with burglaries which he had carried off without any special

implement, but flawlessly though without enthusiasm.
(The world forgot him, but the homicide bureau in
Koblenz could not forget him.) As a fugitive he grew
older; but time did not efface the crime he had committed in the fraction of a second. Since food was not
his only need, he took to reading philosophy: in particular he immersed himself in the Stoic doctrine (and
might pass today for an authority on Seneca). Hidden
but always on the alert, he read and slept in barns and
weekend cottages, where rather frequently, chiefly behind the books of his favorite authors, he found ready
money in bills and coins. And so, while the police
presumed he would be hitchhiking, he traveled by
train. Carefully dressed and reading, with a first-class
cushion behind him, he became familiar with West
Germany from Passau to Flensburg and from Coburg
to Völklingen. As often as he changed his locale, he
changed his costume; the thefts which he performed
with extreme reluctance because they were contrary to
his nature had not only to cover the cost of groceries,
books, train fare, and pocket money, but also to solve
his vestimentary problem: his build—even as he grew
older he might easily have bought suits ready-made—
made it easier for him to find his size. He often
changed suitcases. But since possessions meant little to
him he traveled light: a change of shirts and under-
wear, with books in between.

Did he have his hair cut every three weeks?—Yes,
in airports and railroad stations, wherever he could be
sure of seeing an Italian barber in the mirror. (Interest in warrants is limited by nationality.) The scissor

cut gave way to the fashionable razor cut; in the end
he preferred the American crew cut.

And nevertheless—I read this some months ago in
the *Welt am Sonntag* and saw his picture: a well-
groomed man in his late thirties, who might have applied for an executive position in the cement
industry—nevertheless, he gave himself up.

"For nine years, fortified by the Stoic doctrine, I
was able to endure the inconveniences of a fugitive's
life; but for two and a half years now I have been pur-
sued by toothache. . . ."

("It blocks the receptors of the nerve center, doesn't
it, Doc?") Since Arantil cannot be sold without a
prescription, the fiancée-murderer had to make do
with weaker remedies which soon ceased to give relief.
He was afraid to see a dentist. Dentists read illustrated
magazines. Dentists keep abreast of the news and are
well acquainted with every fugitive murderer, including himself, whom *Quick* and *Stern, Die Bunte* and
Die Neue had honored with photographs. This species
of publication ran in packs like wolves: they had all
hunted him serially and for weeks through the hunting
preserve of the Homebody Readers' Club. Rotogra-
vure pictures with captions. He and his fiancée in the
days when she wore artificial pearls and not a bicycle
chain around her neck. He and she on the shady bank
of the Laacher See. The two of them on the Rhine
Promenade in Andernach under clipped plane trees.
Also with his father-in-law to be—shortly before the
murder—beside the model of an electrical centrifugal
dust remover. And singly in happier days. The fi-

ancée-murderer hatless, hatted, in profile, in three-quarter view. In one picture he is laughing, baring his teeth. (Any dentist would have been struck by that. "You, for instance. It would have stuck in your mind for years: that gap between the upper incisors and that protruding lower jaw, that—everybody notices it—authentic, because congenital, prognathism.")

Deprived of dental treatment, he lived for two and a half years with a pain which had a way of repeating itself and escalating with repetition, a pain which even Seneca's golden words—Only the poor man counts his cattle—could do no more than temper and which overlaid and drowned out that other primordial pain provoked by the thought of his strangled fiancée. Without Arantil and—since Seneca sometimes failed to take effect—cynically consoled by the late Nietzsche—"In moral terms, the world is wrong. But in so far as morality itself is a part of this world, morality is wrong . . ."—he dragged himself from weekend cottage to weekend cottage, sought and found inoffensive little remedies in medicine chests, but never the Arantil for which a prescription is required. (And so, in abandoned stonemasons' shacks on Mayener Feld, I wallowed in pain as though pain were a pleasure, holding my betrothed, a bundle of crackling straw, in my arms—Oh, Lindelindelinde—though at the same time I heard her hiss: You keep out of this. This is between Father and me. I'll prove it to him. It's practically none of your business. Schlottau? What if I have? Stop threatening me with that ridiculous bicycle chain. . . .)

So I went to the homicide bureau in Koblenz and said: "Here I am!" With due respect for the forms, the fiancée-murderer, a native of West Prussia, submitted his "A" refugee card which had meanwhile expired.

The police officers were incredulous. It was only when he laughed, laughed despite all his pain, revealing his unmistakable prognathism and the gap between his upper incisors, that they became affable to the point of chumminess: "It was high time, old boy." •

I shall not go into the scholarly achievement of the so-called fiancée-murderer. (He surrendered to the police a manuscript which in twelve years had grown to impressive size: "The early Seneca as educator of the future Emperor Nero.—Philosophical notes of a fugitive murderer." Here there is room only for his affliction as recorded in the official proceedings: "As a prisoner awaiting trial I hereby request permission to consult the prison dentist. Treatment, possibly the extraction of the aching teeth, is in order. In case treatment should be delayed, I respectfully request Arantil. For Arantil is not dispensed without a prescription. . . ."

Thanks to Arantil—twenty tablets at two marks thirty—I was free from pain and inspired by the side effects as I wrote: Our defeats lie behind us. Now let us reflect and gain. . . .

Shortly before my round of morning beers I was still basking in lamentation—Oh, Sunday . . . Oh, the wallpaper . . . I pondered old happenings, the eternal whisperings on the Andernach Promenade. But then two tablets helped me to deliver my Sunday soul-

searching to a female colleague's private problem:
(Oh, how we take ourselves unawares . . . Oh, how
the past strikes back . . .)—for if Irmgard Seifert
hadn't found those letters, she would be happier and
would know next to nothing about herself: but she
found them and now she knows. . . .

A weekend visit to her mother in Hanover, the
necessity of partaking, repeatedly and with compliments, of her favorite dish, sauerbraten with potato
dumplings—"Come, come, child, take a proper helping. There was a time when you could never get
enough . . ."—her mother's afternoon nap (as though
she were dead for an hour) suddenly finding herself
alone amid furniture and wallpaper that ought to have
made her feel at home, the ubiquitous, immemorial
smell of floor wax, a sudden quarrel among the sparrows in the front-garden hedge, and at lunch, before
the cloying sweet aftertaste of the preserved pears had
worn away, a word dropped by her mother about report cards, class photographs, copybooks and letters
belonging to her daughter, junk done up in bundles in
a trunk in the attic—in short, a concatenation of for-
tuitous happenings led Irmgard Seifert, who like myself teaches German and history (plus music) to don
Mother's apron in anticipation of dust, climb up to the
attic, and open a fiber trunk that was not even locked.

Catchwords line up on my paper: Sunlight slanting
through the skylight. The rusty runners of her child-
hood sled. Family history: her late father was head of
the shipping department at Günther Wagner's. (To

this day she gets her pencils at a discount.) Irmgard's aquarium; zebra fish, goldfish, and guppies that eat their young.

Irmgard Seifert and I are the same age. At the end of the war we were seventeen, but already adults. Whatever may stand in the way of a more than professional relationship between us, we are agreed in our judgment of the recent German past and its aftermath that is still with us. But we react in different tones to the Grand Coalition and to Kiesinger's chancellorship: I with disabused cynicism, while Irmgard Seifert is given to protesting.

From her, certain television utterances and newspaper headlines exact a standing comment: "That calls for protest, energetic and uncompromising protest."

Her students and mine—she purveys music to my junior class—good-naturedly call Irmgard Seifert the "archangel"; her manner of speaking often evokes the flaming sword. (And only when she is feeding her ornamental fish can she be suspected of charm.)

To give a rallying cry. To set an example. Only two years ago she marched with the Easter marchers. Because the German Freedom Union was not on the ballot in West Berlin, she boycotted the regional elections in protest. In addressing her class, and mine as well, she occasionally invoked Marxengels and puzzled radical students with sharp criticism of Ulbricht, whom she termed an old-Stalinist bureaucrat. Though not on my student Scherbaum, she exerted a lasting influence on his girl-friend, little Vero Lewand.

At that time Irmgard Seifert was a fanatical debater. She engaged in fruitless discussions on school reform with conservative colleagues and even with our principal who regards himself as a liberal; for he buried every argument with the "archangel" under a sentence that has become proverbial: "Whatever you may think of the Hamburg pioneer full-time school, there is one thing, my dear colleague, that unites us, and that is our uncompromising anti-fascism."

Then suddenly, amid the usual school papers and class photographs, Irmgard Seifert found a packet of letters she had written in February and March 1945, when she had been a squad leader in the League of German Girls and deputy director of a camp for evacuated city children. In Sütterlin script her thoughts revolved on lined paper around the figure of the Führer, whom she several times called "noble." She regarded Bolshevism as a Judaeo-Slavic alliance and was resolved to oppose it with flaming protest (even then an "archangel"). And the well-known quotation from Baumann: ". . . There is a hunger in our eyes: new lands, let us conquer new lands . . ." provided one of the letters, written in March—the Soviet armies had reached the Oder—with its motto. (In general the extreme right-wing offshoots of Late Expressionism had shaped her style; to this very day my colleague Seifert is strong in flamboyant adjectives, but now they support a left-wing creed. "The goal which all unswerving friends of peace must set themselves clearly for the future is the yoke-breaking victory of socialism. . . .") "My blond hatred," wrote Fräulein Seifert in whom silver threads have since taken their place among the gold, "knows no bounds, and soars amid the music of the stars!"

I tried to laugh when, shortly after her weekend visit to Hanover and still in a state of agitation, she quoted these extravagances to me; but with wide eyes she said: "There are passages in those letters that I should not like to disclose even to you."

("In a word, Doc, Irmgard Seifert had suffered a shock.") Of course she had not forgotten that she had been a squad leader in the League of German Girls. She had remembered many details of that period in the Harz and was able to tell about them: her worry about the evacuated city children from Braunschweig and Hanover; the crushing burden of responsibility as it became increasingly difficult to procure food; the daily fighter-bomber raids on the nearby village; the digging of foxholes and her indignation at the Local Group Leader who at the beginning of April wanted to remove the thirteen- and fourteen-year-old school-boys from the camp and enroll them in the Volkssturm.

On our walks together around the Grunewaldsee, or over a glass of moselle in my apartment, we had often chatted rather than talked about that episode of her younger years—as we had about my days in the Dusters Gang. She remembered having protested in tones that could not be ignored against Local Group Leader's mistreatment of the children. "I registered a flaming protest." Word for word she repeated her speech of self-defense. "In the end he cleared out.

One of those repulsive party bosses. You surely remember the type. . . ."

Irmgard Seifert even made pedagogic use of the situation into which she had been forced in that remote past: she spoke to her students and mine (in music class) "of courage as the overcoming of cowardice."

She turned the contents of the trunk over and over but couldn't find what she was looking for: rebellious, or, as she called them, "antifascist" statements which she claimed not only to have made at an early date but also written down. All she found was these letters. And in the last letter she read of her triumph at having, at her request, been made a bazooka instructor after completing her own training. There it was: "Our preparedness is a self-evident fact. Every one of the boys whom I, working with the Local Group Leader, have trained in the firing of the bazooka, will join me in defending the camp to the last. Stand or fall at their posts. Nothing else matters."

"But you didn't defend the camp at all."

"Of course not. We didn't get a chance."

I digressed, spoke of my Duster days: "Think of it, my dear colleague: me as a gang leader. With so much organized national solidarity around me, what else could I do but attack society, often in ways that verged on crime?"

Nothing could halt my colleague's collapse. "There are other letters, worse . . ."

She told me about a peasant who had refused to allow a tank trap to be dug in his field that bordered on the children's camp: "I reported that peasant to party headquarters in Clausthal-Zellerfeld. In writing."

"Did anything happen? I mean, did they . . .?"

"No. They didn't."

"Then why worry?" I heard myself say. (This conversation took place in my apartment. I poured more moselle. And put on a record.) My Telemann was also powerless to prevent Irmgard Seifert from stating her self-indictment in full: "I remember being disappointed, no indignant, that nothing was done about my denunciation."

"Sheer speculation!"

"I'm going to leave the school system."

"You'll do nothing of the kind."

"I have no right to go on teaching. . . ."

And already I began to line up words of Sunday admonition: "My dear colleague, your share of guilt is precisely what enables you to show the youngsters the way. Some of us spend our whole lives with an existential lie, failing to suspect. . . . Someday I'll tell you about myself and an action whose consequences have only today become apparent to me. Suddenly a word like 'pumice' or 'tuff.' Or children playing with a bicycle chain. And our peace of mind is gone. Naked and vulnerable we . . ."

At this she wept. And because I thought I knew Irmgard Seifert's self-control, I ventured to hope that tears could perform the function of Arantil.

"Oh, Doc, what a name! (I take two more.) Arantil might have been the sister of Tanaquil, the Etruscan princess. Because of her early betrothal, Arantil, the younger sister, was hated by Tanaquil, the elder, and consequently—but also because Arantil's betrothed had suddenly succumbed to Tanaquil's charms—was hurled to her death from the walls of Perugia. Later a singer adopted her name. You remember how, like la Tebaldi, like la Callas, la Arantil sang her way into innumerable hearts and discothèques. But probably her face had more to do with it. (No, not pretty, but beautiful.) Could it have been the position of her eyes, that ramified gaze? Who among us can remember her body? Her talent was her face. Magnified on billboards as high as churches, it reduced itself to dots which our eye, taking its distance, endeavored to put together. In some provincial hole, Fürth, I think, I saw it on an advertising column: rain-spattered torn outmoded three weeks after the performance. (Someone had scratched out both the poster's eyes.) And her photograph! How it got around! Tucked away in prayer books. Framed on the desks of mighty captains of industry. Thumbtacks fastened it to the lockers of our Bundeswehr recruits. There it was: in postcard size and on the wide screen. It looked at us, no, through us. Swept bare, compelling, soothing, it ignored all grief and pain. (And this power to appease pain may later have impelled a pharmaceutical firm to market a homonymous analgesic, specially designed to combat pain in the teeth and jaws, a product which you, Doc, prescribe day after day: "I've prescribed a family-size package of Arantil . . .") Yet her face was terrible and her end tragic. . . .

"For a long time, incidentally, nothing more was heard of the young man whom the yellow press called her murderer. He was said to have been engaged to her. It was the evening papers and the illustrated magazines, especially *Quick*, you can always count on *Quick*, that released the photographer's snapshot to the public. And the press, which had been responsible for her death, now called him a murderer. What alleged crime had he committed? A photographer engaged like all of us in the struggle for existence.

"In spite of the difficulties he got into her hotel suite. There he hid under her bed with his camera and waited in an uncomfortable position for her return. Nay more: he waited until she had changed to nightdress and at last—he trusted his hearing—had fallen asleep. Only then did I issue from my hiding place. (She had always been a sound sleeper.) I aimed my Arriflex at her from a short distance and took one, only one, flashlight picture. By the time the old girl rang (and probably screamed) I was already in the elevator on the way to my darkroom. To judge by my knowledge of her—and I knew her well, only too well—she was already dead by then. For any snapshot not only brought me a sum in several figures (which is helping me today to finance our porcelain bridges), my snapshot also cost her her life. From that moment on she could find no sleep. (I had flashed it away.) Being her fiancé, I was privileged to leaf through the record of her illness: seven months, two weeks, and four days after I had photographed my fiancée Arantil's sleeping face at the Berlin Hilton Hotel, she dimmed, she faded away in Zürich: eighty-nine pounds."

Yet her sleeping face was beautiful, though beautiful in a different way than her waking face. It offered itself to all to make use of as they chose; and rigid and goatlike as her usual waking face may have been, my fiancée Sieglinde Krings also achieved this childlike, devil-may-care relaxed look when I found her sleeping amid her volumes of military rubbish in the Gray Park. But I never photographed her sleep. I possess no photograph even of the waking Linde with her eyes always focused on some goal. And why should I? All that is past. Life goes on. Irmgard Seifert is still teaching. I had quite a time talking her out of the public confession she had planned. "Why do you want to burden the boys and girls with all that? Everyone has to amass his own experience."—At the end she gave in: "At the moment I shouldn't have the courage to lay myself bare before the class. . . ."

My Sunday ended when I tried to drink a glass of beer at the bar at Reimann's. His assistant, who had warned me against eating too hot and drinking too cold, was right: the metallic foreign bodies—four aluminum shells on my ground-down stumps—conducted heat; my glass was still half full when I paid up.

My dentist, who is my friend, explained the pain to me: "Don't you know? In every tooth there is a nerve, an artery, and a vein."

His voice carried and measured his office—sixteen by twenty-three, and ten feet high: "And something else you should know: under the enamel, which is not sensitive, run the dentinal tubules containing nerve ends which we cut into obliquely when we drill or grind."

(After a long-winded weekend I pictured my dentist as a rather colorless figure, and even that morning my attempt to explain to my junior class that there was nothing more impersonal than a friendly dentist who inquires about your health the minute you step in, brought forth unanimous laughter; they thought I was funny.

He hardly greeted me. From beside the accessory table he informed me without transition: "Your affected tooth necks ache because that's where the dentinal tubules come together."

His graphic method of explaining things (even pain)—I ought to adopt it in class: "See, it's like this: the nerve fans out in the crown and passes into the pulp chamber."

When I dropped a passing remark about the Lower Eifel and the village of Kruft in the pumice-mining zone, he abandoned the subject of dental nerves in order that Krings might finally return home.

"To make a long story short, Doc, he took possession of the villa behind the Gray Park and assembled the family—Aunt Mathilde, Sieglinde, and me—in his workroom, which had been closed the whole time but had been described to me as 'Father's Sparta': a camp bed, bookshelves, rolled-up plane-table section maps. On a trestle-supported tabletop the loop of the Vistula before the breakthrough at Baranow. And on the wall, facing the window, a mounted map of the Kurland basin with pins indicating the front line at the time Krings had taken over. . . ."

My dentist recognized the situation at once: "That's the place! October forty-four. Southeast of Preekuln. That's where I . . ."

"Not a speck of dust. Aunt Mathilde has waxed and aired the room for the homecoming Krings. With Kurland behind him and the trestle-borne Center Sector between himself and us, he makes it clear that he wants no family sentimentalities. When his sister gives vent to her pleasure at the General's by no means run-down but on the contrary sturdy appearance— 'I'm so glad, Ferdinand, that these dreadful long years haven't undermined your . . .'—he interrupts with: 'I've been away. Now I'm here again.' Linde says nothing but remains silently present. I venture to ask whether the loneliness of the Russian countryside changes a man, especially a man in captivity. At first it looks as if I should have no answer. With movements of the compass Krings examines the situation in the loop of the Vistula, points to Baranow—'That should never have been allowed to happen!'—and then looks at me: 'Seneca says: All the good things of life belong to others—time alone is ours—I commanded my brain to enliven the admittedly monotonous landscape to the southeast of Moscow with offensive movements. . . . He might equally well have said 'There is no loneliness,' just as he had said 'There is no Arctic!' "

My dentist beside the accessory table was playing with the four loaded syringes. His remark—"As you know, Seneca was deported to Corsica under Claudius; it was Nero's mother Agrippina who finally put an end to his eight years' exile"—reminded me that it was eminently under conditions of captivity that the Stoic doctrine achieved maturity and disciples. (My dentist was not discharged from captivity until the middle of forty-nine.) I waited in the dentist's chair for the nasty little pinprick, fearing that local anaesthesia might tempt him to deliver a variation on Krings' theme—there is no pain!—but he kept his feet on the ground and praised me in the presence of his assistant: "You are one of my few patients to take a more than passing interest in the causes and pathways of pain: the nerve of a tooth leads into the mandibular nerve, or third branch of the facial nerve, and then into the cerebral cortex, which occasionally conducts pain to the back of the head. . . ."

Milky shone the television screen. Should I bring on the fiancée-murderer . . .? Or Colleague Seifert fishing for old letters in Mother's fiber trunk . . .? Or Arantil the insomniac prima donna . . .? Or the four of us driving to Normandy in the Borgward . . .? "Because you see, Doc, though we said nothing of our vacation plans before the General's arrival—I wanted to go to Ireland; Linde said: 'I'm staying here'—no sooner had Krings moved into his Sparta and unrolled a map of his invasion front over the situation map of Center Sector than he issued firm instructions to all: 'As soon as my passport comes, we set out. I want to take a look at the sector between Arromanches and Cabourg and size up this Herr Speidel who seems to

be coming up again.'—With Krings' oven-fresh passport we drove off. The French raised no objection,
his role in the French campaign had been strictly sub-
ordinate. . . ."

"Anyway we cross the border without difficulty,
Linde at the wheel. A day and a half later we reach
our destination. In view of our Krings-ordained haste
I find little opportunity to pursue my art-historical interests; nevertheless, taking advantage of my position
beside Linde in the front seat, I permit myself to comment on this and that cathedral, on the large number
of castles in France, and later on the special features
of Norman architecture; a zeal which Krings (and
Aunt Mathilde as well) tolerate. Linde squelches me.
She knows my compulsion to give impromptu lectures: 'Leave us alone with your crummy art talk.' "

(In a way she's right. I should have reserved my
commentary until we reached the coast and then
faded in the monuments of the German cement industry. That ought to interest my junior class as well.
"Believe me, Scherbaum, they were still there, they
still are: giant pillboxes knocked off kilter by naval
gunfire and some of them pierced clean through. Concrete installations that have become part of the landscape. Reason enough for any cameraman to set his
sights: quiet gray surfaces with a reality of their own.
Incisive shadows. Saturated hollows. Stark revetment
structures revealed in the light. What we today call
concrete finish. Perhaps you will condemn my obser-
vations as mere aestheticism; nevertheless, I am in-

clined to speak of the Stoic serenity of pillbox contours. I should even go so far as to call the concrete pillbox the Stoic's ancestral home.")

And in all seriousness I proposed to Krings, who had listened with interest to my lecture on the development of German trass cements during the last war, that the new type we had developed for steel and concrete superstructures should be named after the late-Roman philosopher Seneca. The idea didn't appeal to him. (Maybe he detected a note of mockery.) Because when—we were standing on the right bank of the Orne estuary—I began to praise the concrete fort as the twentieth-century architectural art form, when I struck up a hymn to the sincerity of uncoated concrete and the truth of defensive architecture, he called me to order with a "Come back down to earth!"

Later my dentist said: "You speak of Krings with an enthusiasm that you try too hard to mask with irony."

While we inspected the cliffs along the coast near Arromanches, he spoke on the phone with a colleague about a series of lectures on caries that he had begun to deliver at the Tempelhof People's University: "Poorly attended, I'm afraid, poorly attended."

I left the Norman pillbox landscape and met Hilda and Inge under the cement-bearing beech tree. The girls jabbered about their vacations in Italy.

"And what about our Hardykins?"

I described our stay in Cabourg and the side trips

on which we had questioned the concrete witnesses to past military engagements.

"Thrilling."

"They've still got real pillboxes? And you can fool around inside them?"

I told them that one could not only visit the interiors—much littered by lovers—but also climb up on top, if only to make a speech.

"Show us. Papa Krings on top of the pillbox . . ." I baptized a garden chair pillbox, mounted the wobbly pedestal, and did a pretty fair imitation of Krings: "I'd have thrown them into the ocean! What do you mean control of the air? Did we have control of the air in Kurland? Headquarters and quartermaster units—I'd have had them all at the front. That Speidel with his General Staff—aesthetes! Always safe in the rear. Break 'em to captain and send 'em up front. Same as in the polar circle, same as in the lower Dniester, same as in the third battle of Kurland. They wouldn't have gained an inch of ground. . . ."

At this point—but no sooner—Linde appears. My fiancée had been very silent on the trip (Krings: "What's the matter, Linde? Do you take a different view of the situation?"), but now she speaks up, joins in the game: "If I remember correctly, you evacuated the Nikopol bridgehead. The first thing you did in the Kurland basin was to withdraw the Narva Army Group. There's no reason to believe that you could have prevented the invasion, because on the east front you failed to hold Center Sector. I remember Konev's breakthrough between Muskau and Gubin. Without it the offensive against Berlin by way of Spremberg and

Kottbus wouldn't have been possible. Nothing but lost battles. You'd better give up, Father."

Neither I nor the girls in the Gray Park know this Linde (Sieglinde). I get down from my chair and break off my parody of Krings. Hilda and Inge gape, giggle, and shiver. They gather up their fashion magazines. But Linde bars our embarrassed exit: "What's so surprising? My father wants to win battles that other people have lost. Since our aesthete friend Eberhard has decided to admire him like a historic fossil, it's up to me to defeat my father—on every front he can think of."

I let that shot stand. (Linde slightly tense, silent in accordance with her decision. Her blinking girlfriends. An intimation of trickling cement dust.) "You see, Doc, Linde's decision opened my eyes to something very painful."

"I wouldn't use the word 'pain' so lightly if I were you."

"But this change is my fiancée, the way she suddenly and deliberately moved away from me—from that time on, she regarded me as a nuisance—was to me a source of enduring pain."

"Let's stick to our example of the dental nerves. . . ."

"Who tells the stories here, Doc . . ."

"The patient as a rule, but when a counter-story is in order . . .

". . . The crisis in your engagement is very much like a crisis of the dental nerves: once the pulp is infected bacteria produce gases than can be released only by drilling. But if the sufferer puts off going to the dentist, the gases seek escape by way of the root apex. Abetted by a purulent discharge, they attack the jawbone. A swelling develops, culminating in an abscess or—to get back to your engagement—a neurotic growth of hatred. Often it bursts into action years later (compensation), in other words, it continues to fester; admit it, this self-important brandishing of bicycle chains and flash lamps amuses you. The cause: an old failure. The usual minor ache. That's why I must ask you to exercise restraint in using the word 'pain.' You couldn't take a really painful operation. Just think of the genre scenes of the lesser Dutch masters. Adriaen Brouwer, for instance. In his paintings the barber—as dentists were called in the Middle Ages—reaches into a peasant's mouth with a pair of tongs such as today you won't even find in our tool kit, to break out a molar. In those days teeth weren't pulled, but broken. The root slowly rotted away when it didn't become dangerously infected. We have reason to believe that death from rotting roots was frequent three hundred years ago. Even a hundred years ago the extraction of a molar was a serious undertaking. Here in Berlin, at the Charité, four men were needed to pull a fifth man's molar without local anaesthesia—at the most his gums were painted with cocaine. I remember the stories my father told, he was a doctor: one man held the patient's left arm, the second wedged his knee into the pit of his stomach, the third held the poor devil's right hand over a candle flame so as to divide the pain, and the fourth man worked with instruments that I'll be glad to show you pictures of someday. In our enlightened century, thanks to our highly developed techniques of anaesthesia, we have left such acts of violence behind us. Our first injection is waiting. The foundation of all local anaesthetics is liquid novocain, an alcohol derivative. But to take your mind off the nasty little pinprick, I can call on our television set for help. . . ."

(The First Program was running a film in which a famous dog was sniffing about in some shacks.) "Makes no difference whom he's looking for. Makes no difference what there is in the shacks. Because the very first shack, as though for our convenience, is empty. And in just such a cleaned-out shack Krings had a sandbox set up, long enough for the Arctic Front, wide enough for Center Sector, and equipped with the help of an electrician: all rather complicated, like one of those labyrinthine toy railroads that cost an incredible amount of money and patience, with electric switch towers, four-pole main switches, group switches and master switches, for every feature of the front, every offensive and counteroffensive, every withdrawal or straightening of the front line, every breakthrough, every second line of defense and every barrier was indicated by variously colored light bulbs; and each of the two contending parties had a set of switches governing this system of light bulbs. Very impressive. And guess, Doc, the name of the electrician who just drove the TV dog out of the shack and is now building Krings' toy?—Schlottau. Krings sent for the plant electrician and said: 'Can you do it?' And

Schlottau, the man with the unsettled account, saluted: 'Yes, sir, Herr Field Marshal General.' "

My dentist said: "Now we'll do a mandibular block, in other words, the nerve will be temporarily anaesthetized at its point of entrance. . . ."

(I am still proud to say that the nasty little pinprick didn't interfere with my film: Linde stood beside Krings, while I stood beside Linde who had taken up a position facing Schlottau. She had recommended him to her father. "Take the electrician. He's good. . . .")

"Now we shall need local anaesthesia to deaden your gums. . . ."

(For practice they tried the Metaxas Line which Krings had broken through with his Alpine Division on April 6, 1941: two offensive wedges, shock-troop tactics.)

"And now the same procedure on the lower left. . . ."

(Schlottau built a first and a second line for the old man to break through. He had the dive bombers of the Richthofen squadron saturate the positions of the Greek light brigades and then, when the green light went on, sent in the 141st Alpine Regiment—terrific!)

"Well done, Schlottau. And now we'll have to try at Demyansk. . . ."

Schlottau said: "But for that we'll need clockwork . . ." And my dentist bade me move into the waiting room while the anaesthetic was taking effect.

"Just a minute, Doc, just a minute! Demyansk

owed its favorable position as an offensive base to the successful operations 'Bridgehead' and 'Gangway'. . . ."

"But now if you'd kindly step into . . ."

"For the first time Linde manned Schlottau's second set of switches. She cut off the prongs of her father's offensive and opened a four-mile breach in the front. . . ."

"But now, my good friend, I must really ask you . . ."

"I'm going, I'm going. . . ."

"You'll find reading matter . . ."

(All I had wanted to say was that Krings began to come up against his daughter's will. With great difficulty—by stripping his rear echelon and even sending field kitchens to the front—he managed to stop the gap in his line. Even so he was unwilling to evacuate Demyansk. But who's interested in Demyansk today? My junior class?) As I was leaving the office, Lassie the TV dog was sniffing through the shack again, looking for—hm, whom was she looking for?

Quick, Stern, Bunte, Neue. (Quickly, getting ahead of myself because I was expecting something, I leafed through the offerings of the Homebody Readers' Club. Paper sounds ranging from limp to dry and monosyllabic splashing, as though he wished to promote bladder pressure. His indirectly lighted fountain, which is supposed to soothe the patients. I won't narrow it down to claustrophobia for the present, although paper was battling more and more vociferously with the fountain. I still had my hearing. Only my palate, my tongue all the way into my throat, and my whole nose were galvanized with mutton tallow.) Headlines: For or against the pill. Cancer is curable. One more version of the Kennedy assassination. Keeping up with the world in a waiting room, sharing in the anguish of the world: will she, Sophia Loren, lose her child again? It is a matter of concern to us all that after twelve years even this most tortuous miscarriage of justice—it was . . . hm, who was it?—has been righted. Photographed injustice cries out to high heaven and is quickly leafed away. Leafed away the black tide. Leafed away the South Sudan. But he lingers on and memories purr: Schirach says, was misled, repents and warns, lies with a certain sincerity, rectifies. When, for the first time in Weimar. A five-course dinner at the Kaiserhof. Bayreuth boiled shirt front and limelight. Fond memories. In shorts. "This, Scherbaum, is what my Reich Youth Leader looked like. Sturdy calves in white knee socks. And it wasn't till they sent him to Spandau that he became a Stoic. (Didn't Seneca himself advise his disciple Lucilius to leave the government service: "No one can swim to freedom with baggage on his back. . . .") So he writes away his ballast indefatigably; Krings might do the same: always start way back with that difficult boyhood. While still in high school the well-known Field Marshal General Krings—"At your age, Scherbaum!"—was obliged to defend the stonemason's shop, which his father had ruined, against the onslaughts of creditors. He had been a defender ever since. That is how he became a fight-to-the-finish general. From the basalt quarries on Mayener Feld to the Arctic Front and the Oder Barrier: always on the defensive. Never, except when he broke through the Metaxas Line, did he carry off an offensive. Poor Krings!—If I wanted to write for *Quick* or *Stern,* I might describe the Krings complex in installments in roughly such terms. Or perhaps I could compare it with other examples (Napoleon's Joseph complex, for instance) and raise questions: what misery might the world have been spared if the Imperial Examining Commission of the Vienna Academy of Art had not rejected the application of Adolf Hitler, whose real ambition it was to become a painter, but . . . For rawly dealt-with failures and rejects do not agree with our people. They are everywhere, lurking in wait for revenge. They invent enemies and histories in which their invented enemies actually occur and are liquidated. They think in one straight line, with a machine gun. They devise variations on the death of always the same adversary. They paint the word "revolution" on their mirrors. In books, they find nothing but themselves. They lie down in beds and keep getting up again. And never forget that trifling ancient rebuff. And cultivate their dark desires. Their desire to exterminate eradicate silence. And with masked toothaches leaf rapidly and hungrily through illustrated magazines. . . .

There!—There he is, wanting to punctuate with an Army revolver of the type used by the Wehrmacht in the last war for close combat and martial gestures. With the famous zero eight, now utilized in the Near East and in Latin-American countries, the good old six-shooter which I as a taxi driver had purchased at a rather steep price after three taxi drivers had been murdered in a single month in Hamburg; with this illegal instrument of self-defense—because you couldn't and still can't rely on gas pistols, and I've never had much faith in bulletproof partitions; with an honest-to-goodness shooting iron I left our bedroom shortly after 5 P.M. in pajamas (first reaching under the pillow; it jumped right into my hand) and barefoot in my pajamas shot first my three-year-old son Klaus, whose persistent whining and screaming had several times interrupted, then definitely put an end to my sleep, begun at 4 P.M. after a twelve-hour shift. The bullet struck the child near the right ear, whereupon he turned in falling and I saw, behind his left ear, the exit wound, which was the size of a tennis ball and began immediately to overflow. Only then did I pump three shots in swift succession into my twenty-three-year-old fiancée Sieglinde, whom I and all our friends called Linde. When I shot the child, she jumped up and was hit in the belly, in the belly and in the chest, whereupon she slumped into the chair where she had been sitting before jumping up, reading the illustrated magazines *Quick, Stern, Bunte,* and *Neue* provided by the Homebody Readers' Club, neglecting to pacify little Klaus with soft murmurings, so that I was obliged to reach under my pillow, leave our bedroom in my bare feet, and shoot the child and then her, my fiancée who had jumped up. Now not only my mother-in-law to be, but I too screamed: "Let me sleep! Understand? Let me sleep!" Whereupon I mortally wounded Mother with the remaining two shots (there was nothing left for me), shooting her in the left shoulder and then in the neck, but missing the carotid of the fifty-seven-year-old widow who had been sitting at the sewing table, so that after the shots Mother's head with its curlers struck first the cover of the sewing machine and only then the rug. She slid sideways from the chair, dragging her sewing along with her and emitted (after my shot at Klaus and my three shots at Linde she had several times cried out "Hardy!") gurgling and whistling sounds which I tried to drown out with repeated cries of "Let me sleep! Understand? Let me sleep!" This happened on the second floor of a new housing development in Berlin-Spandau. The rent for the two-and-a-half-room apartment came to 163.50 deutschmarks without heat. I have been engaged to Linde for three and a half years. The apartment actually belongs to Mother and to Linde and child. (They treated me and gouged me like a subtenant.) First I worked for Siemens, then I switched, because I hoped to make more as a taxi driver so I could marry Linde, you see I'm attached to the child. The light is fairly good in the rooms. And sometimes on summer evenings we sat on the balcony and looked out over the roofs of the development and saw flares going up in the East Sector, it's that close. My record is clean. I met Linde at Siemens'. She wound induction coils there for a while, but she had to stop because she was learning to be a hairdresser and her hands were always moist from doing permanents. We seldom had a fight, I mean a real fight. And when we did, it was always about the apartment, because it was far from soundproof. (But I always controlled myself. I haven't been violent since I was seventeen. But that was wartime and the kids were all wild.) When I was still working for Siemens, Linde even said to me: "Don't knuckle under. . . . Stick up for yourself." She was right. Actually I'm reserved and thrifty. For instance, I only read newspapers the customers leave in my cab. (And none of your two three beers at closing time like my fellow workers.) My favorite territory is Spandau and vicinity, but now that the freeway is open, I like it downtown too. And never an accident. I'd have liked to go on with my education but never could make it. Living conditions, and the kid always whining. And no real vacation in two years. Only once, just before we were engaged, we went to Andernach in West Germany for a few days, because Mother knew the place and thought it was lovely. We stood on the Rhine Promenade and watched the ships. That was just before our kid was born. I got a toothache because it was windy on the Promenade. But Linde insisted on having the child. After the war I wanted to go into the customs. But they flunked me on the test. After that it was simple. With the car keys but still in my pajamas (though I found my slippers in the hall), I left the apartment and the house with my empty six-shooter; I didn't meet any neighbors. The car was parked outside, which wasn't intentional, actually I should have taken it to the garage. I drove until shortly after midnight, first to Neu-Staaken, then via Pichelsdorf and Heerstrasse to Westend and up from Charlottenburg through Jungfernheide, Reinickendorf, and Wittenau to Hermsdorf, then back again. Anyway I had my radio on reception the whole time, because at nine the office began to call me. And the other drivers tried to reason with me. The patrol cars stopped me as I was trying to drive back home from Theodor Heuss-Platz, back up Heerstrasse and then Havel-Chaussee. I'm supposed to have said: "It wasn't me. They kept me from. My fiancée let the kid whine on purpose. They wanted to sink me, always did. Why did they turn me down at the customs? So my nerves cracked. Besides I've got a toothache. Had it for days. With a zero eight, that's right. Must be in Stössen Pond. Tossed it off the bridge. You can look for it." To tell the truth, I wanted to go back to Andernach this summer. We liked it there. I still owe the company for my mileage. Let them dock me and leave me alone. For the same money (and don't ask me what the zero eight cost) I could have gone to the dentist. Mine has TV to take your mind off . . . Why wouldn't they run my story, on the Today Show for instance, Low-Cost Housing and the Consequences? I'll act it out for them, the way I reached under the. Or for *Quick* or *Stern*. They take stuff like that. Then you could read it wherever you go, even in the dentist's waiting room as you sit by a fountain that's supposed to soothe you with its splashing, leafing and forgetting until the injections take effect, your tongue swells up, and the assistant appears in the waiting-room door: "Now let's try again. . . ."

My dentist complimented me: "Your observation is correct. In a mandibular block the tongue loses its feeling almost immediately because the anaesthetic penetrates the lingual nerve."

(Eased, tapered off, hardly to be remembered. One more twinge—but that may have been a reflex—then silence.) Outside it was snowing from left to right on Hohenzollerndamm. (Not the TV, the street side of the office.) The screen was uninhabited. Like myself: all fuzzy and, I may as well say it, deaf. ("I'm told that anaesthetized tongues have been maimed by the experimental bites of incredulous patients.") His voice was wrapped in tinfoil. ("And now we'll take off the aluminum shells. . . .") And my question—"What do you mean, take off?"—was also muffled as it rose up to fill blubbery balloons. Not until he breathed at me from close, too close, up: "They are removed with tweezers. Kindly open wide," did I surrender and make my big Ah.

There they were again, the carrot fingers. Hung the aspirator in place, forced my tongue into the back room. (A desire to bite. To be active. Or should I seek leisure with Seneca: "What do you think, Doc, don't you think toothache may have played a part in historical decisions? Since we know that Moltke had a bad cold when he took Königsberg, mightn't it be worthwhile to inquire whether Frederick the Great was hampered or spurred on by gout toward the end of the Seven Years' War, especially since we know that in Wallenstein's case gout acted as a stimulant. As for Krings, everyone knows that stomach ulcers encouraged that outwardly robust man to carry on. I realize, of course, that this interpretation is contrary to the usual German view of history, because even my students, especially the little Lewand girl, condemn any reference to the private life of historical figures as an unscientific personalization of history—'You and your personality cult!'; but all the same I can't help wondering whether toothache in particular and pain in general may not . . .")

"Shouldn't we turn on the TV?"

Not only outside, but on the television screen as well it is snowing softly from left to right. (Ah, the children don't want to go to bed. They're always thinking up something new: want to see Sandman! See Sandman!) In a weird cottony landscape pain-free animals were grazing. It was snowing cotton. No need to hear the little bells. Soundless movements. (Sandman West and Sandman East pass through twenty-five phases of motion in one second and refuse to recognize each other.) Sandman is a modest little helper. Sandman's only desire is to bring happiness. With cotton he daubed the pain-forsaken face of my poor fiancée, who lay thrice-shot on her bier. (Want to wake her with a kiss! Wake her with a kiss!) And when my dentist said "Now rinse please, rinse well," I didn't want to, I only wanted to see Sandman, Sandman. . . .

And so my vision was flung into the cuspidor:

"No, Linde, you shouldn't have done that. . . ."

"What shouldn't I?"

"With that electrician, in return for information about Papa's next offensive in the . . ."

"Intelligence work."

"And for that you lie down on cement bags. . . ."

"He clams up if I don't."

"I call that mercenary. . . ."

"Nonsense. I think about something else: About Petsamo—or the breakthrough at Tula, across the Oka to Orekhovo."

"Disgusting!"

"But it's all on the surface. . . ."

(At this point my dentist announced the end of my rinsing: "Still a little crumb over here. And here. And now we'll try the rough platinum-gold crowns. Would you care to hold them in your . . .")

The weight seemed right and the trial fitting was successful. Linde (on cement bags) did not enter the picture as long as I was dandling the platinum crowns in the palm of my right (unanaesthetized) hand. ("You see, Scherbaum, at your age you can't suspect the significance of a dental prosthesis in the appraising hand of a quadragenarian schoolteacher.")—"Nice and heavy, Doc."

When my dentist announced his intention of making an impression in special pink plaster of my lower teeth (and stumps)—"After it hardens the plaster is broken out and put together again outside the oral cavity"—I fastened on to two words: "Did you say broken out?"

"Unfortunately we can't avoid . . ."

"What do you mean, broken out? Like this?"

"There's no other word for it."

"But what about me?"

"We won't feel a thing. Only a certain pressure and

an unpleasant though illusory feeling that your teeth are being broken out with the plaster. . . ."

"No. I can't go on."—("You're right, Scherbaum. I'm not up to it. Let the class decide by vote whether to let me give up. . . .")—"Now my assistant is mixing the plaster. . . ." "I've suffered enough. . . ." (But my junior class turned its thumbs down. And Vero Lewand counted the votes.) "If you had known my fiancée . . ." (Only Scherbaum voted in my favor.) "Unburden yourself if you wish. . . ."

"She took up with that electrician. . . ."

"Wasn't his name Schlottau?"

"Like in a spy picture: The pleasures of the flesh in return for military secrets. There, Doc! Don't stir the plaster. She drags him away. Into the cement depot. In among the skids. He lets his pants, she her panties, down. She only lets him lay her standing up. She looks over his shoulder and sees the two stacks of the Krings Works and their discharge of cement dust. Finished. He's finished!" (My dentist broke in with practical remarks. He asked me to open wide and to breathe through my nose while he with a graceful little spatula spread pink plaster over the teeth and stumps of my lower jaw: "And please don't swallow. The plaster sets quickly.")

Poor Schlottau. No sooner finished than he has to talk: "Where on the Tula Front? With what divisions? Who's covering the flanks?" Linde takes notes. (And my dentist also retired to his card file: "You'll have to wait two three minutes. You'll hardly feel the heat of the setting plaster. Relax and keep breathing through your nose. . . .")

Meanwhile a commercial was on; and amid trass skids Linde says: "Mazda—sunlight in the home!" She digs out his last remaining information: "Where did he get winter clothing for the Fourth Army? Where is the 239th Siberian Infantry Regiment?" And over Linde's "Dippily-Doo, Dippily-Doo, the new hair-set . . ." Schlottau spreads Krings' sketch of the enveloping movement to be launched from the Tula area. In the midst of the Vesuvius Life commercial his electrician-fingers explain the itinerary of Krings' forward prongs to the Moskva River by way of Kashira. Linde laughs, sucks at a blade of straw, and cries out in offensive jubilation: "Fanta so cool, Fanta so cool, Fanta so cool to the taste . . ." The next product is none of your common soap powders: "Soak your clothes clean with Ariel!"—And now she proclaims: "I won't let him through the Tula-Moscow Line!"—Now she points to the railroad line on the sketch and advises: "Try Medicus shoes and you yourself will say: Medicus forever!"—Now she is photographing Krings' secret document with her Leica (as though she were advertising Leica as well): "I thought you wanted to get even with my father." Schlottau grins and makes propositions: "I think I can do it ag . . ." But Linde has the information she needs. She wipes Schlottau off the screen—"Margarine—what's our daily bread without it?"—pushes the deep freezer into the picture, and lies down amid spinach, chicken, and milk in insulated containers.

How she preserved herself. How true and fresh she kept. And how briskly she advertised frozen goods, in other words, herself: ". . . yes, still expensive, fresh vegetables for instance, but when you remember that our ready-to-cook meats contain neither bones nor waste and that the nuisance of cleaning—think of the bother of preparing red cabbage?—is largely avoided, then even our prepared dishes, freezer-fresh and ready to pop into the oven, are relatively cheap. And you yourself, Madam, don't forget to drop into our keep-fresh chamber if only for a few hours. Make it your fountain of youth. . . ."

With athletic vigor she jumped out of the freezer and started unpacking the deep freeze products: "Here, for instance, you see my former fiancé. I keep him way at the bottom, covered with chopped meat, string beans, and red perch fillets. At the moment he looks a little icy and white-haired, but once we thaw him out you'll see how well preserved he is for his forty years. Pretty soon he'll start spouting: date and peace treaties, art styles and fundamentals. Because his gift for delivering off-the-cuff lectures about historic turning points and Art with a capital A, about pedagogy and the absolute, about Archimboldi and Marxengels, but also about trass cement and centrifugal dust removers is still with him, and so are his lousy charm and his hypocritical love of truth. Only the state of his teeth ought to give even him food for thought. His so-called chopper bite has been preserved all these years. He has to go to the dentist and have bridgework done. His students—for he's a teacher, a typical teacher—agree with me and have voted against him. Now he has to keep still and breathe through his nose. If only he weren't so cowardly and sorry for himself. . . ."

My dentist placed his evenly breathing thorax in front of the screen and said: "And now if you don't mind, we'll . . ." and seized my jaw in both hands. (Why didn't he strap me down?) His assistant had to hold me down in the chair: Come on, boy! (No more talk of automatic devices and warm-water spray; the Middle Ages, palpably returned, transformed doctor and patient into two wrestlers measuring their strength.) Because I had no pain, I began to dream up pain: a pelvic presentation through the mouth, they're trying to deliver a plaster embryo. To break out and give birth to my seven months' secret. (It's all right, Doc!) I'll confess, I'll tell them everything: While Linde was doing it with Schlottau I lay listlessly with her girlfriends, first with Inge, no Hilda, then with Inge, in various resting places. But it didn't help: when I said to Linde: "Tit for tat," she understood me perfectly: "I'm glad you've finally found something to keep you from meddling with Father and me. It's none of your business. It's between the two of us. Anyway you have no idea, when he talks about the Terek River, where this Terek is and the Mozdok bridgehead that he wants to leave behind him to march on Tiflis and Baku over the old military highways of Georgia. He wants oil. Caucasian oil. You keep out of it. Or better still: Let's split. I have your interests at heart. Do you need money?"

His assistant pressed the palm of her hand against my forehead: no demon of hell, only the reconstructible impression of my lower ground-down and unground-down teeth lay on the glass top of the accessory table and, because it was full of contradictions, looked witty.

"Tell me, Doc, what do you think of the Soviet system?"

"What we need is worldwide and socially integrated Sickcare.—Don't forget to rinse."

"But in what system is your international Sickcare to . . .?"

"It is to replace all existing systems and . . ."

"But isn't your Sickcare, which I relate to my own project for a pedagogical province expanded to world-wide proportions, itself a system?"

"My worldwide Sickcare has nothing to do with any ideology; it is the base and superstructure of our human society."

"But my pedagogical province, in which there are only students and no teachers . . ."

"It will adapt itself without difficulty to the new therapy. . . ."

"But Sickcare is only for sick people. . . ."

"Kindly rinse in between.—All people are sick, have been sick, get sick, and die."

"But what's the good of all that if no system educates man to surpass himself?"

"Why do we need systems that prevent a man from finding the way to his sickness? All systems take health as their aim and standard."

"But if we want to eliminate human failings . . ."

"We eliminate man.—But now shall we . . ."

"I don't want to rinse any more."

"Think of your aluminum shells."

"But how can we change the world without a system?"

"Once we abolish systems, we shall have changed it."

"Who's going to abolish them?"

"The sick. To make room at last for the great all-embracing world Sickcare, which will not govern us but care for us, which will not try to change us but will help us, which, as Seneca has already said, will give us leisure for our infirmities. . . ."

"The world as hospital . . ."

"In which there will be no more healthy people and no obligation to be healthy."

"And what's to become of my pedagogic principle?"

"Just as you want to do away with the distinction between teachers and students, so we shall abolish the distinction between doctor and patient, definitively and—systematically."

"Systematically."

"But now we shall put the aluminum shells back on."

"Put the aluminum shells back on."

"Your tongue must be used to the foreign bodies by now."

"Bodies by now."

(A furry dumpling. Couldn't his Sickcare serve me an apple? But even tender sage-fed lamb would have been rubber to my cataleptic palate. I, so sensitive to foretaste, taste, and aftertaste, couldn't even taste the plaster. ("Oh Doc. To demonstrate a crisp apple, to bite, to be young again, curious and with clamoring palate . . .")

Instead, I saw a TV cook flaming veal kidneys. Relevant chitchat about recipes—"I hope none of us is prejudiced against innards!"—mingled with remarks on the protective function of my aluminum shells: "And don't forget. Neither hot nor cold. And especially no fruit, because the acid . . ."

Eye to eye with my absent palate the TV cook cut into the kidney. He tasted one morsel and then another, and if my dentist hadn't concluded the session and eliminated the cook by pressing a button, veal kidney would have become repugnant to me for all time.—Doubly relieved, I attempted a closing remark: "Anyway Krings started fighting one battle after another in the sandbox. His daughter became his natural enemy. . . ."

Then I gave up (for the present) and took refuge in the pain which is the right of every patient: "It aches, Doc. Well anyway, I feel something. . . ."

My dentist (who is still my friend) donated Arantil: "This will take care of you.—But before I let you go, suppose we consult the dental color chart and select a suitable tint for the porcelain of your bridges. I believe this yellowish-white with a suggestion of warm gray will do the trick. How does it strike you?"

Since his assistant (who couldn't help but know me) nodded approval of his choice, I agreed: "Fine, we'll take that one."

My dentist dismissed me with the (solicitous)

words: "And close your mouth tight when you go out."

I bowed to reality: "Yes, yes. It's still snowing."

A light beer, waiter, a light beer!—and an idea not soluble in water, an idea to which blue light gives right of way, a brand-new idea that will cut a clear path through the tooth-geared smog, so that we all— waiter, my beer!—all of us who flirt with the past and stir up dregs may return home over the military high-way, through the Red Sea piled up—waiter, my beer—to the left and right . . .

"Because, Doc, what and how much can we learn from history? All right, I admit it: I was disobedient, I ignored transmitted experience; because it was snow-ing outside and because I was making footprints in the snow, I drank a cold beer on the way home and had to take two more Arantil tablets with lukewarm water. . . . We learn nothing. There's no progress, at the most footprints in the snow. . . ."

Within my four walls my dentist was still present. He strung pearls, the triumphs of dental medicine, into a chain. He countered my ironic interruption— "When did the first toothpaste appear on the market? Before or after the toothbrush?"—with critical objec-tions to chlorophyll: "All right, it's refreshing. But does it prevent cavities?"

When he reviewed the development from the low-speed drill to the high-speed Airmatic—"And Siemens is coming up with five hundred thousand r.p.m. at the next dental equipment fair. Compared to that, my machine is a lazy old fossil"—when he held out the prospect of ultrasonic scaling and ultimate victory over caries, I admitted: "Maybe things are going ahead in your field, but history—despite the infallibly logical development of its weapons systems—can teach us nothing. It's all as absurd as sweepstakes numbers. Accelerated immobility. Wherever you look, unsettled accounts, face-lifted defeats, and childish attempts to win lost battles in retrospect. When, for instance, I think of the former Field Marshal General Krings and how consistently his daughter . . ."

Even behind my desk, surrounded by private bric-a-brac—fetishes that were supposed to protect me—he smacked several spoonfuls of pink plaster into my mouth the moment I said "Linde." (And right now he's asking me not to swallow and to breathe through my nose as long as the plaster is setting in my oral cavity. . . .)

Something is flowing evenly: Father Rhine. Carrying ships in both directions. And the two of us in wide-billowing spring coats strolling back and forth on the Rhine Promenade. (Having it out again under the close-clipped plane trees on the ramparts amid the Mary-thank-you notices.)

"What did you say? Say it again. I want to hear that again."

Two profiles whose substructure has found a bench. (Sitting and having it out.) Heads rigid. Only the hair gives an illusion of movement. Plus freighters passing through the picture from left to right and right to left.

"Don't make such a fuss. All right, if that's what you want to hear: You do it better. Satisfied?"

Now the ships count. Four coming upstream from Holland. Three have found their way through the Binger Losh and are floating downstream. That much at least is correct. And the reason: March. Gray-brown drips the tender springtime. (Leuterdorf still across the river.)

"What do you think, Doc, should I organize a trip to Bonn for my junior class? Visit Parliament? Interviews with leading political figures. And then on to Andernach . . ."

(Now the two of them are silent upstream and down.)

The traffic in both directions was stronger than my objections: Long-drawn-out perseverance with laundry fluttering on the stern and slowly hardening plaster over ground-down tooth stumps in which the nerves were silent. What I was really going to say—Schlottau wanted to get even with Krings because Krings had broken him from staff sergeant to private in Kurland—floated out of the picture with the barges. I've always been easily distracted. (Fade in any old thing: Irmgard Seifert feeding ornamental fish.) Long before there was a fiancée . . . (Difficulties in procuring school equipment.) Before I went to work for Dyckerhoff-Lengerich . . . (Heckling from my student Veronica Lewand: "That's subjectivism!") As a student in Aachen I earned my living delivering ration cards upstairs and down. My territory was Venloer Strasse. . . .

Once there was a student who delivered ration cards for a fee. He was engulfed by a nine-family apartment house that had remained standing between vacant lots. On his left the student of engineering clutches his oilcloth briefcase with the bread, meat, fat, and sugar-and-flour stamps, with a list to be checked off, and a few books on statics; on his right the bell responded to his thumb. "Won't you come in a moment?"

In a widow's apartment the freshman lost some of his timidity and the habit of straying from the subject. From those days, however, he retained—for now and then his vision was clear—the picture of a smiling, carefree sergeant in a standing frame on the bedside table in among the bric-a-brac.

The widow's name was, no, not Löwith, that was the party across the hall, who, when the student's right thumb pressed the bell, said: "Come right in, young man, my sister has gone to the rationing office for extra coupons, but I can probably." Soon—and better from week to week—the student learned to take the curlers out of her hair, which was on the red side.

No, reddish-blonde was the daughter on the second floor, whom the student had to help with her homework until she was successfully promoted. Across the hall the daughter flunked because the student wasn't allowed to help her. He had to debate with the mother until the son intervened in the discussion with a "Just wait until Father comes home from the prison camp . . ."

But even as a student I enjoyed arguments, especially as Frau Podzum always had real coffee and other little delicacies such as pork fat with cracklings and apples in it, of which the student without Frau Podzum's noticing—or did she wisely overlook it?—little by little carried off several pounds to the third floor of the house.

There a girl student lodger, whom pork fat didn't agree with, got pimples from my booty. She was squeamish in other respects as well, blushed at nothings, and kept a diary which the student had no qualms about reading and diagnosed as "a scream" until she burst into tears.

Heide Schmittchen, across the hall to the right, was something else again. She owned a typewriter and let the student use it whenever he pleased. Though she was only a few years his senior, there was something motherly about her, perhaps because she was childless and her husband (whom to this day I can see leaving every time I see myself coming in) took no interest in such things.

The fourth floor, on the other hand—as one could already hear on the third—abounded with children and smelled of Brussels sprouts. There two women in different phases of exhaustion and wrappers with different patterns said: "Come right in, young man." And the student learned and learned: to say yes, to say no, to temporize, to look away, to think of something else. The time passed under a wall clock and beside a grandfather clock, which had both survived the war. Where were the fried potatoes better? Where was there a parakeet? (On the left, I maintain, on the left where the grandfather clock was, because on the right nothing appears on the screen but the wall clock and the severe bespectacled face of a woman in her middle forties.) The student must have wasted a good deal of time at Frau Szymanski's, in the first place because the parakeet started out in good health (now I see him sick, huddling ruffled and woebegone on his perch) and when after a long illness he was back in his cage again, chipper and in excellent feather, Frau Szymanski wanted, in the second place, the student to stay and live with her; but he had ration cards to deliver on the top floor left. To whom? What did it like? And the wallpaper?

("You'll admit, Doc, I had opportunities that lent themselves to exploitation.") Soundlessly the door opens on the screen. Wearily a hand with three overloaded rings beckons the student into the hole. How adroitly he had learned to hesitate. He sniffs at the hand. He takes off the third ring: his fee. The hand is entitled to crawl down his neck. Now it is entitled to fondle his curly, always rather tangled hair. Now it unbuttons him. Now it pours something. Now it tears up paper. Now it slaps the student's face with the two remaining rings. Now she masturbates with one ring. And he takes off the second ring: his fee. Now she pours something again. Now comes sleep. Time passes. Now she puts water on for coffee. Now she cries before the mirror and shows a cracked face. Again time passes. Now she fiddles with the radio button. Now she lays down the last ring, now she signs (and I check off: sugar, flour, bread, meat, and fat stamps). Now she opens the door and pushes the student out: he is a grownup now and knows differ-

ences and nuances. He knows everything in advance
and feels his weariness afterward. He can compare
and is no longer a novice. Someone has graduated.
Leaving the attic, the student goes downstairs from
floor to floor and leaves the house. (I recapitulated,
for I was beginning to forget characteristic features,
such as certain patterns and flaws in the plaster.)

"No longer a student, no, Doc, the graduate
mechanical engineer Eberhard Starusch is amazed to
see how many new buildings have shot up in Venloer
Strasse which only a minute ago was half destroyed by
bombing. On both sides of his apartment house the
gaps have been filled (or as you say, bridged over).
The shop windows are bursting with goods shortly before clearance sales. The Consumer Society has set in.
(And, now that you want to break the plaster out of
my face again and for evermore, my oilcloth briefcase
that I carried on my left when this fairy tale began is
made out of new pigskin and swollen with my accepted thesis on dust control in cement plants; for
while I supplied my nine-family apartment house with
ration cards and the plaster was taking time to set, I
worked hard, passed all my examinations, and grew to
manhood, even if my fiancée did say later: "You're
still wearing short pants.")

"What do you think? Wouldn't that be a good subject?" My student Scherbaum is asked to imagine that
he's a student in 1947 and has to deliver ration cards
in an apartment house in Neukölln.

(When I left my apartment house in 1951, Scherbaum was just cutting his milk teeth.) Or I take two more Arantil tablets and call up Irmgard Seifert; but before I chew over old letters with her, I slip away to Kretz, Plaidt, and Kruft, I roam through the Nette Valley with Linde, climb (still in love) the Korrelsberg with her, crawl further back (there is always something before) and read my paper on trass at the cement producers' congress in Düsseldorf, go to work again for Dyckerhoff-Lengerich, skip Aachen (the apartment house) and, as long as Arantil helps (and Irmgard Seifert doesn't call up with her lamentations), sedulously pursue my crabwalk: When I was eighteen in a heavily chlorinated American camp near Bad Aibling in the Allgäu, a close-cropped prisoner of war who, with his nine hundred and fifty calories a day and full set of teeth (Oh, Doc, you should have seen my teeth!), had left behind him all fear of clearing mines without covering fire and was conscientiously attending classes.

For we Germans have a way of organizing even the most monotonous camp life profitably. (Some of my colleagues go so far as to call me an expert at drafting smoothly functioning school schedules.)

The prisoners doubled up in order that a school barracks might offer room and opportunity to supplant ordinary hunger with the hunger for knowledge: Language courses for beginners and advanced students. Double-entry bookkeeping. German cathedrals. With Sven Hedin through Tibet. The late Rilke—the early Schiller. A short course in anatomy. (And you too would have found a larger audience for your lectures on caries in the camp at Bad Aibling than today at the Tempelhof People's University.) At the same time the do-it-yourself movement started up. How can we make, if not bazookas, at least vacuum cleaners out of tin cans? The first mobiles (cut from American sheet metal) moved in the hot air over our drum stoves. Quartermaster sergeants gave lectures introducing us to philosophy. (You're right, Doc, especially in captivity Seneca can provide consolation.) And every Wednesday and Saturday a former hotel chef—now esteemed by all as a TV chef—gave a beginner's course in cookery.

Brühsam claimed to have learned his trade with Sacher in Vienna. Brühsam came from Transylvania. His lessons began: "In my homeland, in beautiful Transylvania, the kitchen-loving housewife takes . . ."

The curriculum was determined by shortages and absences: Brühsam cooked with imaginary ingredients. He evoked brisket of beef, veal kidneys, and roast pork. Word and gesture preserved the juices in a shoulder of lamb. His pheasant on wine cabbage and his carp in beer sauce: reflections of reflections. (I learned to imagine.)

While wide-eyed and spiritualized, our features sharp-cut from undernourishment, we sat in the school barracks listening to Brühsam, our copybooks—an American gift—filled with recipes that made us put on weight ten years later.

"In my homeland," said Brühsam, "in beautiful Transylvania, when the kitchen-loving housewife goes to market, she draws a sharp distinction between free-range geese and force-fed geese."

There followed an edifying digression about the natural freedom of the Polish and Hungarian free-range geese and the sad lot of the force-fed geese in Pomerania: "In beautiful Transylvania, which was my home, the kitchen-loving housewife chose a free-range goose."

Then Brühsam demonstrated how first the breast, then the rump must be tested with thumb-and-ring-finger grip. "One must be able to feel the glands in spite of all the fat in which they are embedded."

(Surely you will understand that your assistant's three-finger grip, which commands me to keep silent, reminds me of Brühsam's rump-testing grip; or to reverse the image as in a mirror, that while instructed by Brühsam I locate the glands of an imaginary goose, your assistant's fingers block my oral cavity.)

"On returning home," said Brühsam, "one must remove the goose's innards to make room for the stuffing."

And with our pencil stumps—one pencil for three men, everything was shared—we noted: "Whatever stuffing the kitchen-loving housewife may select, no goose can be said to be stuffed without artemisia, without three sprigs of rustling, aromatic artemisia."

And addressing us who were glad to find a bit of dandelion between the barracks to make a little extra soup with, addressing us humble pot scrapers, Brühsam listed stuffings. We learned and noted: "Apple stuffing, chestnut stuffing . . ."

And someone who was fifteen pounds underweight said: "What are chestnuts?"

That's how Brühsam the TV chef ought to exuberate today on the First Program: "Glazed chestnuts. Candied chestnuts. Chestnut purée. Never red cabbage without chestnuts. In beautiful Transylvania that was my home, there were chestnut vendors with charcoal stoves who . . . In the winter, on the frosty market places when the chestnuts . . . Chestnut stories: When my uncle Ignazius Balthasar Brühsam moved with his chestnuts to Hermannstadt, which is in Transylvania and was my home . . . And so in November, on St. Martin's Day, our free-range goose demands, no, cries out for chestnuts which, honey-glazed together with cinnamon-powdered apple wedges, rustling artemisia—never a goose without artemisia—and the raisin-stuffed goose heart, fill our free-range goose, whether Hungarian or Polish, to bursting and give the breast meat that little something which top heat and bottom heat, for all the golden-brown crispness they confer, can never give the delicious goose skin: that note of mild chestnut sweetness. . . ."

(Ah, Doc, if we'd only had your aspirator in those hollow-cheeked times!) Brühsam wouldn't let us out of his clutches, he refined the torture: "And now for the force-meat stuffing. The kitchen-loving housewife in my homeland takes ten ounces of ground pork, weighs two onions, three apples, the innards of the goose except for the precious liver—sprinkles artemisia over these ingredients, stirs in three soft rolls previously soaked in warm milk, adds grated lemon peel and a mashed medium-sized clove of garlic, and breaks two eggs over the mixture, salts moderately, mixes thoroughly, and, to give the stuffing body, binds with three level tablespoons of wheat flour. Then she stuffs the goose, stuffs the goose . . ."

(Thus began the re-education of a misled youth.) We learned and learned. From ruins and hardship rose undernourished pedagogues, proclaiming: "We must learn to live again, learn to live right. For instance, one doesn't stuff a goose with oranges. We must choose between the classical apple stuffing, the meridional chestnut stuffing, and the forcemeat stuffing. But in hard times when the supply of geese is large, but of pigs small, and when the foreign chestnut is unavailable on the domestic market, a potato stuffing"—so spoke the former hotel chef and later TV chef Albert Brühsam—"offers an excellent substitute for apple, chestnut, or forcemeat stuffing, especially since potato stuffing, with grated nutmeg to enhance its flavor and artemisia—never a goose without artemisia!—to lend that certain something, becomes a great delicacy."

In the autumn of fifty-five my fiancée and I—it was our last trip together—went to Posen for the autumn fair, where I took the opportunity to convince a few Polish engineers in the employ of the cement industry that centrifugal dust removers were a paying proposition. After the fair we went to Ramkau near Karthaus southwest of Danzig to visit my Aunt Hedwig, who, after long-winded conversations about agriculture in Kashubia and after a nice little family reunion had developed, spoke to me of the advantages of Polish free-range geese with potato stuffing in terms very similar to those employed ten years before by Brühsam; except that my aunt was not too familiar with nutmeg; she seasoned with caraway seed.

My fiancée dreaded the tiring trip, the arrangements for which involved considerable bureaucratic obstacles, but she grumblingly consented when I pointed out: "If I adapt myself to your family, which is rather strenuous, you'll have to admit, it won't hurt you to show a little good will." And so we visited my simple and rurally hospitable relatives. (And since they were the last remnants of my family, it was not without emotion that I embarked on the journey. We also went to Neufahrwasser, the waterfront suburb of Danzig; you remember, Doc, the place where, across from the Island, I once lowered my milk tooth into the still sludgy harbor sludge.)

"Well, my boy, you've certainly grown!" said my aunt, who was actually my grandaunt, sister of my maternal grandmother, née Kurbjuhn. She had married a small-holder by the name of Rippka, whereas her sister, my grandmother, had moved into the city and married a sawmill foreman by the name of Behnke; my mother, you see, grew up in town and married a Starusch, whose family had been residents of the city for three generations but who, like the Kurbjuhns, originated in Kashubia: early in the nineteenth century the Storoszes were still living near Dirschau.

"Now tell me what you do for a living?" said my grandaunt and took my fiancée into her field of vision.

(Over absurd resistance on the part not only of the

Polish but also of the West German authorities, I managed, immediately after our return, to ship ten bags of cement to Ramkau. That was Linde's idea.)

My fiancée promised Aunt Hedwig the cement needed to rebuild the barn which had been shot up during the war and still showed it, but my aunt was not to be deprived of her lamentations: "All we've got is a little rye, a cow, a calf, sour apples if you want some, spuds of course, some chickens, and a few free-range geese. . . ."

But these last were not for us. Ancient chickens out of preserving jars were put on the table; it seemed to Grandaunt Hedwig that canned fowl was more high-class than freshly slaughtered birds whose cackling had been heard shortly before the ax fell behind the tool shed. Perhaps it was out of consideration for my fiancée, because later on in the vegetable garden amid cabbages she said to me: "My, what a fine lady you've nuzzled up to."

Naturally a lot of pictures were taken. Especially the children of Uncle Josef, a cousin of my mother's, had to stand repeatedly in front of the shot-up barn, because Linde wanted them to. And toward evening we took the bus to Karthaus to visit my aunt's Great-Uncle Clemens, a brother of my late maternal grandmother, and his Lenchen, née Storosz: doubly related. What a reunion! "Well, my boy! And what a pity your poor mother had to die like that! She collected your milk teeth, she was just crazy about them. Everything lost. I lost everything too, except my accordion and the piano; Alfons, our Jan's youngest, plays it. Maybe he'll play for us later. . . ."

Before the family music there was more canned chicken and potato schnapps which, because my fiancée was such a fine lady, had been rendered loathsome with peppermint. (And yet the Kashubians are a people of ancient culture, they are older than the Poles and related to the Serbs. Kashubian, an Old Slavic language, is gradually dying out. Aunt Hedwig and Uncle Clemens with his Lenchen still spoke it, but Alfons, a phlegmatic young man in his late twenties, mastered neither the old language nor the Kashubian variant of the West-Prussian dialect, and only put in an occasional and grudging word or two in Polish. Nevertheless, students of Old Slavic would find it worth their while to compose a Kashubian grammar, because to date there is none. Copernicus— Kubnik or Kopnik—was neither of German nor of Polish, but of Kashubian origin.)

Because dinner had gone off rather quietly— Linde's High German was a wet blanket and my relapse into the dialect of the Danzig suburbs lacked assurance—my Great-Uncle Clemens, from whom, via the distaff side, I inherited my knack for pedagogical encouragement: "Look here, my boy, what's the use of being miserable? We got to be happy and learn how to live. And we got to sing too, till the cups rattle in the cupboard."

And we did just that in family style: my Grandaunt Hedwig, her daughter Selma—my mother's cousin— her husband Siegesmund, consumptive (he had a slight cough) and unfit for work, Great-Uncle Clemens with his Lenchen and their grown son—my half-cousin—Alfons, who didn't want to play the pi-

ano because he had a boil on his rear end, but had to:
"Wake up, boy. Don't be bashful. Bang those
keys"—gathered into their midst, the one as a relative,
the other as almost an in-law, my fiancée and myself.
Accompanied by Great-Uncle on the accordion and
Alfons, seated half-assed at the piano, we sang for
about two hours, mostly "Forest glade, forest glade!
Oh, how lonely and afraid . . ." and drank potato
brandy drowned in peppermint.

(In every sip of this Kashubian beverage the chemical extract of peppermint clashed with varying outcome with the musty smell and taste of a potato
cellar; just as you started on the taste of cloying sweet
liqueur, the crude spirits crashed through, and when
your palate tried to accustom itself to the peasant rot-
gut, the extract reminded you of the wonders of
chemistry. But over the conflict of taste lay, recon-
ciling and reuniting, the forest-glade song.)

"My boy," said my grandaunt as she was filling the
glasses, "do you think the Führer's still living?" (This
sense of intimacy with past history is forbidden to us
who endeavor to take a cool, scientific view; and when
recently I was so thoughtless as to quote my Aunt
Hedwig in class, my students held my grandaunt to be
deficient in political consciousness, as though I should
have answered her with Hegel.) "Of course not, Aunt-
ie," I ventured to say. And my fiancée, whose arms
had been attached by Uncle Clemens' Lenchen and by
Siegesmund the consumptive railroad worker—we
formed a swaying chain as we sang Forest Glade—
nodded in confirmation: Linde and I were of one
opinion.

"There you have it!" my grandaunt pounded the table. "He talked and talked—and look what happened!" (Even Scherbaum could not side-step this logic: "She's okay, your aunt. . . .") And once again we, my family and Linde, sang "Forest glade, forest glade! Oh, how lonely and afraid . . ." to the dregs.

At the end we were joined by an authentic family doctor, who had been called in by my ma's Cousin Selma to write out, very very legibly, a list of the medicines my family needed: a tonic for Aunt. Something for Siegesmund the railroad worker's lungs. Something for Uncle Clemens' trembling. (Though he didn't tremble at all when he played the accordion.) And for all of them except the railroad worker something to combat obesity.

Aside, the doctor said to me: "They only want all those things because they come from the West. It won't do any good. They should eat less and sing more Forest Glade. You ought to come here some November when they start in on the geese. . . ."

My grandaunt took the doctor at his word. "That's it, my boy. Come again soon with your fine fiancée. At St. Martin's you'll eat yourself sick. A Kashubian free-range goose. You saw them in the meadow today. And do you remember how we stuff them?"

I listed what I had learned in the Bad Aibling prison camp from the former hotel chef and present TV chef. "There's apple stuffing, there's the fine chestnut stuffing, and there's the forcemeat stuffing. And every stuffing calls for artemisia. Never a goose without artemisia."

My Grandaunt Hedwig was pleased: "Artemisia is

right. But we stuff our goose with raw potatoes and we pour off the juice. You're in for a big treat when you come for Christmas with your fiancée. . . ."

But Linde had had enough. The canned chicken backed up on her. She got pimples, heartburn, and stomach cramps on the trip back. (I even thought she was going to pass on, not an unusual thought for me.) She didn't feel better till we got to Berlin. It was almost over between us anyway. Because in spring 1956 she paid me off: "Do you want the money in installments or all at once?"

I decided in favor of a lump sum. Financially we were quits. And today I freely admit: I learned the art of stuffing geese from Master Brühsam. In a nine-family apartment house I became a man: knew everything in advance and felt my weariness afterward. Great-Uncle Clemens gave me my final polish and savoir-vivre as I was leaving: "We got to learn to be peaceful again and to live!" But it was my fiancée who financed the pedagogue in me.

(All the same I hesitated a long while to take money and let things come to a break.) When we were having it out on Mayener Feld at the edge of an abandoned basalt pit (because immediately after our trip to Poland Linde had resumed her so-called espionage activities with Schlottau), I said: "If you don't break with him I'll kill you."

Linde didn't laugh, she expressed concern. "You oughtn't to say those things so lightly, Hardy. Of course they won't kill me, but the word 'kill' might settle down in your little head and produce episodes that would produce episodes. . . ."

"Ah, how we overflow. Ah, how we are beset. Ah, how superabundance smothers us. . . ."

Housecleaning on TV. Bulldozers, first at play in an open field. Then they set themselves in motion, attack gadgets and cosmetics, crush upholstered groups and camping equipment, sweep second cars, home film projectors, and built-in kitchens into great heaps, undermine the foundations of high-piled boxes of Zymo (washes whiter), topple the children's bar and then the freezer, out of which—along with vegetables fish fruits—fall quickly thawing consumers: my fiancée, presumably dead, old Krings in uniform, reluctantly Linde's aunt, Schlottau with hand on penis, also my students colleagues relatives scramble with four five nine women over commodities and gadgets (with Polish free-range geese in between), roll and are rolled. . . . Furiously clatters the empty clothes drier. Rhythmically clap the students.

And the bulldozers push this excrescent superfluity from the background through the middle ground close up to the screen; bursting through curved glass, they empty it all into the room; the dentist's office is full up. I take flight, forcing my way through tumbled rubbish, through a serried group of people who want to talk with me—"What's up, Scherbaum?"—Where to? To the television screen that has been suddenly healed by faith: there my dentist is waiting with his assistant and bids me be seated; today two porcelain bridges are to be put in place, an acoustically rewarding procedure, interrupted only by rinsing sounds, while the dialogue between dentist and patient, to be edited a bit at some later date, begins to arise in austere Platonic balloons: the dentist advocates moderation, confidence in the continuous evolutionary process, while the patient (a schoolteacher egged on by chanting students) demands radical changes and a revolutionary approach.

For instance, he wants bulldozers to clear all the crap away, the accessories and spare parts, the duplications (second car, second TV set) and easy-payment plans—"Pay as you go! Pay as you go!"—the chromium and the advertising budgets, and remove it all from the consumer's field of vision to make room (as his student Vero Lewand wrote on the class blackboard) for new foundations on which to build a pacified existence.

But the dentist is equally well read: he traces every abuse of power back to Hegel, whome he refutes elaborately, largely on the strength of the peaceful evolutionary progress of dental medicine. "Two many mutually contradictory doctrines of salvation and too little practical advantage . . ." he says, and recommends that all government be replaced by his worldwide Sickcare.

Here the teacher discovers common ground: "Basically we are in agreement, especially as we both are conscious of an obligation to humanism, *humanitas.* . . ."

But the dentist wants the patient to withdraw his incitements to violence: "At the very most I'll tolerate the radical abolition of chlorophyll toothpaste with their unwarranted claim to provide effective protection against caries."

The teacher hesitates, swallows, is unwilling to retract. (Grinning, my junior class looked on.) Promiscuously he quotes Marxengels and even old Seneca who in condemning superfluity was of the same opinion as Marcuse. . . . (I went so far as to give the late Nietzsche the floor: "Ultimately, with the transvaluation of all values . . .")

But the dentist insists on my abjuring violence and threatens, if no retraction is forthcoming, to treat my lower jaw without anaesthesia. No more tender Sickcare. The instruments of torture are displayed. A dentist's threat: "In other words, my friend, if you continue to advocate violence, I shall remove your aluminum shells without local anaesthesia, and install your bridges, both of them . . ."

At this the liberal, and only inauthentically radical, schoolteacher (my junior class booed me down) capitulates and asks the dentist not to take his suggestion of housecleaning bulldozers literally, but rather to take a symbolic view of these essentially useful ("vital" was my actual word) vehicles: "Naturally I'm not an iconoclast, I'm not in favor of a totally destructive anarchism. . . ."

"Then you retract?"

"I retract."

(Immediately after my capitulation the dentist's office rid itself automatically of all the consumer goods and superfluous figures the freezer had vomited.) Muttering, my junior class withdraws. My fiancée takes her leave with a cutting remark: "And they let that creep teach!" (The Polish, artemisia-stuffed free-range geese have to clear out of the office.) It's properly rectangular again, sixteen by twenty-three and ten feet high. All the dental equipment is standing or lying in its place: the patient in the reclining chair is permitted, between the dentist and his assistant, to leave the television screen upon which, no sooner evacuated, consumer goods, upholstered groups, driers, camping equipment, and also—between advertising spots for mortgage companies and detergents—publicity is being made for deep freezers in which lies, covered over by fruit, veal kidneys, and ready-to-eat dishes, the schoolteacher's former fiancée, sending up balloons: "You super-yellowbelly . . ."

Now, as the dentist is poised to administer the first injection lower left but the television screen dwells on the deep freezer and its provocatively repetitious contents, the patient in the dentist's chair attempts once again to clean house. "Bulldozers . . . ," he says, ". . . . several thousand bulldozers ought to clear all that truck away, remove it from our field of vision."

But the violent word has lost its effectiveness. The freezer, to be sure, is pushed out of the picture by a telegenic spirit hand, but no bulldozers enter from left to right, playfully animating the background, then occupying the middle ground and undertaking the radical transformation of our environment. The screen has nothing to offer. (My junior class also refuses to appear.) Milky flickering. The nihilating Nothing. "Do you see anything?" asks the dentist as he weighs the syringe in his hand.

"I see nothing," the patient answers.

"In that case let's pretend this time that you haven't been so thoughtless as to advocate violence again. Of course you've spoiled the current program completely. We'll have to go without the evening news. To make up for it I'll switch to room monitor. Better than nothing."

The great consensus: framed by assistant and dentist the patient in his Ritter chair sees the assistant shape her hand into the left-handed three-finger grip and, beside the television screen as on it, help the patient to lock his jaw: her middle finger holds his tongue down, her ring finger blocks his upper jaw, and her index finger presses a cotton roll against his gums. Beside the screen and on it the dentist administers the first injection in the lower jaw.

The sound reproduction is excellent: both office and screen speak at normal listening volume: "We start with a mandibular block, anaesthetizing the nerve at its point of entrance."

(I saw what trouble he was having inserting the needle.)

"Your gums, as you can imagine, have been pretty badly bruised by our previous injections."

A camera—there's got to be a camera somewhere!—brings the patient's gums into close-up: the three-finger grip and the searching needle take up the entire picture. Now he has found a spot that has not yet been punctured: premonition catches up with actuality. The releasing pinprick strikes me (has struck me) in the picture and in reality: Myohmy . . .

"And do you remember what happens now?"

The secret camera abandons the detail transfigured into a mythological landscape and once again shows the patient in the Ritter chair between dentist and assistant.

"Now comes the local anaesthetic. . . ."

"Correct. Then we know what to expect. . . ."

"Look here, Doc, the rest of the injections are nothing new. We could get along without your sound, I mean not just on the TV. . . ."

"If I catch your meaning, you want to get on with your war games. . . ."

"My fiancée, Sieglinde Krings . . ."

"Wouldn't it be better if you gave your Krings a recalcitrant son. . . ."

"No advice, please, Doc. . . ."

"Suit yourself. . . ."

"I won't say bulldozer any more and you won't ever again try to talk Krings into a son."

"Agreed in the presence of a witness. . . ."

(Though, as the picture shows, without handshake.)

"I could draw you a portrait of Linde: a tough mountain goat that keeps her footing on steep slopes. Her plan demands sacrifices. She gives up her medical studies. (She wanted to become a pediatrician.) And later on she is also obliged to drop her fiancé. The new discipline takes posession of her. (I was asked to bring her thick tomes about strategy and tactics.)

We've got to show her like this: bending over war diaries, divisional histories, photostats of military secrets, plane-table maps. Dug into her room which gradually loses all its maidenly attributes and comes to resemble Father's Sparta. Occasionally all alone in the Gray Park. Often exhausted and depressed by data and contradictory information. Linde has just learned from Schlottau the electrician—we already know how—that her father is planning to fight the tank battle at Kursk over again—and to win it. Krings also finds himself obliged to engage in espionage and to recruit his future son-in-law. (I told him what I knew; what the hell did I care?) The family goes on the offensive: Linde's aunt is employed by the General and his daughter by turns to leak false information to the enemy. Pawns are displaced on the map. Feints. Veiled remarks at the dinner table. I am able to hold up my end only by playing the double agent and providing Linde too with information. Not without reciprocation. (I did the same as Schlottau. Or rather, she made a Schlottau out of me and let me only when I knew more than he did.) Sometimes I buy his information. Just as Krings buys me. Only Aunt Mathilde delivers gratis and in all innocence. Sieglinde Krings becomes a regular visitor at the Koblenz military archives. Registered letters are handed personally to Fräulein Sieglinde Krings. Which is not only her name according to her certificate of baptism, but also the name of a diversionary offensive on the Narva Front, baptized at the end of 1944 Operation Sieglinde. Afterward, to be sure, the success of this minor offensive was attributed to Colonel General

Fleissner, Krings' predecessor as commanding general of Army Group North, but that does not prevent Krings, after the recapture of Lauban, from naming a key position held at the price of great losses the 'Sieglinde position.' (Already in the tundra he had tried to have his gradually congealing Sixth Alpine Division rewarded with a victory rune identifying it as the 'Sieglinde Division'; but the Army High Command rejected his petition.) The sandbox offers late compensation: the tank battle at Kursk, lost by Model, Manstein, and Kluge under the code name 'Citadel,' is won by Krings under the name of 'Sieglinde March,' because his daughter couldn't get hold of the plans of the Soviet mine fields.

"Cut it out, Linde. You're not getting anywhere. This isn't a snipe hunt, it's a phantom hunt. Just ask yourself not once but a hundred times: What is a general? Or say it very fast: General general general general . . . What have you got left? A piece of cardboard. A term like 'layers of loess.' But 'layers of loess' means something at least, whereas the word 'general' . . .

"On the Korrelsberg she cuts short my definition of the general as such: 'Have you finished? Each general is a different story. This one refuses to admit defeat.'

" 'I'll prove to you that there's nothing left of this general but court costs. Tell him to clear out of the shack. The storage space is needed. Let him write his memoirs. Now at last I know what a general is: somebody who after a life full of death-dealing vicissitudes writes his memoirs. All right. We'll let him win battles—in his memoirs. . . .'

"I speak in the direction of the Laacher See. She speaks in the direction of Niedermendig. (And yet we were well suited to each other. She was capable of being entirely different. Frankly silly and not so uptight. And she liked to eat well. She could even be sentimental: she read trashy novels in the illustrated magazines. And she picked her movies for the love interest. She dug Stewart Granger. And she wasn't dumb. Politically we were on the same wave length. She agreed with me that humanity is terrorized by overproduction and forced consumption.) What today my student Vero Lewand demands as junior class spokesman was envisaged ten years ago by my fiancée on the Korrelsberg—there she is, look, Doc!—'All this truck, this superfluous rubbish—ten thousand enormous all-demolishing bulldozers ought to. . .' "

My stratagem of proclaiming the need for radical changes through third persons didn't go down. When I tried to compromise—"Actually, before the First War, Krings wanted to become a teacher"—my balloon was soundless. The room-monitor image was still there. My balloon was there too, but swept empty it said nothing more. His balloon filled: "See here, my friend. While I was giving you the benefit of four injections, I listened without a murmur. Since the beginning of your treatment I've let you indulge in the wildest fictions. But now you've gone too far. I will not tolerate incitements to violence, even if put into the mouth of a former fiancée or of a minor girl student. I will not stand by while the fruits of slow—often ridiculously slow—progress, and that includes my practice built on the principles of preventive dental medicine, are destroyed, just because your fiancée has run out on you, just because you're a failure, a washout, who draws on insane fictions to show that the whole world is a failure and justify him in destroying it. I know you. One look at your tartar tells the story. I suspected it the moment I saw your X-rays: Here's somebody, another somebody, who wants the transvaluation of all values. Here's somebody who wants man to surpass himself. Who wants to take measurements with an absolute yardstick. I know, he pretends to be modern. He's not planning to dust off the moth-eaten Superman, he's foxy enough not to speak of a new socialist humanity, but everything: his way of sneering at small but useful improvements, his passion for cutting knots with swift but unaimed blows, his hankering after the most pompous possible doom, his outmoded hostility to civilization, which for all its progressive trappings is nothing but nostalgia for the days of the silent film, his inability to work quietly and conscientiously for human welfare, his educational methods which oscillate between utopia and resounding nothingness, his restlessness, his capricious birdbrain, his malicious joy when something goes wrong, and his repeated incitements to violence—everything gives him away. Bulldozers! Bulldozers! Not another word. Off to the waiting room with him. I don't want to hear from you again until the anaesthetic has fully taken effect. . . ."

(I gesticulated. It amused him to leave my balloon without content. That was his way of building up a patient before writing him off. But I was absolutely unwilling to go back to the fountain sounds and the illustrated magazines *Stern Quick Bunte* and *Neue* ... I never again wanted to read what my Reich Youth Leader could remember and what evaded his memory. Every corner of the earth is ripe for the Great Refusal, so why not a dentist's chair? I braced myself for an upcompromising no. Let him call the police!—But the dentist punished his patient with tolerance and with his little finger gave him back his sound.)

Dentist: "Did you wish to say something?"

Patient: "I'm afraid of the waiting room."

Dentist: "Wouldn't it be more accurate to say you're afraid of escaping into still more fictions?"

Patient: "You don't understand. My occasional need to overthrow the existing order, if only in words, has a history behind it. ..."

Dentist: "Which, you must realize, is well known to us. At the age of seventeen, shortly before the end of the war, you led one of the teen-age gangs that were springing up everywhere."

Patient: "We were against everything and everybody."

Dentist: "But today as a quadragenarian school-teacher ..."

Patient: "At present my junior class is going through a similar process of clarification. My permanent dialogue with my student Scherbaum can't help touching on the subject of violence. ..."

Dentist: "It's my duty to take care of you. All the same I must warn you ..."

Patient: "So please believe me that my students and

I look upon revolution merely as the prerequisite for a better order, a pedagogical order. After a relatively brief period of violence . . ."

Dentist: "Perhaps I shall have to insist on your recovering a certain perspective in the waiting room."

Patient: "Please, no."

Dentist: "You make it very hard for me to take care of you."

Patient: "Fundamentally I am in favor of peaceful development, though I find it hard to believe in progress. . . ."

Dentist: "You benefit by progress!"

Patient: "That I will gladly admit, if only I don't have to go to the waiting room. . . ."

Dentist: "Dental prosthesis has a development behind it which I should term revolutionary—though not in your obsolete sense."

Patient: "Granted. If only I don't . . ."

Dentist: "All right. You may stay."

Patient: "Thanks, Doc. . . ."

Dentist: "But the sound has got to go, or else you'll start playing with that stupid word again."

(And so I sat silenced in the dentist's chair and saw myself: silenced in the dentist's chair. I thought the mandibular block and the local anaesthesia of my lower jaw had made my tongue and both cheeks swell up, puffed my lips and given me a bloated look, but the television screen knew better: nothing swelled, my cheeks were normal, and my tongue—I showed it to myself—had remained narrow, long, mobile, curious, and affectionate. I stuck it out. What my student Vero

Lewand could do at seventeen I could still manage at forty. My tongue lured: Come, Linde. Come. . . .)

In a fashionable suit dress, under a teased hairdo, she put emphasis in the right places: "Dear quiz friends! Today's 'Do we still remember?' show will be devoted to battles that helped to shape the destinies of Germany, of Europe, in fact of the whole world. . . ."

Her solemn undertone cartwheeled to a brighter pitch: "I shall now introduce our guests. This time they come to us from a Berlin high school. A terrifying young lady: Fräulein Veronica Lewand . . ."

Amid audience applause an intercut: There sat the three top classes of our school; and in the first two rows sat representatives of the P.T.A.

"Well, Fräulein Lewand—you don't mind if I call you Vero?—why are you interested in history?"

"I believe that history, especially the history of the recent past, is enormously important for the development of our awareness. My friend is of the same opinion. . . ."

"Which, dear quiz friends, gives us a chance to introduce Vero's friend, young Philipp Scherbaum, known to his schoolmates as Flip. How old are you, Flip?"

Scherbaum's "seventeen and a half" was drowned out by laughter. The familiar nickname "Flip" aroused merriment which Linde immediately squelched: "And who aroused your interest in history?"

"It's always been my hobby. But our history teacher, Herr Starusch . . ."

"I see. It was your teacher.—And now the opposing side, consisting of one. It gives me pleasure to welcome former Field Marshal General Krings."

After polite welcoming applause Linde dropped the "General": "Herr Krings, toward the end of the war you commanded Army Group Center . . ."

"I did. I succeeded in stabilizing the Oder Front. Koniev, my then adversary, said: If it hadn't been for Krings I'd have broken through to the Rhine. . . ."

"Which puts us in the thick of battle and brings us to my first question. Let's all think back two thousand years: After what battle did Caesar find letters belonging to his enemy, and what did he do with them? Well, Philipp? Thirty seconds . . ."

"The battle of Larissa in Thessaly. Caesar defeated Pompey, found letters in his camp, and burned them without having read them."

"Perhaps Herr Krings can tell us who informed us of Caesar's noble conduct."

The former Field Marshal General's answer—"We find a brief reference in Seneca"—met with as much applause as Scherbaum's reply. Linde put down the score: "And now for the battle itself. What position, Fräulein Lewand, did Caesar occupy?: Thirty seconds . . ."

My fiancée—in excellent form—led from battle to battle with adroit words of transition. I own that every correct answer given by my Philipp filled me with pride. (Why so amiably communicative here and so hostile in class: "What do we care about your Clausewitz, Ludendorff, and Schörner?") Marvelous how pertinently he spoke. Several times I was tempted to break in on my dentist who was filling out file cards:

Look, Doc! My student. He's beating Krings. His account of the weather conditions at the battle of Königgrätz left the old boy speechless . . . but soundless I kept my peace, especially as Scherbaum dropped quite a few points when my fiancée asked about the twelfth battle of the Isonzo. Krings described every phase of the storming of Hill 1114 in detail. The audience—even Irmgard Seifert clapped moderately—consented to give him a fair amount of applause. The tally keepers announced the provisional score: the former Field Marshal General was leading twenty-four to twenty-one.

My fiancée launched on a witty introduction: "There is a powerful animal which nowadays is to be found only in zoos and national parks: but since we have not come here today for a quiz about animals, I'll spill the beans: that animal is the buffalo.—Now what troop movement took place in March 1943 under the code name Buffalo?"

Krings smiled from the vantage point of his knowledge echeloned in depth: "The withdrawal of the Ninth Army and half of the Fourth Army from the advance offensive base of Rzhev." Linde's supplementary question betrayed her misgivings: "In connection with the Buffalo Movement the Field Marshal has spoken of an offensive base. What is your opinion of Rzhev, Philipp?"

"To call Rzhev the 'cornerpost of the European Front' strikes me as an exaggeration. Like Demyansk it was always in danger of being cut off, and if Zeitzler, then chief of the General Staff . . ."

Breaking the rules of the contest, Krings jumped up

and partly out of the picture: "That damn slacker, that rear-echelon lounge lizard! Zeitzler, Model—traitors, the whole lot of them! Break 'em to captain and ship 'em to the front! We never should have evacuated our Volga bridgehead. I'd have thrown in all available reserves and . . ."

I admire the elegance with which my fiancée stopped the General, whose offensive was becoming offensive, and appeased the youthfully hissing audience. The next round of questions permitted Vero Lewand to prove that Krings was planning to commit divisions that had shrunk to battalion strength or were unavailable at the time of his projected offensive: "You are operating with false premises!"

And Scherbaum said: "You've forgotten the thaw which set in in mid-February that year, and moreover, you've committed a division of Air Force ground troops that was already engaged in antipartisan operations in the forests south of Systchevka."

When my student Vero Lewand made it known that the Vyazma-Rzhev highway had been cut on March 2, Linde the quiz chairman announced with the knockdown gesture of an auctioneer that the Krings offensive had failed with heavy losses. "The final score is in. Our high-school students are the winners. Congratulations!"

Of course I was glad that Scherbaum had done well. The prize was a steamer trip on the Rhine for him and his girlfriend, with a visit to the Koblenz military archives thrown in. Part of Linde's face smiled: "But we must not forget our second winner." With words of good cheer—"All that happened so long ago, Herr Field Marshal General"—she handed Krings his consolation prize, an edition of the *Letters to Lucilius* on Bible paper. Immediately he quoted from it without opening the book; and the cameramen were polite enough not to fade out the quiz program until he had recited: "We are born into this life without prospect of mercy."

Oh, how disappointed I was to see nothing but myself again, still in the dentist's chair. Even my grimaces, benumbed and out of control, displeased me. Station break. It wasn't even snowing outside. Behind me I heard my dentist's pen racing over file cards. His assistant was feeding him figures, diagnoses and dental formulas, in an undertone. I was sick of looking at myself. ("Doc, please, Doc, won't you agree that the capitalist system inevitably . . .") But both in the office, sixteen by twenty-three and ten feet high, and on the screen my balloon remained empty. (I should have attempted the word "bulldozer.") Instead there was this babbling behind me: ". . . true overbite with Class 2 malocclusion . . . Correct plane by grinding occlusal surfaces . . . Extraction of first bicuspids . . . Open bite front . . . cross bite on the side . . . anterior inocclusion . . . true prognathism . . ."—And it was time for Sandman. Self-pity kept striking the same chord. (The lonely patient tries to oppose the emptiness with two homemade tears.) But the screen let me blink in vain. I tried the tongue test again, I displayed my benumbed dumpling to myself and to all the tired little children, but it was still able to do graceful acrobatics on the heavenly frosted curve, and played decoy bird: Come, Linde, come. . . .

And she came in a simple blouse and created herself in the electronic wishing globe, taking the form of the storyteller in the Children's Hour. In a folksy little voice, she thawed out deep-frozen products and for my benefit took the place of Sandman: "Once upon a time there was a king. He had a daughter and he did everything he could to please her. He started a war against his seven neighbors, for he wished to give his daughter their neatly chopped-off tongues for her birthday. But his generals did everything wrong and botched battle after battle until the king had lost his war against his seven neighbors. He returned home tired and sad, with ruined shoes and without the promised birthday present. Gloomily he sat down to a glass of wine and made gloomy looks until the wine turned black and sour. His daughter tried to comfort him—It doesn't matter, Papa. I'm happy and contented even without the seven tongues—but nothing could cheer the begloomed king. When a year had passed, he lined up several boxes of tin soldiers—his real soldiers were all dead, you see—in a sandbox that he had specially built at great expense, and won all the battles his generals had lost. After every victory in the sandbox the king began to laugh a littel louder, but his daughter, who had always been cheerful and gentle, grew sad and also a little angry at her father. She made a face, put away her knitting, and said: Your sandbox war is so boring because you haven't got a real enemy. Let me play the seven neighbors.

After all you did promise me their seven neatly chopped-off tongues for my birthday.—How could the king have said no? He had to fight all the battles over again, but his daughter defeated him every time. Then the king wept and said: Oh, how badly I've fought this war. I'm even more useless than my generals. From now on I'm just going to stare into my glass until the wine turns black and sour.—Then his daughter, who only a moment before had been a little angry, became gentle and cheerful again. She comforted her father, removed the glass from his gloomy look, and said: Let other kings fight wars, I'd rather marry and have seven children.—Fortunately a young schoolteacher was just passing by the castle where the expensive sandbox was, and he took a shine to the king's daughter who was after all a real princess. So a week later he married her. And the king had a lovely school built for them from the wood of the sandbox. The children of the dead soldiers were delighted. And the seven neighbors were glad too. Because from that day on they had no need to fear for their merry red tongues. . . ."

(. . . and if the teacher hasn't strangled the king's daughter with a bicycle chain or some such notion, she is alive to this day.)

Scarcely had she announced the end of the fairy-tale hour and wished the juvenile television audience a good night, scarcely had I rediscovered myself on the screen, when she—both in the room and on the screen—reappeared. It was she who briefly announced: "The anaesthesia has taken full effect." It was she who with her practiced three-finger grip commanded me to keep quiet. She hung the aspirator over my furry lower lip. And he, back from his file cards, struck me, regardless of whether I squinted to the left and right or questioned the screen, as strange and yet familiar. (Why, of course, you know that goat smell.) "Doc, is it really you?" They seemed suspiciously intimate with each other. (Didn't he chuck her under the chin before barking for the tweezers?) A shady pair. I caught glances between them—such as my dentist and his reserved assistant would never have permitted themselves. (Lecherous intimacies. He's just given her a pinch in the behind.) "Why don't you do something about it, Doc?"—No balloon appeared and nothing filled with my protest. Then I tried the direct approach: "See here, Schlottau, if you're going to palm yourself off as my dentist, at least let me watch the tube. The news will be on in a minute. I want to know what's going on in Bonn. Or whether the students . . ."

Victory! The sound has come on! (Or rather, partial victory. The screen was still on room monitor.) But my balloon is there and the sound waves carry my broadcast at normal listening volume: "Linde, stop fumbling around. Immediately!" (She obeyed.) "And you too, Schlottau, I've had enough of your byplay. The news, please."

(Schlottau yielded grumblingly: "The commercial's still on." But Linde pressed the button: "Let him look while we're twisting off the aluminum things.")

Twist off, she said. (I'll still bet that she spoke of twisting off.) Before I can correct Linde, Schlottau tosses my dentist's tweezers out of the picture on the right and from his pocket produces his tool, a pair of common combination pliers. The commercial is on and spares me the sight of a busy electrician in a dentist's smock. ("Go on, kid, do your stuff. I'll live through it.")

While my right eye takes in the hydromechanical action of a pulsating jet of water on my gum tissue— ("Say, Doc, was that you doing publicity on the screen: Water Pik cleanses and vitalizes!")—my left eye perceived Schlottau the electrician, heating his combination pliers to red heat over the Bunsen burner. Say, he's not going to?

"Schlottau! What is this nonsense?"

With dry grip she presses me back in the chair. What I feel between my ribs, feel intensely (because I don't feel anything else), is her sharp right elbow. Now Schlottau applies the red-hot pliers.

(And then you, in the shape of a plugger, said: "Water Pik is a precision instrument. It is equipped with an electrically activated pump. . . ."

—But already there was a burnt smell.)

"Something smells, Schlottau!" (Only plate, lip, gums, and tongue were anaesthetized, not my sense of smell.) "I smell burnt flesh. My dangling lip. Those red-hot tongs! Have you . . . ?"

But no pain, only rage. He's doing it on purpose. Wants to brand me. Because she wanted him to. (My rage was looking for expression.) While Water Pik and my dentist were displaced by whole-wheat bread, the smell subsists: rage. While the large-sized dishwasher relieves the smiling housewife of work, my rage mounts and wants to smash built-in furniture. Rage that wants to slash Dunlop tires and use Mazda light bulbs for target practice. Rage rising from my smooth-wrinkled socks through both trouser legs and bunching above my well-hung parts. Pure rage. Foretaste of rage that drowns out the aftertaste. Silenced rage. Rage silent to high heaven. (Never—though Vero Lewand has gone to great lengths to provoke me—has my junior class succeeded in putting me in such a rage.) Forty-year-old, stored-up, accumulated, cork-popping rage. It's got to come out. Ink rage. Rage unappeased by color, black and white hatching, layer on layer. Rage about and against everything. Brush-stroke rage. Rage projects: bulldozers! I draw, create ten thousand enraged bulldozers, which clean up on TV, no, everywhere, which attack, crush, pile up the rubbish, the superfluity, the lethargic comfort, topple it over and push it from the background, across the middle ground, up toward the screen—and then?—dump it into the dentist's office, no, into space as such, no, into nothingness. . . .

Once again I succeeded. They obeyed. Brigades on brigades of bulldozers flattened shopping centers, warehouses, spare-parts depots, cold-storage plants filled with sweating mountains of butter, conglomerate production areas, intensely humming research laboratories, flattened I say, assembly lines and conveyor belts. Department stores fell to their knees and set each other on fire. And over it all a chant: Burn, warehouse, burn*—and the voice of my dentist, who was trying to make me believe he had removed the aluminum shells, that there had been a little accident, that his red-hot tweezers had branded me.

"I'm very sorry. It's practically never happened before. But we have a special ointment for burns. . . ."

He wasn't the least bit sorry. Anyone who is so quick to say ointment-for-burns and has it ready at hand knows no pity; he's pleased with what he's done. Well, I was pleased with what the bulldozers had done. My grand housecleaning had been so successful that even Linde and Schlottau had disappeared. I own I was glad that not he but she was removing the last cap. I preferred to have my mouth stopped by his clammy-fingered assistant. And after my dentist had apologized over and over again, I gave in: "Such things happen, Doc. . . ."

I forgave him, but the evacuated screen was not to my dentist's liking: "You've done it again, you've conjured up the nihilating Nothing."

"It's always tempting, Doc, if only theoretically, to start again from scratch."

"Then you're pleased with your . . . your Nothing?"

"As a starter I've made a clean sweep . . ."

"By violence, my friend. By violence!"

". . . and now something can be built, something radically new. . . ."

"What, may I ask?"

* German *Warenhaus* = department store. The slogan "Burn, warehouse, burn" was coined by German students who believed "warehouse" to be the English word for "department store."

"The truly classless society. Its superstructure, I hope, will be a worldwide educational system not unlike your worldwide Sickcare. . . ."

"You're mistaken. Worldwide Sickcare is a product of slow reforms, so slow that they often come too late, not of stupid violence that can only create Nothing. We have taken the liberty of recording your demolition process. While my assistant and I are getting ready to install your two lower bridges—and just look at the fine work—you will see how after Nothing—and from Nothing—the status quo ante Nothing is created."

(When I tried to acquaint him with the demands of the radical wing of my junior class—smokers' corner, a voice in policy making, the right of the student council to dismiss reactionary teachers—he wore me down with clinical reports on EBA No. 2, the dental cement which was to hold my porcelain bridges in place.) "Since EBA No. 2 did not spring from Nothing but may be regarded as the product of many, often unsuccessful series of experiments, we can have full confidence in it; moreover, thanks to its quartz component EBA No. 2 offers insulation even against ice water, which cannot be said of every dental cement that appears on the market. But you despise the evolutionary process. You want to create by decree. Ex nihilo. Ridiculous. But suit yourself. Now we'll take a look at these ideas of yours about Nothing. . . ."

He put me off with a trick. Run off in reverse, Nothing became a consumer's paradise. The burned-out department stores (Burn, warehouse, burn . . .) caught fire again. The fire died down and left department stores full to bursting. My bulldozers, only a moment ago busily flattening production areas and butter silos, crawled backward and did construction work. They, which had been so skillful at overturning and crushing, built vertically and horizontally. Demolition specialists · shed their skins and became master restorers. Splintered built-in furniture, gutted upholstery, crushed second cars and punctured light bulbs fitted into place, upholstered, took up space, and glowed again. The research laboratories hummed intensely. The deep freezer recovered its old subtenants. (At the very bottom my fiancée kept fresh.) The publicity paean ran backwards as well as forwards. And when whole-wheat bread advertised itself, I was already looking forward to Water Pik: "Down with reactionary toothbrushes! Abolish those parasite germ carriers once and for all! We proclaim the end of the brush era and the beginning of the revolutionary age of the pulsating jet of water. A new classless era has been born. Water Pik is for Everyman and is also adapted to office use. . . ."

My dentist was already holding the handy, graceful appliance: "And with this beneficent gift to mankind I shall now, while our dental cement is being mixed on a chilled glass plate, give your oral cavity a thorough cleaning. For Water Pik reaches into every crevice, groove, and pocket."

He cleaned and healed simultaneously. Then he dried with hot air and set the expensive porcelain bridges in place, first on the lower left, then on the lower right.

"A net gain, I hope you'll agree: we have prepared four teeth for abutments—and now we install six new teeth."

While I wished I were out on Hohenzollerndamm, he termed his porcelain bridges "progressive" and spoke of "conventional" jacket crowns.

"Do you even know why they're called that?"

I was already pleading with Scherbaum: "Doesn't it tempt you even a little—to take over a run-down students' newspaper and make something of it?"

"A ledge, or shoulder, is ground in the tooth, for the jacket to rest on. . . ."

"It's a challenge, Philipp."

"But jacket crowns don't stand up under extreme pressure."

"You'll be able to publish your project for replacing religious instruction with a course in philosophy. . . ."

"In the fall, for instance. Are you fond of wild duck, partridge, and hare? There you have it. You bite into a piece of shot and the porcelain cracks." But Scherbaum was evasive. He had other plans. Couldn't speak of them yet. ("They're on ice for the moment.") My student left me sitting at the dentist's.

"With our type of porcelain bridge, however, the so-called Degudent bridge, there's no danger of cracking, because the porcelain is bound with the platinum-gold by an oxide. It's a special alloy, the Degudent people won't tell us any more: top secret!—All right, we'll turn back to room monitor.

But be careful in your choice of words. The newly installed bridges might be damaged. All our work would be for the birds. We'd have to start all over, from scratch, as you like to say.—Well? There you are. Now tell me: aren't they magnificent?"

Yes, definitely. How pearly and hungry they look. And how skillfully he had matched that color tone, that yellowish-white with a tinge of gray. An artist! They are more real than real. ("What do you think, Scherbaum? Has it been worthwhile? Or should I call in certain vehicles with caterpillar treads and power shovels . . ."—"I haven't said a thing, Doc. Not a thing!")

(Only then did I see, under the glassy film of ointment, the capital L imprinted on my lower lip. He wanted to brand me. I was branded. Oh, Lindelinde-lindelinde . . .)

"You've endured like a Stoic."

Promptly his assistant served me two Arantil tablets.

"Now we'll give you a week's rest and then attend to your upper jaw."

Temptation to lick the ointment. "It would mean a good deal to me if we could extend the rest period to two weeks."

They were waiting for me to leave.

"Appointments are available in two weeks as well."

"I've got to devote myself to my class. There's one student I'm especially worried about."

"Call me if you have any trouble. We've been

pretty hard on your gums. They show a tendency to inflammation."

"Scherbaum really ought to take over the school paper, but for the present he declines."

"I've prescribed ointment for the burn. And here's the usual little offering."

"Scherbaum is gifted, though. He's got something up his sleeve."

"The family size ought to see you through. . . ."

I left. And as I turned around in the doorway to provoke him one last time with an allusion to radical bulldozers, I saw on the television screen that in leaving I had turned around to say something: I said nothing and left.

Part Two

When Eberhard Starusch was obliged to consult the dentist, a course of treatment was undertaken which involved both his upper and his lower jaw and was designed to correct his faulty occlusion.

After the treatment of his lower jaw, the dentist and the schoolteacher agreed on a two weeks' rest period; and with the words "rest period" on his swollen tongue the teacher left the dentist's office as the local anaesthesia was beginning to wear off. Semiacquittal, vacuum limited in time, two weeks gained. "You know what lies ahead. Get a little rest."

When the schoolteacher approached his home in a taxi, the two Arantil tablets he had swallowed in the dentist's office had not yet taken effect. As he stepped out of the cab he was in pain and took to squeezing his house keys. Outside the house, beside the eight times six bell buttons, a student was waiting for the schoolteacher and wished to speak to him. As sometimes happens when students wish to speak to teachers, it was "urgent."

In freezing temperature the teacher had to open his mouth: "Not now, Scherbaum. I've just come from the dentist's. Is it very pressing?"

The student Scherbaum said: "It can wait until tomorrow. But it is urgent."

He had a dog with him, a long-haired dachshund. Both were gone before I entered the house.

He teaches, goes for walks, does his homework, nourishes hopes, recapitulates, thinks up something else, cites an example, evaluates, educates.

It means something to be a teacher. Something is expected of a teacher. There is a shortage of teachers. Students sit down at desks and look toward the front of the room.

When the teacher was obliged to submit to dental treatment, he said to his students of both sexes: "Please treat your poor teacher with forbearance. He's been to the tooth plumber's, he's suffering."

The teacher as such. (He sits in a glass house and corrects papers.) The teacher broken down into compartments: elementary-school teacher, boarding-school teacher, classical-high-school teacher, scientific-high-school teacher, not to mention vocational-school teacher. The educator or pedagogue. (When we say teacher we mean the teacher in Germany.) He inhabits a pedagogical province which is not yet fully mapped, which even in the draft stage is in need of reform, which for all its narrowness is held to be universal.

The teacher is a figure. He used to be an eccentric. Even today's students thoughtlessly say "screw" when they mean teacher; just as I spoke to my students of a tooth plumber when I wished to lend my dentist a sadistic note. (In our chats together we forgot about plumber and screw and did not let those crude classifications dismay us.)

He said: "Of course there are any number of anecdotes representing dentists as modern torture masters."

I said: "Regardless of what school or class a teacher enters, or what P.T.A. meeting he is obliged to answer to, the teacher figure stands in his way. Teachers always remind people of teachers. Not only of teachers they've had, but also of literary teacher figures; by and large the teacher figure is taken as a standard. The teacher in Jeremias Gotthelf. (We are always being measured against the joys and sorrows of some village teacher.) Raabe's teacher as the son of a teacher in his *Chronicle of Sparrow Street,* and ah, all those high-school teachers who have been said to be outstanding philologists—we are condemned to carry them all around with us, to be measured against them: Mine was entirely different. . . . Mine reminds me of . . . And mine, have you read?—And so I say: Just as my teachers entered into my memory and, measured against literary or even cinematic teacher figures, seem almost fictitious—how could my poor Professor Wendt expect to compete with a Professor Unrat, especially since he reminded one of Unrat, not Unrat of him—so I too shall become a memory for my students and be compared with—what?"

My dentist remarked that I was short on contemporary teacher figures: "Don't let it worry you. There aren't very many dentists in literature either, not even in comedies. (Except perhaps in spy novels: The microfilm in the porcelain bridge.) We're not interesting. Or we've ceased to be interesting. Secondary roles at the most. We work too painlessly and inconspicuously. Local anaesthesia prevents us from being weirdies."

Yet his reform projects struck me as adequately weird; just as he regarded my revolutionary stirrings as comical if not silly. His worldwide Sickcare—my worldwide pedagogic province. Two utopians blinded by their professions, he eccentric and I silly. (Am I? Must a teacher, dwarfed by his subject matter that he cannot help splitting up into tiny morsels, call forth the ridicule of his students?)

My students smile as soon as I throw doubt on the textbooks: "There's no meaning in all this, only organized chaos.—Why are you smiling, Scherbaum?"

"Because that doesn't prevent you from teaching, and I'd bet money that you do look for meaning in history."

(What should I do? Give up teaching, stand up in the yard or at the next conference and shout: Stop! Stop!? "I admit I don't know what's right, I don't yet know what's right, but this has got to stop, to stop. . . .")

On my slip of paper it says: I like this student. He worries me. What did he want just now? What can wait until tomorrow? (Does he want to take over the school paper after all? Does he want to become editor-in-chief?)

Often Scherbaum treats me with indulgence: "You oughtn't to take this business about history so tragically. Spring has no meaning either, or has it?"

Maybe I'm a weirdie after all. I should have closed my ears to my favorite student's plan.

To my dentist I said over the telephone: "One of my students has a plan. Listen to this. He comes up to me after class and says: 'I'm going to do something.'

"To which I reply: 'May I ask what? Going to emigrate?'

"He: 'I'm going to burn my dog.'

" 'Oh,' I said, but it might just as well have been: 'You don't say so.'

"He went into details. 'On Kurfürstendamm, outside Kempinski's. In the afternoon when they're busy.'

"At that point I should have washed my hands of it. ('Your affair, Scherbaum.') Or walked off. ('Nonsense.') But I stayed. 'Why there of all places?'

" 'The ladies in hats. Stuffing themselves with cakes. Give them something to see.'

" 'A dog isn't for burning.'

" 'Neither are people.'

" 'Granted. But why a dog?'

" 'Because Berliners love dogs more than anything else.'

" 'But why your dog?'

" 'Because I'm attached to Max.'

" 'A sacrifice, you mean?'

" 'I call it enlightenment by demonstration.'

" 'A dog doesn't burn so easily.'

" 'I'll douse him with gasoline.'

" 'But an animal. You're speaking of an animal.'

" 'No trouble getting gas. I'll notify the press and the television people and paint up a sign: This is gasoline, not napalm.—That's what I want them to see. And when Max catches fire, he'll start running. At the tables with the cake on them. Maybe something will catch fire. Then maybe they'll understand. . . .'

" 'What do you want them to understand?'

" 'Well . . . What it means to burn.'

" 'They'll kill you.'

" 'Possibly.'

" 'Is that what you want?'

" 'No.' "

I spoke to Scherbaum for about ten minutes. Actually I felt sure that nothing would happen to his dachshund. And to my dentist I said: "What do you think, should I take it seriously or only pretend to . . ."

He asked whether the inflammation in my gums had gone down and whether the little burn on my lower lip was starting to heal. Then he lectured: "First we must ask ourselves: Why ought something to happen? Something should happen because nothing is happening. What does Seneca say about the circus games? 'Is there an intermission?—Then cut people's throats in the meantime, then at least something will be happening.'—Fire is just such a filler of intermissions: Public burnings are no deterrent, they merely satisfy base instincts." (I'll tell Scherbaum that, I'll tell Scherbaum that. . . .)

Go ahead and do it. If no one does it, everything will just go on as before. I certainly would have. It's nothing to the things I. When, for instance, the submarine tender. That was in wartime. It's always wartime. There are plenty of arguments against it. And were. True, I'm not sure whether we or our dockyard apprentices who had formed a gang of their own un-

der Moorkähne and had admittance to the docks, because the tender was going into drydock but was still
manned when the fire first broke out on deck and then
penetrated to the interior, so that the ensigns and
cadets tried to squeeze through the portholes, and the
story was they were screaming so terribly that they
had to be shot from launches. They couldn't prove
anything against us (or against Moorkähne either).
We did different things. But we really did them. And
we had our little mascot. We called him Jesus. Jesus
was against fire. . . .

In the yard I said to Scherbaum: "Public burnings
are no deterrent. They merely satisfy base instincts."

He tilted his head: "That may be true about burning people. But a burning dog will be more than our
Berliners can take."

My pause was longer. (Vero Lewand was pushing
her bicycle deviously across the yard.) "You've made
up your mind?" (Then she pushed it between us.)
"Think of the papers, the *Morning Post,* for instance."

"So what?" That was Vero. "We know all that."
That was Scherbaum.

"They'll say: A coward. Why doesn't he burn himself if he wants to show what napalm is like?"

"You just said that human burnings satisfy base instincts."

"I still say so. Think back. The cruel Roman circus
games. Seneca says . . ."

(She stopped me with her "So what?") And Scherbaum spoke softly but with assurance. "A burning dog
will shake them. Nothing else shakes them. They can

read all about it and gape at pictures through a magnifying glass, or have it right under their noses on TV. All they say is: Bad bad. But if my dog burns, the cake will fall out of their faces."

Bucking Vero Lewand's resistance—"Careful, Flip. Now comes the old historical objectivity"—I rummaged about in the storeroom of history: "Listen carefully, Scherbaum. During the war, the last war, I mean, saboteurs set fire to a submarine tender in the harbor of my home town. The crew, all ensigns and cadets, tried to escape through the portholes. Their hips got stuck and they burned up from inside—well, you get the picture. Or in Hamburg, for instance, the planes dropped phosphorus bombs that set fire to the asphalt streets. And the people who ran out of the burning houses ran out onto burning asphalt streets. Water was useless. The firemen buried them in sand to keep the air off. But as soon as air got in, they started burning again. Today no one can imagine what that's like. Do you understand?"

"Exactly. And because no one can imagine, I've got to douse Max with gas on Kurfürstendamm and set fire to him—in the afternoon."

The link between us: the telephone. "Shall I report him?" My dentist asked me not to.

"I couldn't do it anyway. Me, me of all people, reporting anybody. I'd rather . . ."

He interrupted with an amalgam of dental medicine and ironical footnotes: "We can learn from the Catholics: a long ear and a silent tongue."

Scherbaum hurried away after class. I bent over my notebook. From the faculty room I had a view of the yard: he was mingling with groups he had formerly snubbed. Later he stood off to one side, near the bicycle shed, with Vero Lewand. She spoke. He tilted his head.

I invited a conversation with Irmgard Seifert. "Do you know," she said, "sometimes I hope something will happen that will purify us; but nothing ever happens."

Her departure from the Lutheran Church—she dated it from the beginning of German rearmament and termed it a spontaneous answer to her Church's acceptance of the Bundeswehr—that angry act of renunciation had only made her yearning for redemption more intense. ("Something has got to happen now. Now!") She trusted blindly in her seventeen, eighteen students: "This new generation, free from the burden of guilt—believe me, Eberhard—will put an end to the moth-eaten nightmare. These boys and girls want to start afresh; they refuse to go on squinting backwards and lagging behind their potentialities like us."

(Then and now: always flinging her words into great echoing spaces.) "We must set our hopes in the fresh, and yet so gratifyingly practical courage of the younger generation."

What else could I do but dish up a sour stew that nobody wanted: "Look back. What has become of us? How sobered and skeptical the war left us! How determined we were to be on our guard, to distrust the words of adults, the adult word!—How little of that is left! Settled citizens in their middle thirties and forties find little time to remember their defeats. We have learned to appraise the situation. To elbow our way. To adapt ourselves when necessary. To keep an open mind. Above all not to commit ourselves. Shrewd tacticians, able specialists, who strive for the possible and actually—when no unexpected obstacles arise—attain it. But nothing more."

This conversation began in the faculty room and was continued in my apartment. In my "bachelor's antrum," as Irmgard Seifert calls it. Objects stood listening. My desk with its beginnings. The bookcase full of Celtic shards. In among them Roman pieces from the Lower Eifel. Books, records. There were also books and records on my new Berber rug.

We were sitting, as usual with a glass of moselle within reaching distance, on my couch, coming close to one another neither in the literal nor in the figurative sense. Irmgard Seifert spoke over her glass: "You're right, though I hate to admit it. Undoubtedly our generation has failed. But those who put their hope in us, who expected us to become liberators— weren't they evading their own responsibilities? They had sacrificed us and now we were incapable of sacrifice. Marked by a criminal system when we were only seventeen, we were powerless to bring on the new era."

That was it—and still is, I suppose: The new era. Redemption. The act that purifies and liberates. The sacrifice. But when I spoke of Scherbaum and his plan, she listened with only half an ear, picked up books and records and strewed them over the rug. Impatiently she waited until I had completed my exposé of Scherbaum's plan and its consequences. Then she resumed her chant about herself and the depravity of our generation: "We were washed up before we even tried to lay the first stone. Now it's too late. Now they'll sweep us away."

"Who'll sweep us away?"

"The new, the unprecedented, the coming generation . . ."

"When I think of my student Scherbaum . . ."

". . . will sweep us away . . ."

". . . who is your student . . ."

". . . like so much useless litter."

". . . when I think of him and his radical plan . . ."

"You've got to realize, Eberhard. When I was seventeen, a loyal member of the League of German Girls, a Hitler bitch as you call it, I was already marked, already branded . . ."

"All the same, we've got to prevent Scherbaum . . ."

"Yet I thought I was doing right when I saw that peasant as an enemy and tried to destroy him. . . ."

Before Irmgard Seifert could lose herself in her camp for evacuated children I changed the subject: we chatted until shortly after midnight about school matters. First about staggered instruction and aptitude tests, then about subject matter as a challenge to emulation; not without irony we spoke of education as dialogue, but we also discussed the new, reformed version of the second state teachers' examination.

Inevitably we told anecdotes about our days as teachers in training. High spirits, rather strained to be sure, enabled us to see certain of our colleagues in a comical light. I parodied one of our faculty meetings at which as usual the problem of procuring equipment was discussed. Irmgard Seifert laughed. "Yes, we poor soldiers of the school front . . ." And when we had come to our favorite topic, the Hamburg attempt at an integrated pluridisciplinary school, when we agreed that this plan offered the only hope of doing away with obsolete entrance examinations and promotion requirements, when we found that we saw eye to eye as believers in reform, I thought I had given my colleague some encouragement. But as she was leaving—between apartment door and elevator—she looked again for redemption: "Don't you too occasionally feel this insane desire that something should happen, something new, something that can't yet be put into words, something—you mustn't laugh, Eberhard—that will bowl us over, that will bowl us all over. . . ."

(On a slip of paper I wrote: How bashfully-stammering my otherwise so cool-headed colleague courts her own destruction.)

Who keeps ornamental fish anyway? Careful feeding, precise regulation of water temperature, plenty of oxygen, the constant battle against parasites—and even so, today a fantail, tomorrow a zebra fish is floating belly up. The guppies eat their own young. Repulsive-looking in spite of indirect lighting. "It's absurd, Irmgard. Why don't you give it up?"

"Does your junior class behave any better?"

I phoned my dentist. When he asked about my health, I said "Fine" although my gums ached and I had to rinse every four hours. Then I developed my plan; he called it a typical schoolteacher's plan, but nevertheless said I was on the right track and gave me succinct practical advice as though speaking of a root treatment. He spelled out for me the address of a rather demented old number, whom I called on in Reinickendorf: in his private collection of faded horrors in the Ullstein Archive, and at the state photo office I found some twenty-five slides, some black and white, others in color, which I projected one afternoon in our biology room for Scherbaum's benefit.

At first he declined: "I can imagine what you're going to dish up. I know all that."

Only when I appealed to his sense of fairness—"You've told me about your plan, Scherbaum, now you must give me, your teacher, a chance"—did he give in and promise to come: "Well, all right, so you'll be able to say: I did all I could."

He came with his long-haired dachshund. ("Max wants to see it too.") So I showed the two of them my program: first primitive woodcuts featuring the burning of witches and Jews in the Middle Ages. Then mortification of the sinful flesh by boiling in oil. Then the burning of Jan Hus. Then the burning of natives by the Spaniards in South and Central America. Then the burning of widows in India. Then documentary photographs: the effects of the first flame throwers, of phosphorus bombs in the Second World War, victims of fires and plane crashes in close-up, Dresden, Nagasaki. And in conclusion the self-immolation of a Vietnamese nun.

Scherbaum stood beside the projector and asked no questions while I commented rapidly on the type of wood used for burning witches (gorse, because of the yellow smoke), on the concept of purification by fire (purgatory), on burnt offerings as such ("We can learn from the Bible, but not only from the Bible"), on the burning of books from the Inquisition to the barbarities of the National Socialists, on St. John's fire and suchlike hocus-pocus, and on cremating ovens. ("You'll forgive me, Scherbaum, for not wanting to dwell on Auschwitz.")

When I had run all my slides, he said, with Max in his arms: "That's just people. This is going to be a dog. Don't you see? Everybody knows about people. They've swallowed that. They just say: Bad bad. Or: Like the Middle Ages. But a living dog, right here in Berlin . . ."

"What about the pigeons? They were poisoned. Operation Civic Spirit they called it. Right here in Berlin . . ."

"Of course. That was a mass action. They were in the way. The whole thing was planned and announced in advance. Everybody had time to look the other way. Nobody saw it. That made it all right. . . ."

"What are you talking about, Scherbaum . . . ?"

"The massacre of the pigeons. . . . I also know they used to set fire to rats to drive rats away. I've also heard of incendiaries using burning chickens. But a burning running howling dachshund in a city like Berlin where the people are crazy about dogs—that's something new. Only when a dog burns will they realize that the Yankees are burning people down there—doing it every day."

Scherbaum helped me to pack up the slides. He fitted the oilcloth cover over the projector and thanked me for the special showing. "It was really very interesting."

When I returned the borrowed slides (I sent those belonging to the old gentleman in Reinickendorf by registered mail) I saw the absurdity of my defeat. (So that's how Irmgard Seifert feels day after day when her aquarium defeats her.)

I phoned my dentist and couldn't avoid listening to his regrets about my unsuccessful experiment: "But we won't give up and we won't let idiotic fate run its course." There followed a few quotations from Seneca and a few asides—"Protrusion of the upper incisors . . ." (His assistant was filling out filing cards.) Then he returned to the subject: "Does your student show any signs of pity for the dog?"

"Yes. Certainly. Scherbaum and his dog (really an endearing little animal) took me to the bus stop. Just before the bus came he assured me that the thought of Max's—that's the dog's name—sufferings didn't leave him cold, because he'd had him for four years after all."

"Then there's still hope," said my dentist.

"The companion of hope is fear."

He interpreted my quotation: "Seneca got that from

Hecaton, who said: 'If you have stopped hoping, you are no longer afraid.'—But since we're worried about your student and, all in all, there is reason to fear, I should say we were entitled to hope."

"I only hope the kid comes down with a good case of flu that keeps him in bed. . . ."

"Even that is hope. Even that."

My dentist gave me to understand that several dozen file cards on his desk were still incomplete. "You know that I attach special importance to the dental treatment of children at pre-school age. Caries is on the rise. The incidence in deciduous teeth is terrifying. Our statistics point to ninety percent after puberty. Admittedly a byproduct of civilization, but the virgin forest is no solution either. . . ."

Before we hung up, he did not neglect to ask about my supply of Arantil: "Have you still got enough?"

(I still had plenty of Arantil.) And plenty of slips of paper that I inserted among other slips of paper.—The boy is ruining his life. He's ruining my life. Where does that leave me, if he does it? He should have consideration. As if I wouldn't want to. Demolish. Clear away. (Ten thousand bulldozers . . .) Start all over from scratch. The primal revolutionary urge just before tooth brushing, just after breakfast: Down with the sanctimonious reformists, unleash the hot wind of revolution in order that a new society . . . This would be a good time for a school trip. To Bonn, for instance. We could sit in the gallery and hear what they have to say about medium-term financial planning. And when we get back, themes: Parliament at work. Or: "If I were a member of Parliament.—Or on the provocative side: Parliament or hot-air factory?—And of course I could call up from Bonn. "Linde, it's me. You know—me. Your former.—Yes, I know. That was a long time ago. And it's not only my voice that has changed. Yours not at all. Should we? Where? The best would be Andernach on the Rhine Promenade. I'll be waiting on the bastion among the Mary-thank-you notices, remember? I'll be able to get away for two or three hours. Not alone with me? The manager of the Hotel Traube? Oh. Should I bring a student along as chaperon? Very talented, name of Scherbaum. I've told him a little about us. I mean about you and me in those days. This morning we visited Parliament. Pretty depressing. And imagine, the kid wants to douse his dog in gasoline and burn him. Publicly. In Berlin on Kurfürstendamm, outside the famous Hotel Kempinski. Because the people in Berlin are crazy about dogs, so he says. . . ." But I could suggest it to Scherbaum if he doesn't give up his plan: Scherbaum, my former fiancée advises you not to burn your dog in Berlin where you'll only be shocking a few cake-crazed ladies, but in Bonn, the seat of political power. In just the right spot, before an important session of Parliament: just as the Chancellor and his ministers are driving up. . . .

When I suggested the main entrance to the House of Parliament to Scherbaum and his girl-friend Vero, he said he had already considered it.

"Why here and not in Bonn?"

"Too much confusion. The effect would be lost."

"Those guys would only laugh if they saw Max burning. They'd say: So what?—They'd call it a public nuisance."

"But Bonn is the seat of power."

"But it's only in Berlin that the people are so crazy about dogs."

I tried to cast ridicule on Scherbaum's local fixation. I spoke of an obsession and of a general tendency to overestimate the situation in Berlin.

Vero Lewand produced figures. "Do you know how many registered dogs there are here?—Well!"

She knows everything, almost. She talks didactically through her nose. She expresses demands in the plural: "We demand a voice in drawing up the curriculum. . . ." She belongs to a group that Scherbaum doesn't belong to. She wears absinthe-green tights and demands a course of study in sexology, not confined to biological facts. Only yesterday she went around with a metal saw: gathering star flowers—today she has stopped playing. A clinging vine, though: a burr in Scherbaum's sweater. ("Scram, kid. You have that musty group stink.") He tolerates her good-naturedly; just as he good-naturedly lets me speak: "Scherbaum, I earnestly advise you to drop this irrational project. . . ."

Irmgard Seifert listened to me with an expression of open-mindedness, tilting her head in a way that ordinarily gives promise of attention. She nodded in the right places as I unfolded the Scherbaum case. I felt justified in reading surprise understanding consternation in her eyes. When I asked for her opinion and if possible her advice, she said: "Maybe you'll understand: these old letters have changed my whole life. . . ."

When I tried to wedge in a sentence ("It's a relapse into ritual") that would rescue the Scherbaum affair, her only reaction was to raise her voice slightly: "Maybe you remember. During a weekend visit to my mother in Hanover I rummaged through the junk pile in our attic and came across a lot of school notebooks, some drawings I had done as a schoolgirl, and finally some letters I had written shortly before the end of the war when I was deputy directress of a camp for evacuated city children. . . ."

"You've told me. A camp in the western Harz. You were the same age as our Scherbaum is today. . . ."

"That's right. I was only seventeen. Let's even admit that blind faith in Führer, Folk, and Fatherland was general at that time. Nevertheless that hysterical scream—"Bazookas'—still calls my whole existence into question. I had the gall to arrange for fourteen-year-old boys to be trained in the use of that instrument of murder. . . ."

"But my dear Irmgard, your combat group was never used. . . ."

"No thanks to me. The Americans just rolled over us. . . ."

"And there your story ought to end. Who today would dare to accuse a girl who was then seventeen when our new Chancellor is held to be acceptable in spite of his past . . ."

"I have forfeited the right to judge the Kiesinger case. No one can acquit me. To think that I reported a peasant, a simple peasant, to Party Headquarters because he refused, staunchly refused, to let us dig a tank trap in his field."

"That worthy peasant, as you've recently told me, died a natural death ten year later; if you can't manage it yourself, then I'll acquit you."

This acquittal gave me an opportunity to become acquainted with Irmgard Seifert's wrath. A moment ago she had been seated, now she was standing: "Friendship or not, I forbid you to try to resolve my conflict by such superficial means."

(Later, still disgruntled, I noted a few caustic remarks about the chaotic conditions prevailing in her aquarium: "And how are your vivacious little fishes getting along? Who's eating whom at the moment?") In the faculty room I was still polite: "Your involvement, your sense of guilt, should give you the strength to guide these young people today who are unable to formulate their increasing distrust."

She was silent and I spoke into the void: "Let's both of us bear in mind that our Philipp Scherbaum is barely seventeen. He's suffering. The world makes him suffer. Injustice, no matter how far away, comes as a blow to him. He sees no way out. Or rather, he sees only one: he wants to burn his dog in public and so give the world—or at least the dog lovers of Berlin—a sign."

There she was again: "That's nonsense."

"Of course. Of course. However, we must learn to understand the inextricable situation the boy is in."

Surrounded by the order of the faculty room, she said: "It's irresponsible nonsense."

"No need to tell me that. However, I've been unable to dissuade him."

The archangel said: "Then it becomes your duty to report him."

"You think . . . ?"

"I don't just think. I definitely advise you to."

"To the principal?"

"Bah! Threaten him with the police. Then we'll see. And if you can't make up your mind, I'll have to do it."

(Irmgard Seifert has a thing about the police. Must I now say: still has?) My dentist disapproved over the phone: "Look who wants to call in the guardians of the law. Keep your dialogue with the boy. Dialogue prevents action."

Me an accomplice of law and order! He treats everything like caries: "Prevention is the cure. Not revolution but dental prophylaxis. Treatment at the preschool age. Campaigns against sucking and against breathing through the mouth. Blowing exercises to combat distal bite. Too much action, too many one-eyed victories. Grabbing at the moon when there's still no effective toothpaste. Too many men of action, too many knot cutters."

Can it be that action is active resignation? Something is trying to develop; it moves ever so slightly, and there comes your man of action and bashes in the hothouse windows. "Then you deny that fresh air is always beneficial?"

"Interrupting a process of development whose early stages gave ground for hope . . ."

Action as evasion. Something has got to happen. The agent, a juridical concept. What does it mean to gird for action, to convert something into action? (If my dentist wants to prevent action by dialogue, he must believe that dialogue is not action.) I remember what he said when he first saw my tartar: "Looks bad. We'll have to remove it, radically." What if I liken capitalism to this tartar that has to be removed?

And even so. What about my dentist's assault on my prognathism which he called congenital and therefore authentic? Wasn't that action? He will say: Knowledge plus skill, whereas the precipitate extraction of teeth, this mania for creating gaps that no longer hurt, is action without knowledge: active stupidity.

Therefore hard work, doubt, reason, the acquisition of more knowledge, new beginnings, scarcely perceptible improvement, mistakes allowed for in the over-all plan, step-by-step evolution: two steps forward and one back; whereas your man of action skips the intervening steps, rejects the knowledge that would slow him down; he is lightfooted and lazy: Laziness is the promoter of action.

And another is fear. Development, so it seems (and is), can no longer be read off. No bell rings to announce the small day-to-day steps forward. Immobility engenders a terrifying stillness, the stillness of the tomb, into which my colleague Irmgard Seifert sighs her "Oh, if something would only happen." Stillness as the losses mount. An anguished, cringing stillness, which Scherbaum wants to dispel with his action: Fear is a goad to action.

My dentist laughed into the telephone: "Children whistle in the dark. Even the creation of the world was a series of acts issued in installments, an anxiety reaction camouflaging itself as creation. A bad example that has perpetuated itself. Men of action call themselves creators. We should have had a talk with the old gentleman upstairs before he started acting. You know my thesis: dialogue prevents action."

After having written speeches for his Nero and supplied action with words, Seneca recommended inaction as the sum of experience. (Bits of advice he gave me.) Should I assign a theme entitled: What are acts? Or should I turn Scherbaum into Lucilius and thwart his action with dialogue?—It's easy for an active dentist to talk, a man who removes tartar or evil, who indulges in one radical assault after another. Men of action recommend inaction.

They were standing in groups. Scherbaum moved quickly from one to another. The dry cold had held since the beginning of the year. They stood in close-knit groups. (Talking their abbreviated Donald Duck language.) Vero Lewand made circular movements with her cigarette. ("So what?") And in between the groups sparrows in groups.

When I stopped Scherbaum in the yard, literally stopped him by cutting him off as he was going from one group to the next, I said with deliberation: "I'm sorry, Philipp. If you won't drop your project I shall have to report you—to the police. You know what that can mean."

Scherbaum laughed as only Scherbaum can laugh: not even insultingly, rather with a kind of good-natured arrogance and a note of concern, as though wishing as usual to spare me: "I'm sure you won't do that to yourself. You have far too much self-respect."

"All the same I've been thinking seriously how to formulate such a report if it becomes necessary."

"You'll never make it, going to the police station, and. . . ."

"I'm warning you, Philipp . . ."

"It doesn't go with the cut of your jib."

(She left the group what remained of her cigarette and approached in chartreuse-green tights.) Unmethodically I began to list: the absurdity, the arrogance, the danger, the bestiality, the stupidity. I lined up words like on the one hand, for that very reason, lacking in plausibility, ineffectual, unrealistic. None of my words satisfied Scherbaum. "I know all that," he said. "As a teacher, you've got to talk like that." And when I referred to an act of madness that would be applauded by the wrong people for the wrong reasons, Vero Lewand said: "So what?"

"Fräulein Seifert would say the same thing if she were informed of your plan."

"Oh, so the archangel knows."

Before I could smooth things over, Vero Lewand was at it: "Hell. She can't say a thing. She's always talking about resistance. Says it's a duty."

She parodied Irmgard Seifert, not by imitating her tone but by putting her delivery in quotes: "Yes, time and again, in our nation's darkest hours, there have been men who rose up and took action. They gave the signal. They faced up to injustice." With a snap of her fingers Vero Lewand let me know that it was my turn.

Across bridges such as "Now you must think . . ." and "Now you might say . . ." I built up a long-winded house-of-cards dialogue which Scherbaum, grown suddenly impatient, demolished: "Why don't you say: Do it? Why don't you say: You're right? Why don't you build up my courage? Because it takes courage. Why don't you help me?"

(The ensuing pause was hard to bear. No rhetorical enclosure to hide in. Go on. Take the leap!) "Scherbaum, my last word. I shall acquire a dog at the Lankwitz Kennels, I'll get him used to me, then at the exact spot you indicate I shall douse him with gasoline and set him on fire. I'll display your sign too. The press and television will be there. We'll make up a leaflet together, giving the cold facts about the effects of napalm. After I've been arrested or possibly lynched, you and your girl-friend can hand it out on Kurfürstendamm. Okay?"

The yard emptied. Sparrows returned. My tongue explored the two foreign bodies: Degudent, a special process. Vero Lewand breathed with her mouth open. And Scherbaum looked into the spaces in the chestnut foliage. (I, too, stood there looking, but I did not invent fixed points in the air, I put them in the sand: Störtebeker planning again. He has a plan. He has a plan. . . .) The last bell. Overhead a Pan Am plane on its way to Tempelhof.

"Okay, Philipp, okay?"

"Watch yourself, Flip. Mao warns us against the motley intellectuals."

"You keep out of this.—Got to think it over."

"No, Philipp, now. Okay?"

"I can't decide without Max."

They both walked away. In my pocket my hand looked for Arantil: that safety island.

"I see, I see." My dentist said: "You're playing for time. Acquire dog. Accustom dog to master. Let Scherbaum's plan go to seed. Maybe something will happen in the meantime. There's always the hope of a truce. Or the Pope will give the world another peace encyclical. Stock market irregular. Special peace ambassadors meeting on neutral grounds. Not bad, your tactics, not bad."

"I simply refuse to stand idle while the boy runs the risk of being lynched."

He was unconvinced.—"Just what I've been saying: your tactics may succeed"—and I myself never believed for more than half a sentence in my attempt to save my student. (And as I shaved before the mirror I was determined to do it, to do it. . . .) He knew me in and out. He had analyzed my chipped-off tartar: "Try to find a covered bitch in Lankwitz. That will give your student a chance to release you from your promise. He'll never expect you to burn an expectant mother."

"The cynicism of your suggestions betrays their medical origin."

"Nonsense. I'm only carrying your own idea to its logical conclusion. In any case it will be interesting to know what the boy and his dachshund decide together."

Suppose he says yes. Suppose it falls on me? Suppose between quote and unquote he simply says "Yes"?—It will relieve me of the need to make decisions. (Including those of a personal nature.) I shall be able to write finis: West Berlin schoolteacher, 40, protests war in Vietnam by publicly burning spitz dog . . . But not on Kurfürstendamm. Better reconsider the Bundestag. More effective as a gesture of protest, more serious. Have to plan carefully. Press release to all the agencies. Before an important interpellation. I could write my former fiancée: "Dear Linde, come, please come to Bonn, outside the Bundestag, main entrance. And do bring the children. Your husband too, if you must. There's something I want to show you, no, prove to you. Now at last you'll realize that I'm not the affable, self-pitying underdog you insisted on turning into a schoolteacher, but a man, yes, a man of action. Come, Linde, come! I am going to give the world a signal. . . ."

My teaching benefited by the tense student-teacher relationship. I tried, always on the basis of facts, to acquaint Scherbaum with the chaos of history. (Except for him and Vero Lewand the class doesn't amount to much: middling muddlers.) I set out to show the absurdity of supposedly rational actions. Departing from the curriculum, we discussed the French Revolution and its consequences. I began with the causes. (The ideas of the Enlightenment: Montesquieu, Rousseau. The Physiocrats' critique of the mercantilist system and of the hierarchical society.) I wore myself out calling Scherbaum's attention to the debates between the exponents of liberal democracy and of "total" democracy. (Leading to the subsequent conflicts between parliamentary—formal—democracy and the Soviet system.) We discussed the moral justification of terror. For a whole hour I dissected the timeless slogan "Peace to the huts, war on the palaces!" Finally I demonstrated how—and how insatiably— the Revolution devours its children. (Büchner's Danton as a witness to absurdity.) And it all ended in reformism. With a little patience, they could have had the same thing at less cost. That's where Napoleon came in. Revolution as repetition. Short excursions: Cromwell, Stalin. Inevitable absurdities: revolution creates restoration, which has to be eliminated by revolution. Similar processes outside of France: Forster in Mainz. (How the wind goes out of his sails. How he dies in misery. How Paris takes him in and spits him out.) And taking Switzerland as an example I showed Pestalozzi turning away from revolution because it bogs down in petty reforms, where he aimed at a great change, the birth of a new man. (Similarly Marcuse. Flight into the doctrine of salvation: pacified man.) Cautiously I cited Seneca before citing the resigned Pestalozzi: "One day better men will call on better men to lead them. . . ."

Previously I noted my misgivings: Maybe Scherbaum will laugh if I attack him cautiously with Seneca and long-windedly with Pestalozzi. Let him laugh. Laughter, too, prevents action.

But he remained attentive and as usual skeptical. No laugh-dimples.

A dog cemetery flanks the driveway leading to the Lankwitz Kennels. Tombstones (child size) tell the story of Putzi, Rolf, Harras, Bianca. Old women come time and again and pluck at the ivy. Here and there a photograph is encased in the marble. Inscriptions speak of fidelity, unforgettable fidelity.

Before school Scherbaum was waiting at the bus stop: "We've thought it over. No dice."

"May I ask you your reason or reasons?"

"Your suggestion almost made us weaken."

"An understandable weakness . . ."

"I have to admit it: we're afraid. . . ."

"Let me do it, Scherbaum. Maybe it sound pretentious at this point, but I'm not afraid."

"Exactly. That's why it's no dice."

"That's hairsplitting."

"Such a thing can only be done by someone who is afraid."

"I used to be afraid. . . ."

"Because I've come to realize that what's done without fear doesn't count. You only want to do it to prevent me from doing it. You don't believe in it. You're over thirty, all you care about is limiting the damage."

(There I stood, Eberhard Starusch schoolteacher,

unafraid and interested only in limiting the damage, there I stood with my Arantil-masked aches and pains. I'm afraid of toothache, though. That's what I should have said.—And when he prepares to administer the local anaesthetic, I'm afraid of the nasty little pinprick. . . .)

"Then you think that because I'm over thirty I've lost my purity and with it my fear. That because I'm impure I can't make a sacrifice."

Scherbaum looked for dots in the air and probably found them: "Purity and sacrifice have nothing to do with it. Sometimes you talk like the archangel, just as pompous. Sacrifice is something symbolic. What we want to do has a purpose. But it won't work if we're not afraid."

A matter of words. "Scherbaum, if a man is afraid of doing something and does it all the same because he thinks it will achieve a political or if you will humanitarian purpose, he is making a sacrifice, he is sacrificing himself."

"Perhaps. In any case your motives must be absolutely pure." Like Vero Lewand stopping me in the corridor—"If you don't stop undermining Flip's morale with your impure maneuvers . . ."—or Irmgard Seifert waylaying me in our free period: "Eberhard, I resent your answering my problems with flippant suggestions. If there's any solution for me, it must be absolutely pure. Do you understand?!"

My dentist comforted me with scientific refutations of purity that were not new to me. I had dropped in "for a checkup."—He smiled all-knowingly and irritated me by drawing me into his first person plural: "We two impure creatures," he said, referring to the bridges in my lower jaw. "Even this Degudent platinum-gold which is intended to give you a normal articulation is impure by implication; it is a special alloy patented by Degussa, which maintains rather shady business connections in South Africa. Wherever you look, there's a fly in the ointment. But I'm amazed that even your student whom I took to be a levelheaded young fellow, for all his youthful extravagance, should make such absolute demands."

By the time he had checked my bridges, painted my still inflamed gums, and coated the slowly healing burn on my lower lip with a vitreous ointment, we had come to an agreement: "With all its display of realism, this younger generation is looking for a new myth. Watch your step!"

(She anticipates my plans. She counts my wishes on her fingers: today it's this one's turn.) Shortly before midnight she was standing beside me at my corner bar: "I thought I'd find you here or at Reimann's."

She let me order her a coke and a schnapps. (Just don't line up questions. Let her start in. The old peasant rule: If you're out to buy a pig, talk about the weather.) "Formerly, before I had the pleasure of practicing the teaching profession, I worked in the cement industry. The cement workers used to drink one or two schnappses before breakfast, though not with a coke for a chaser. They preferred several bottles of Nette beer. The Nette is a little river in the Lower Eifel. It winds picturesquely through Germany's largest pumice-mining region. Pumice makes people thirsty. Of course I don't know if you're interested in pumice. Be that as it may, pumice, geologically speaking, is one of the Laach trachytic tuffs. With the ejection of these tuffs, volcanic activity in the Laacher See region came to an end. . . ."

"Why don't you leave Flip alone?"

(There she goes, and she doesn't give a damn about pumice.) "I believe, Fräulein Lewand, that you call yourself a Marxist. Consequently I fail to understand why you take so little interest in the conditions of the workers in the pumice industry. I too regard myself as a Marxist. . . ."

"You're a liberal. Know what Mao says about liberals: 'They claim to support Marxism but they're not prepared to put it into practice.' You can't make up your mind."

"Right. I'm a liberal Marxist who can't make up his mind."

"You talk about Marxism, but in your actions you're a liberal. That's why you're trying to talk Flip into a corner. But you won't succeed."

(Wouldn't it be better to play tiddlywinks? And yet she can be pretty in her duffel coat. . . .)

"Waiter, a light beer."

"I'll have a schnapps."

"My dear Veronica. Surely it's also in your interest that I should call Philipp's attention to the consequence of so absurd a sacrifice."

(That nasal intensity.) Vero Lewand spoke softly —with, why not say it, an inner fervor—to the rows of bottles behind the bar: "In *The Foolish Old Man Who Removed the Mountains,* Mao says: 'Be resolute, fear no sacrifice and surmount every difficulty to win victory.'—That's what it comes to. I'll run along now. All you know how to do is interpret, you don't know how to change things. And the third revolution's just around the corner. It's only a handful of reactionaries that haven't caught on yet."

When she had gone, my beer came. I should like to have told her about the sadness of my better knowledge. About my hesitation and my reluctance to put words on barricades. (Also how the word "sacrifice" stops my ears: After months of self-sacrificing combat service, the Sixth Army . . . A little sacrifice for Winter Aid . . . Sacrifice sacrifice . . .) Ah, how is the gold become dim.

Nevertheless my proposal took the luster out of Scherbaum's pure and yet purposive sacrificial project: he rang my bell, declined to come in, had Max on the leash, and said: "We like the idea of the dog from the kennel. It doesn't have to be Max. I'll go out to Lankwitz and buy a white spitz if they've got one. Have you any idea how much they ask for a spitz without a pedigree?"

He wanted to borrow money from me; he was fairly direct about it: "I'm always kind of short toward the end of the month"—and nevertheless refused to set foot in my apartment when I asked for a moment to think it over: "I'll make some tea, Philipp, and we'll discuss the matter calmly."

"Vero's waiting downstairs. It'll be all right if you give me the money tomorrow."

"You're asking a good deal of me. You want me to lend you money so you can buy a spitz, douse him with gasoline, and burn him publicly, but at the same time you refuse to let me examine your, frankly, rather erratic mental processes. That's unfair."

"Well, if you don't want to . . ."

"Only yesterday everything had to be 'absolutely pure,' and today you're cooking up an impure compromise, asking money of an adult who doesn't believe in your project and isn't even afraid. Why are you adulterating your sacrifice?"

"You shouldn't ask questions, you should help."

"Very well. You're afraid for Max's sake. Your fear is understandable. And now you want me and a nameless spitz from the Lankwitz Kennels, if possible a bitch that has just been covered, to pay for your pathetic, yes pathetic cowardice."

"Lankwitz was your idea."

"Which I intended to carry out in your interest."

"But you yourself might have bought a spitz."

"Not to save your Max. It was for you, Scherbaum, for you! But your plan is exploitation, rank imperialism. Spare your own dog and sacrifice some mutt. I don't like it."

"Neither do I. You're probably right."

Scherbaum left me standing in the open doorway, overlooked the elevator and ran, no fled downstairs with his Max.—I poured myself a cup of tea, took two or three sips and let it grow cold.

(I'm pleased with myself. Am I pleased with myself? Slight gains in the afternoon, crumbling away as night falls.)

"You ought to have lent him the money," said my dentist. "Time-consuming complications: The trip to Lankwitz. Selecting and buying a dog. Buying a leash. The presence of the white spitz in his parents' home. Explaining to his mother who is expected to explain to his father—or vice versa. Then, if all goes well, a friendship grows up between dachshund and spitz. Comical scuffles, snapping, and sitting up on hind legs. Maybe your student has a little sister . . ."

"No, no sister."—"Only a hypothesis. And the child takes a liking to the spitz, claims him, with the support of the parents, for herself. All these incalculable consequences would have repeatedly and increasingly messed up your student's plan."—"Speculation, Doc. Pure speculation."—"But that's not all: The new situation would have enabled you to play off the dachshund against the spitz. First with insidious questions: 'Why not burn both dogs?'—Or: 'Shouldn't the dogs draw lots with their muzzles?'—Or: 'Isn't it unfair to play so highhandedly with the life and death of either dog?'—Simple arithmetic, my friend. Two dogs are more than one. Everything gets more complicated and hence more amenable to practical reason. . . ."

Our telephone conversation also touched on dental medicine and marginally on current politics ("This Lübke is really too much . . .") and ended up with the usual exchange of quotations.

He: "You know what Seneca says about ethics:

'Our human society is like an arched vault: it would cave in if the individual stones didn't . . .' "

I: "Kleist took up this vault motif in a letter to his sister. . . ."

He: "And he goes further. Listen to this: 'Only the moral integrity of a life is important, not its length. But moral integrity often consists precisely in not living too long.' "

I: "When Scherbaum hears that, he'll turn Stoic. Your old Seneca, he'll say, was on the right track. Tomorrow I'll burn Max. Seventeen years are more than enough."

My dentist laughed. I let his laughter infect me. (Two laughing men on the line.) He had started first and was first to recover: "You're right, of course. That old-Roman morality jazz reduces the expectation of life.—But getting back to the young man: you should have lent him the money."

(Even now, when I set my beer to my lips at Reimann's, my bridges speak up: Nothing hot! Nothing cold! The foreign bodies conduct. His advice is too reasonable to take before the first injury. I advise you . . .—Better not advise me, Doc.—And you still open to advice?—What should I do, Doc?)

The next day—I had a free period—I called Scherbaum out of the music class that Irmgard Seifert gives my juniors. He put on his look of well-bred innocence.

"I've thought it over, Philipp. You can have the money. I've called Lankwitz. A spitz without pedigree costs between seventy and eighty marks."

"That was a passing weakness yesterday, I want to apologize. It's Max or nothing. . . ."

"But my offer obligates you in no way. . . ."

"Then it might just as well be a stuffed dog. Or several. Vero Lewand has a collection. Not a bad idea, come to thing of it. I'll ask if she's willing to part with her zoo. That could be the start, all perfectly innocent, to make the hats think: Oh well, stuffed dogs. Childish nonsense. One of those silly happenings. Then I'll sacrifice Max—and the cake will fall out of their faces."

I pondered his idea. The thought of stuffed dogs fired his imagination. He mimicked stuffed animals, emitted Donald Duck sounds (Woof Smack Grrr) and suggested the vomiting up of cake: "Moan burp groan." I should have left him on the spot. But with words of elegiac valediction—"Sorry, Philipp, I wanted to help you"—I gave him the opportunity to leave me: "I know you want what's best for me."

My student went back to his music. From the corridor I heard the class singing something Orffic.

He's gifted. (Everybody wants what's best for him.) He's quick. (Too quick.) He only works when it amuses him. (His excellent theme on the symbol in advertising: "The Mercedes star as Christmas tree decoration.") He's my height but still growing. (Störtebeker was a little shorter.) When he laughs, he dimples. Both his parents are living. His father is an executive at Schering's. I know his mother from the P.T.A.: a nice-looking woman in her middle forties, who regards her son as "still very much of a child."

He has two older brothers, both studying in West Germany. (One in Aachen: mechanical engineering.) Despite above-average performance in my subjects and in music (he plays the guitar) he'll have trouble, as usual, getting himself promoted. His friendship with Vero Lewand hasn't made a radical of him. (At the most he demands—quite reasonably—the abolition of religious instruction and the introduction of regular courses in philosophy and sociology.) His satirical bent makes for overstatement. He wrote in a theme: My father, of course, was not a Nazi. My father was an air-raid warden. An air-raid warden, of course, is not an antifascist. An air-raid warden is nothing. I am the son of an air-raid warden; consequently, I am the son of a nothing. Today my father is a democrat just as he was formerly an air-raid warden. He always does the right thing. Occasionally he says: "My generation made many mistakes," but he always says it in the right places. We never quarrel. Sometimes he says: "You too will have your experiences." As a nothing or as an air-raid warden—which, as I have demonstrated, is the same thing. ("What are you doing right now?"—"I'm having experiences.") My mother often says: "You have a generous father." Sometimes she says: "You have a father who is too generous." Then my generous nothing says: "Leave the boy alone, Elisabeth. Who knows what's in store for us?" That, too, is right. I like my father. He has such a sad way of looking out of the window. Then he says: "You have it good. Living in an almost peaceful world. Let's hope it lasts. Our youth was a different story, an entirely different story." I really like my father. (I like myself too.) It seems that as an air-raid warden he saved human lives. That is fine and right. Would I be a good air-raid warden? In the summer when we go swimming in the Wannsee . . .

It was difficult to grade this theme. (I begged the question by calling it derivative.) But he really is gifted.

Irmgard Seifert also thinks Scherbaum is gifted. ("The boy has an artistic nature. . . .") But before I could speak to her of Scherbaum, she had started in again (still in the same nagging tone) on those old letters whose discovery and interpretation she kept on and on discovering and interpreting. This time a particular passage—"At last I am ready for the sacrifice!"—turned out to be a particularly rich strike because the words "at last" had proved to her that previously she had not been ready for the sacrifice, that she had doubted. I pleaded with her to attach importance to her doubt: "It cancels out your subsequent readiness, or at least calls it into question."

This conversation took place between the Hunting Lodge and the Paulsborn Forest Inn. She had suggested a walk around the Grunewaldsee and picked me up in her Volkswagen. We parked at Roseneck and struck out. Nothing unusual, for during my teacher-in-training days we had made a habit of walking around the Grunewaldsee before school. We carried on conversations such as only a female schoolteacher and a teacher-in-training of the same age can carry on: gravely distant or more lightly so, not without excursions into a sophomoric, slightly strained joviality which often threatened to shift into its opposite, frosty embarrassment. (What with nature and the two-someness, I felt obliged to enlarge our academic friendship with the possibility, conceivable after all, of falling in love in my late thirties; the resulting strain could only be overcome by forced wit.) At first, on our walks around the lake, we kept our distance without particular effort; after Irmgard's discovery in her mother's attic—which threw her off balance, she started smoking again—our walks "once around the lake" became a burden on our relationship. I began (half wanting to and half for the hell of it) to look for and bring about situations that might at least make intimate contact possible. We also took chances. We paid each other surprise visits. In the midst of some conversation or other we would suddenly kiss, and after the kiss jump back just as hurriedly into our sober everyday tone. We spoke ironically about our "animal lust" and joked about our incapacity. "It's a false alarm, Eberhard. We may as well spare ourselves the melancholy we already have a foretaste of."

Thus ironically and mockingly, also acrimoniously because of the early hour, we began our walk as arranged the previous evening. Once again I had made a surprise visit. The evening had stretched out interminably.

"Did you get home all right?"

"I indulged in a couple of beers and tried a new combination: Coca-Cola and common schnapps."

"How perfectly giddy! I don't know that side of you. Our relationship, in any case, is distinguished by passionate moderation."

"A situation in which all possibilities remain open. Maybe we're afraid to make a move that might disturb it."

"Nonsense. It's only our vocal cords and a grain of unexpended sympathy that bring us together. You prefer to backtrack, to look for nourishment in the, I must admit strenuous days of your engagement, while I, since those letters have fallen into my hands, bend all my efforts to pursuing a seventeen-year-old girl who did something who in my name did something which I never . . ."

"You forget, Irmgard, that at the time of my engagement I was twenty-seven, that my failure, God knows, was that of an adult. . . ."

"What's a difference of age when we're talking about defeats that neither you nor I can twist into victories. For instance, I've been trying for days to interpret a passage in a letter—that inadmissible little sentence: 'At last I am ready for the sacrifice!'—in my favor. My situation is simply ridiculous: having to be prosecutor and defense counsel at my own trial. What do you think of it? That 'at last' right at the start gives a certain clue. Don't you agree?"

We had the Hunting Lodge behind us and were heading for Paulsborn. A cheerless dawn, the day refused to break. The snow that had frozen overnight gave off sounds. At the end of the Lange Luch, a strip of frozen swamp connecting the Krumme Lanke with the Grunewaldsee, a ranger was chopping holes in the ice for the benefit of the ducks. His breath puffed white over his shoulder. Immediately after we turned off to the left, as, occasionally in single file, we were following the footpath along the northwest side of the lake, diligent Sunday reflections occurred to me: "Don't you see: your fruitful doubt, everything that preceded your 'at last,' has stayed with you, whereas your stupid action, which as we know had no consequences, lies behind you and ought to be buried for good."

But Irmgard Seifert was already as busy as a beaver: all the way to the end of the lake, more precisely to the wooden bridge connecting our lake with the Hundekehlesee, she added timbers to her defeat. And on the bridge, amid the noisy ducks in their ice holes, after kissing her furiously to shut her up, that's right, shut her up, I was subjected, the moment I let her go, to the end of an interrupted sentence: ". . . and the worst of it is I'm more and more certain that I must have been disappointed when nothing came of my report. I'm forced to assume that I sent in a second report, or why not say it, denunciation. I doubled my guilt."

We were late by then and I hurried her on toward Roseneck: "But the peasant survived your first as well as your second hypothetical report. . . ."

"That's not the point. Won't you understand?"

"I understand perfectly."

"Words. Alleged relations between cause and effect."

"Exactly. The peasant, you've told me yourself, died ten years later after a second stroke. You're alive, I've survived too by pure chance, and my student, no ours, Philipp Scherbaum is in trouble. . . ."

"When will you stop talking about that idiotic

school rubbish? Nothing can take away my guilt. Those letters, especially that one terrible passage . . ."

(Entries were made: This morning shortly after eight thirty, after I had kissed her and in doing so torn open the slowly healing sore on my lower lip, I slapped my colleague Irmgard Seifert in the face. In below-freezing temperature, amid snow-covered firs and birches, at the top of the icy steps leading through the woods to the path connecting with Clay-Allee, I lopped off her sentence with a left-handed slap in the face. Despite the sharp report no birds flushed. In my days as an Air Force auxiliary, when I was called Störtebeker, I once slapped a girl in the face, but never since. I wished, the moment it was done, that someone, no, that Linde, had seen me. . . . A slap in the face may be ridiculous, but it's still an act. A stone strikes the surface of the water and foments circles: in quick sequence I struck Irmgard Seifert once again one-sidedly, but then over and over again left right, left right Linde, now on the Rhine Promenade, now in the cement depot, now on Mayener Feld amid basalt blocks, now in hotel rooms—and once in the presence of her father: an endlessly repeatable act. "Splendid!" he said. "Splendid. Only way to bring her to reason.")

Irmgard Seifert reached at once for a cigarette: "You're right. Forgive me."

With the same hand I gave her a light. "I'm sorry. But I couldn't help it."

She took three puffs and threw it away. "You wanted to talk about Scherbaum." And back in the

Volkswagen, no sooner had she started the motor: "I agree with you, the boy is extremely gifted, or at least he has an artistic temperament."

"Doesn't even Dr. Schmittchen, who has reason to complain of Scherbaum's unco-operativeness, say: Even in my subject his performance would be appreciably improved by a little more concentration; his talents justify greater hopes"?

We succeeded in laughing. She drove with assurance and a little too fast: "Only a few months ago Scherbaum showed me some songs he had written with guitar accompaniment and—at my request—even sang them for me: That intermediate register—a mixture of weltschmerz and commitment. A little Brecht, a good deal of Biermann, which boils down to Villon. But quite original and—as we've said—very talented."

(There was even some talk of publishing Scherbaum's song "Gathering Star Flowers" in an anthology—Poems by High-School Students.)

"But he's stopped writing."

"Then we must see to it that he starts writing again."

"Anti-napalm poems, I suppose, to keep him from burning his dog."

"I wasn't thinking of so direct a connection, but it's true that an artistic preoccupation might give form to his confused and still aimless critique and—since the creative process would take up all his energies—produce the secondary benefit we have in mind."

"Art as occupational therapy. Is that it?"

"My dear Eberhard, may I remind you that you

asked me to help you find a way—a way out—for young Scherbaum?"

"I appreciate it. . . ."

We drove the rest of the way in silence. And still, after she had parked the car, not a word. In the course of the few steps to the school entrance she said softly and almost diffidently: "Tell me, Eberhard, can you imagine me at the age of seventeen sitting at an unvarnished wooden table, writing in Sütterlin script a denunciation intended to cost a human being his life?"

What makes me try so obstinately to distract her from herself? (Let her swim in her stagnant pool.) She had slender intelligent fingers with which, when her guppies are floating belly up, she fishes them out of the aquarium. (I can say that again: I like her hands which are known to me for holding hands as we sit on my couch, talking and talking up top . . .)

The class was writing. (Whispering, writing sounds, throat clearing, subdivided silence.) I stood at the window and practiced against the pane: Look here, Scherbaum. I haven't heard any of your poetic efforts in a long time. Fräulein Seifert also thinks you should concentrate on songs, especially since you play the guitar. Write, Scherbaum, write! You know as well as I do what force, what political force, there can be in the lyrical word. Think of Tucholsky, of Brecht, of Celan's *Fugue of Death*. You have to admit we've had a tradition of political songs since Wedekind. All the more reason why we in Germany should give new impetus to the song of protest. I do hope that with your talents . . ."

And it was roughly in those terms that I spoke to Scherbaum in the yard. He was standing with Vero Lewand near the bicycle shed. I overlooked her smoking. She stayed put and overlooked me. "Look here, Scherbaum, I haven't heard of your lyrical efforts in a long time. . . ."

He interrupted me only when I went into detail about the song of protest: "The message," Joan Baez, If I had a hammer, and flower power. "Only lulls people to sleep. You don't believe in it yourself. No impact. With luck you can make money out of it. It only affects the tear glands. I've tried it on Vero. Right? When I sang you my most militant song—Beggar's Song, it's called, the 'bread for the world' bit— you cried like a baby and said it was great, simply beautiful!"

"It is great. But you get mad when somebody likes something."

"Because it just puts you in a tearful mood. With you it's all a matter of feeling."

"So what? If I like it."

"I'll spell it out. What I wanted to say in my song is that alms only increase misery, that they benefit only the people who give them, the rich, the oppressors. . . ."

"That's exactly what I understand. And I think it's great."

"Teeny bopper."

(It sounded condescending but good-natured. An

affectionate term, come to think of it. When she sounded off about base and superstructure—"Our group's meeting tonight. We're doing surplus value. Why don't you come?"—there was tenderness in his patient refusal: "You'll always be a teeny bopper." The ease with which he thought up nicknames—it was Philipp who introduced "Old Hardy"—proved to me that he was talented; it wouldn't have occurred to anyone but Scherbaum to call Irmgard Seifert archangel; and Irmgard Seifert—or the archangel—had several times mentioned Scherbaum's Beggar's Song with praise.)

"Fräulein Seifert also thinks you should go on with your committed poetry. . . ."

"What for? If even Vero doesn't understand . . ."

I agreed on the one hand with Scherbaum and on the other with Vero, and lauded their controversy, calling it a legitimate discussion which in itself demonstrated the power of the committed song to call things into question: "But never mind, Scherbaum. You don't believe in words. You want action. Let's suppose you carry out your plan. You burn your Max outside Kempinski's. If they don't kill you, at least they'll send you to the hospital. That's what you want: Public reaction. Headlines. Prosecution by the SPCA. Despite votes to the contrary, you'll be thrown out of school. Probably I'll have to go too, which wouldn't be so bad.—And two weeks later nobody'll be talking about it any more, because something else has come up and made the headlines, maybe a two-headed calf.—On the other hand, suppose you sit down and write The Ballad of Max the Dachshund. Folk-naïve but hard-hitting. Station by station. Max as a playful puppy. Max growing up. Philipp reads the paper to Max. Max gives him to understand: Burn me. Philipp refuses. (Possibly using my own worthless arguments.) But Max wants what he wants. He won't obey Philipp any more, because he despises him. And so on, and so on. If you make a good job of the song, it will live on, longer than any headlines."

The two of them had listened without reacting. (Maybe the ballad idea had carried me away.) Then Scherbaum lifted his shoulders, let them fall, and explained to his girl-friend: "Old Hardy believes in immortality. D'you hear that? He wants me to write for eternity."

"What would you expect of a teacher of German? He's a paper tiger."

"Suits me. And your paper tiger even admits that as a rule poems produce no immediate effect, that they take effect slowly and often too late. . . ."

"But we want to act now, this minute!"

"You want headlines that will be crowded out by headlines."

"I don't know what will happen tomorrow. . . ."

"That's too easy, Philipp. It's not worthy of you. . . ."

"I don't even know what *is* worthy."

"At least you should try to understand the world in all its variety and contradiction. . . ."

"I don't want to understand. Don't you understand?" (That sudden rigor. A steep crease and no more laugh dimples.) "I know that everything can be explained. Because the vital interests of the Americans are affected. . . ." (Me and my lousy appeasements, condemned in advance.) "Exactly. Unfortunately. When in the Budapest uprising more than ten years ago the interests of the Soviet Union were affected, they ruthlessly . . ."

(His anger built up slowly.) "I know. I know. Everything can be explained. Everything can be understood. If A, then B. Yes, it's bad, but to prevent worse. Peace has its price. Freedom isn't given away. If we give in today, it will be our turn tomorrow. I've read what they say: Napalm makes it unnecessary to use nuclear weapons. The localization of the war is a triumph of reason. My father says: If it weren't for the atom bomb and so on, we'd have had the Third World War long ago. He's right. You can prove it. We should be thankful and write poems that take effect the day after tomorrow if ever, if ever. No. No impact. Human beings are burning every day, slowly. I'll do it. A dog, that'll shake them."

Into the carefully prepared silence Vero Lewand said: "Great the way you say that, Flip. Great."

"Teeny bopper!"

Scherbaum's left hand was blocked by me (only I was entitled to do that) and bent back. I called their attention to the fact that the yard was empty, the intermission over. They went off, and after a few steps Philipp Scherbaum threw his left arm over Veronica Lewand's shoulder. Slowly I followed them and felt my gums, the two foreign bodies.

Since I had a free period, I reported to my dentist. He listened without impatience and asked for details:

"Does your student's girl-friend breathe through her mouth by any chance?"

Surprised, I replied in the affirmative and spoke of adenoids. When I tried to expand my report to take in general ideas—"Only if we succeeded in applying a pedagogical principle on a world scale . . ."—he cut me off abruptly: "I like the youngster."

"But he'll do it. He'll really do it."

"Probably."

"What should I do? As class teacher, I'm responsible. . . ."

"You think of yourself too much. It's not you, it's the boy who wants to do it."

"And we've got to prevent him."

"Why?" my dentist asked over the phone. "What's to be gained by his not doing it?"

"They'll kill him. The women from Kempinski's with their cake forks. They'll trample him. And the TV people will focus their camera and ask for co-operation: 'Be nice. Just step back an inch. How can we report objectively if you prevent us . . .' I tell you, Doc: Nowadays you could crucify Christ and raise the cross on Kurfürstendamm, let's say on the corner of Joachimsthaler, at the rush hour, the people will look on, they'll take pictures if they've got their gadgets on them, they'll push if they can't see, and be happy in the front rows because of the extra-special thrill; but if they see somebody burning a dog, burning a dog in Berlin, they'll hit him and go on hitting him until there's not a quiver left in him, and then they'll hit him some more."

(That was my Golgotha number that I'd taken over from Irmgard Seifert. "Believe me, Eberhard, every day Christ is murdered on some of our street corners, and the people look on, nodding in approval.")

My dentist kept cool. (Religious allusions embarrassed him.) "I presume your student is aware of the intense love of animals prevailing in broad sections of the population and knows what he may be letting himself in for."

"I'm afraid I'll have to report him after all."

"I can understand that you should be worried about your position as a teacher."

"But what should I . . ."

"Call me up again at lunchtime. Office hours, you understand. My work here keeps moving. Even if the earth should stand still, people would come running with mouths full of lamentations and cries of pain. . . ."

Pace my Berber rug: my recent acquisition. Quote Jeremiah: How is the gold become dim . . . Spied upon by my desk where beginnings in their folder would like to hatch out new stories: Well, come on. Come on. Dream up a nice out-of-the-way little murder. You can't let your fiancée and this Schlottau. You could wire a bomb to the electric signal system, and as soon as Linde starts counter-attacking at Kursk, they'd all, she, he, Krings and the shack . . . Or stick strictly to the facts about Schörner . . . Or how about dropping in at Reimann's for a beer or two . . . Or the new combination: coke and schnapps . . .

What should I do? Write my senator on the school commission? "Dear Herr Evers, An unusual situation has brought home to me the limits of my pedagogic possibilities and capacities. If I turn to you for advice, it is because I know of no one more competent than you to utter a word of wisdom in such a case.—Permit me, first of all, to recall a statement you made in an interview with our *Berlin Teachers' Journal*: 'I proceed on the assumption that the human individual and society both exist. Neither is subordinated to the other. They are interdependent; each is imprinted by the other.'—Such a human individual, one of my students, has resolved to give drastic expression to his protest against society: he is planning to pour gasoline on his dog in a public place and burn him, in order that the population of this city, in which he diagnoses an attitude of indifference, may be made to realize what it is to burn alive. My student hopes in this way to demonstrate the effect of modern chemical warfare, and specifically of napalm. He expects to enlighten the public. In response to the justified question—Why must a dog be burned and not some other animal, a cat for instance?—he replies: The Berlin population's exceptional love of dogs is widely known and admits of no other choice; in Berlin the public burning of pigeons, for example, would at most spark off public discussion as to whether it would not be more expedient to poison pigeons as has hitherto been done in our Operation Civic Spirit, since, among other reasons, ignited pigeons fluttering up into the air might well become a public menace.—My attempts on the one hand to bring my student to reason with arguments and on the other hand to warn him of the consequences of his act have been unsuccessful. Although this student admits he is afraid, he is prepared to face the violence of a population which habitually reacts with the utmost vigor to the mistreatment of dogs. He looks upon every possible compromise as an act of appeasement that would prolong the war crimes in Vietnam, for which he holds the American armed forces exclusively to blame. I beg you to believe me when I say that I cannot see my way clear to go through official channels, because the student's spontaneous sense of justice meets with my sympathy. (Grateful as we West Germans, especially the people of Berlin, must be to the Americans for their protection, these same allies are elsewhere offending our moral sentiment day after day; not only my student, I too suffer from this tragic contradiction.)—Last July, my dear Senator, you cried out at a meeting: 'May we have the moral courage of Adolf Diesterweg!' Those words, so meritorious for their frankness, engraved themselves on my mind. It is my earnest request that you join me in accompanying my student on his hard road, in order that your presence may lend the public burning of a dog the pedagogical significance to which we must all aspire, to which my student also aspires, and which must at all times be the aim of a true educational policy, which in your own words is 'always a social policy.' Yours respectfully . . ."

(There are no statistics on unmailed letters. Cries for help that never get postmarked. There is toothache—and Arantil.)

Addenda, because even while failing I began to justify my failure: I am concerned about Scherbaum because he is a human being; but Berliners will be
concerned about the dog because he is not a human
being.

Several attempts to find a substitute for the words
"human being" or the generalization "Berliner" or to
delete without replacing them: I am concerned about
Scherbaum, but the public sympathy will go out to the
dog. (Could my relation to Scherbaum be comparable
to the relation of a dog lover to his pooch?—I have a
photograph of Scherbaum. I cut him out of a class
picture and had him enlarged with his laugh-dimples.
Into a frame that has been standing empty for years I
sometimes slip the postcard-size photograph as if it
were something forbidden: my little Scherbaum, the
way he tilts his head . . . And didn't Irmgard Seifert
say: "You identify too much with Scherbaum. You
can't lead the boy around on a leash . . ."?)

Projections. Compensatory love. Dogs, allegedly
more faithful than people. The cemetery in Lankwitz.
Inscriptions on tombstones: My beloved Senta . . .
My unforgotten only friend . . . loyalty for loyalty . . .
Might (we ask ourselves) statistics on canine losses
during the war in Vietnam stir the population of Berlin more than the losses in human material in the
same war zone? Body count. By official body count . . .

Seneca says of dogs: "The dumb animal also has an
element of the good, it has a kind of virtue, a trace of
perfection, but it never has this good, this virtue and
perfection, in absolute degree. This is the privilege of

beings endowed with reason; to them alone is it given to know the Why, the Wherefore, and the How of things. Hence the good lives only in reasoning creatures. . . ."

It's as simple as that. With the help of Scherbaum's parents I might (should shall) poison Max the long-haired dachshund and so deprive Scherbaum of the object of his demonstration. (React radically to a radical project.)

When I called my dentist during lunch hour, he did not listen to the end of my, as I called it, "proposal for a necessarily violent solution." After a brusque "That'll do!" he became quite rude: "I'd appreciate it if you'd get this idea of capitulating out of your head as quickly as possible. It almost looks as if you were trying to go your student's confusion one better with your childish absurdities. Poison the dog: absolutely ridiculous!"

I pointed out my desperate situation, admitted that I was rather helpless, mentioned my already discarded idea of writing Senator Evers—he laughed loudly and ruthlessly—spoke in passing of shooting, as well as slightly throbbing, pains and increasing Arantil consumption—and then lost my head on the telephone: "For God's sake, Doc! What should I do, Doc? Help me! Damn it all, help me!"

After a certain amount of breathing in and out his advice was: "Ask your student to inspect the projected scene of the crime with you. Maybe something will turn up."

Even before school was out I suggested to Scherbaum that we inspect the scene of the crime.

"Oh, all right. But don't get up any exaggerated hopes. What a guy won't do for his teacher!"

I asked him if he wanted to bring his girl-friend along.

"Vero's got nothing to do with it. Besides, I've drawn her a diagram. Let her keep out of it."

We made an appointment for the afternoon. At home I brewed myself a cup of tea.

Make preparations or take it easy, let things take their course? Pace the floor, measure the rug, open book, read? In shaving talk at the mirror until it steams over? "What more can I say, Philipp? Even if you're right, it's not worth it. When I was seventeen, I myself. We were against everybody and everything. Same as you, I didn't want anything explained to me. I didn't want to turn into what I am now. Even if I am as I am and you see how I am, just as I saw how others were, I know that I've turned into something I don't want to be and that you don't want to be. But if I wanted to be the way you are, I'd have to say: Do it! Why don't I say: Burn him!?"

"Because you're jealous. You'd like to do it yourself but can't. Because you're a has-been. Because you're not afraid. Because it's all the same to you whether you do it or not. Because you're washed up. Because you have everything behind you. Because you have your teeth repaired for later. Because you always want to see things in perspective. Because you figure out the consequences before you act, so the consequences will

fit in with your calculations. Because you don't like
yourself. Because you're rational, which doesn't prevent you from being stupid."

"Very well, Philipp. Do it. Do it for me. I can't any
longer because I already. When I was seventeen, I
could too. Then I was a man of action. That was in
wartime. . . ."

"It's always wartime."

"Very well. Now it's your turn. But it's no use. It
will become a memory for you, enormous. You'll
never get over it. You'll always have to say: When I
was seventeen, I. When I was seventeen I was a man
of action. But never mind. Now we'll be on our way,
so you can see what's in store for you outside Kempinski's. . . ."

Our appointment had not included the dog but
Scherbaum brought the dachshund. The cold, sunny,
windless January afternoon permitted us to carry little
flags: our breaths. All those who passed us in the opposite direction, overtook us, or cut across our path
sent up similar smoke signals: We live! We live!

The wide sidewalk at the corner of Kurfürstendamm and Fasanenstrasse presented itself. The pavement was bordered with black-rimmed piles of snow,
which were marked with dog urine and excited
Scherbaum's long-haired dachshund. (Order and
merriment.) The terrace of Kempinski's was packed.
Under the terrace roof infrared tubes glowed, providing an assembly of opulent stately ladies, who were
spooning in pastry, with that upper warmth that
makes for cold feet. Amid dwindling cakes, sugar

shakers, cream pitchers, coffeepots, filter coffee and—as could be surmised—pots of Sanka stood cheek by jowl. Opulence was accentuated by fashionable clothes, tailor-made, or when ready-made from the best shops. Furs, mostly Persian lamb, but also a good deal of camel's hair, whose café-au-lait color went well with Sachertorte and with chocolate cream puffs, with paper-thin slices of Baumkuchen and the popular walnut layer cake. (Vero Lewand had called them cake-eating fur-bearing animals.) A few dogs, their leashes attached to chair legs, started tugging the moment we and Max located the spot chosen as the scene of the crime. Otherwise we attracted no attention because inevitably the ladies were used to tugging at their chair legs. Many dogs were led by. (In all there are 63,705 dogs in West Berlin, one dog to 32.8 inhabitants. The canine population had diminished: in 1963, 71,607 dogs were kept, one dog to 29.1 inhabitants. That doesn't strike me as unduly many. Actually I expected there would be more. In all domains the same regressive tendency: the wasting away of Berlin. That's what I should have said to Scherbaum: "Perfectly normal, Philipp: In the Kreuzberg section there is almost a shortage: only one dog to 40.6 inhabitants. To speak of a Berlin dog craze in the face of these figures is to foster a legend that has outlived itself.") We stared at the terrace which may have been interpreted as looking for a friend. Cake dwindled. New pastry was served. I began ironically, in order to divest our scene-of-the-crime inspection of any solemn, definitive quality: "If we assume that a jelly doughnut contains two hundred calories, it becomes superfluous to ask how many calories are contained in a portion of Schwarzwald Kirsch Torte with whipped cream."

(Vero Lewand's estimate had been correct: "At least three pounds of jewelry apiece. And what do they talk about when they talk? Phew, about weight and dieting. Ugh!")

The ladies in hats glanced, ate, and spoke simultaneously. An unappetizing, much caricatured, yet innocent picture. In view of so much simultaneous and continuous gluttony, an outside observer, Scherbaum for instance with his preconceived opinion, was bound to infer a corresponding process: simultaneous and continuous bowel movements; for this obsessive abundance of apple strudel, almond crescents, cream kisses, and cheesecake could only be counterbalanced by a contrary image, by steaming excrement. I rose to new heights: "You're right, Philipp. Colossal piggishness . . . Monumentally repulsive . . . And yet, we mustn't forget, it's only a partial aspect."

Scherbaum said: "There they sit."

I said: "It's worry that makes them stuff."

Scherbaum: "I know. They paste cake over everything."

I: "As long as they eat cake, they're happy."

Scherbaum: "It's got to stop."

We stared for a while at the mechanism of the loading and unloading cake forks and registered innumerable little bites with detached and uplifted little finger. ("Pastry hour," they call it.)

I tried to undermine Scherbaum's disgust (and my

own): "When you come right down to it, it's just funny."

But Scherbaum saw interrelations: "There you see adults. That's what they wanted and now they've got it. Freedom of choice and second helpings. That's what they mean by democracy."

(Should I have countered his oversubtle comparison with a complicated disquisition on the pluralistic society? Well, Doc? What would you have done in my position?)

I tried to cheer him up: "Imagine, Philipp, that those ladies in their overflowing plenitude are sitting there naked . . ."

"They won't shovel in any more cake. Afterwards, when they want to start in again, the image of Max, burning and writhing, will stand in their way."

I said: "Wrong. Here where you're standing they'll beat and kick you. They'll kill you with umbrellas and heels. Just look at their fingernails. And other people, who were only out for a stroll, will form a circle, they'll push and shove, and end up arguing about whether that blob of humanity on the pavement burned a schnauzer, a terrier, a dachshund, or a pekinese. A few will read your sign, decipher the words 'gasoline' and 'napalm,' and say: 'What poor taste!' True, after you've been wiped out, most of the cake-eating ladies will pay up, complain to the management, and leave the terrace. But other ladies in similar furs and similar hats will take their places and order apple turnover, cream kisses, and almond cake. They'll show each other with their cake forks where it happened. Here, right here where we're standing."

Since Scherbaum said nothing but merely stood watching as the cake dwindled and a new generation of cake sprouted, I went on with my description of the consequences: "They'll talk of inhuman barbarity and repeat the whole incident, savoring it along with their cream cakes and coffee because your Max won't burn quietly, patiently, and quickly. I see him jumping and writhing. I hear him whimpering."

Still Scherbaum said nothing. Max kept calm under my words. I let inspiration carry me. Talk, keep on talking to him. "It would be perfectly reasonable, though, to try to reduce their cake consumption. But then you'd have to write the caloric values of the various tidbits on signs and parade back and forth on this sidewalk: For instance: A piece of raisin cake equals 424 calories. Then we'd need a breakdown into carbohydrates, proteins and fats. That would be worthwhile, Philipp. A campaign of enlightenment against the society of superabundance . . ."

When I began listing the ingredients of Schwarzwald Kirsch Torte, Scherbaum vomited violently and in several gusts on the sidewalk outside the Kempinski terrace. The mechanism of a few cake forks stalled. Scherbaum retched. Nothing more would come. Before a circle could form—the pedestrian traffic had already come to a halt—I dragged Philipp and the whimpering Max across Fasanenstrasse into the crowd of afternoon strollers. (How quickly one can submerge.)

In the bus I said: "That was more effective than if you had burned the dog."

"But they don't know why I threw up."

"It was a good joke all the same. The look on their faces, Philipp, the look on their faces . . ."

"I'm not supposed to throw up, they are, when Max burns."

"Sure. Sure. Maybe they will. Inner agitation . . ."

"You just don't want to admit it: I'm a failure."

I suggested that he shouldn't go home right away but have some tea at my place. He nodded and kept silent. In the elevator—he held Max in his arms—there was sweat on his forehead. I put on water; but then he didn't want any tea, only to rinse his mouth. When I suggested: "Take a little rest, Philipp," he complied and lay down on my couch. "A blanket?"—"No, thanks." He fell asleep. I sat down at my desk but did not open my folder of beginnings. (The empty picture frame. Fragments of mortar for paperweights.) Around the title on yellow cardboard—"Lost Battles"—I made gloomy doodles with my magic marker. (Ah, the cake . . . Ah, the delicate pastry . . . Ah, the beaten egg whites . . . Ah, that sweetness they offer for sale . . .) Scherbaum awoke at about six. Only my desk lamp shed its circumscribed light. He stayed in the half-darkness: "I'll be going now." He put the leash on Max, who had slept on my Berber. In his overcoat, he said: "Now I suppose I have to say thank you."

Did he go to Vero Lewand's? ("I'm a washout. Go on, say it, say I'm a plain washout.") And did she comfort him with her untiring nasality? ("Come on, Flip. You've just got to do it. I don't dig it. Why don't you do it? It'll be clear and simple. It'll be a fact.

You'll be getting away from theory. It'll be *praxis*, Flip. Just do it.") And did the two of them lie down amid Vero's stuffed animals?

My dentist obliged me by not laughing when I told him about Scherbaum's public vomiting. His telephone diagnosis was: "That weakness will only strengthen your student's determination. Reactions of defiance, you know. How about bringing the youngster to see me?"

That's the way he is: open. I can tell him anything I please. He listens serenely even to my most preposterous suggestion—this one, for instance: that my student Scherbaum should burn a dog to make him realize what it means to burn a dog, even a strange and preferably unprepossessing mutt—and then dissects it with a few questions: "What dog?"—"Who's going to buy this dog?"—"Where and at what time of day is this to happen?" My dentist split my idea (one among many) into so many parts that I couldn't put it together again. He helped me, reconstructed the undertaking until it was theoretically flawless, called it "reasonable in conception," praised my gift of pedagogical invention—"Admirable how doggedly you keep on looking for a solution"—and then crossed the whole thing out, my inspiration and his own realistic appraisal: "Nonsense, let's just forget it; because what proves to us that this relatively promising experiment won't have the opposite effect? It's perfectly possible that your student will pass the test and, thanks to the training which we have encouraged, go through with the public burning of his own dog. Your proposal is feasible but relatively dangerous."

He had a thing about the word "relative." To him everything (not only pain) is relative. When I described the scene of Kurfürstendamm and—in passing—criticized the exaggerated cake consumption, he interrupted: "I can't see what you're driving at. For all the unreasonable quantities of cake and pastry they may consume, those ladies, taken individually, are relatively likable and quite intelligent. You can talk with them. Perhaps not about everything. But with whom can you talk about everything? My mother, for instance—a sensible Prussian lady, but not devoid of humor and charm—got into the habit of going to the Café Bristol twice a month after shopping. I went with her relatively rarely, I'm sorry to say. After her death two years ago I felt guilty about it, because what she liked best was to go to the café with her son: 'To slander and sin,' as she put it. She only ate one piece of cake, almond cake without whipped cream. A relatively trifling sin, even you will admit; she was less moderate in her slanderous gossip."

He told me how during the war, during air raids and later at the time of the blockade, his mother had practiced the art of slander: "But in the last years of her life it was that short hour in the café that provided her best opportunity of sparing nothing with her sharp tongue. I remember: once she brought a school friend along, a charming old lady with a lingering touch of girlishness, who smoked cigarettes in an amber holder. You should have heard the two of them.

Any spy would have come to the conclusion that they were two anarchist poison mixers about to blow up the land office and the Moabit courthouse. No, no, my friend, your generalizations don't hold much water. Society, even the society that crowds onto café terraces, is relatively diversified. Stop making a bugaboo out of stage props like cloche hats, cake mountains, and compulsive eating: Your adopting his narrow perspective won't do your student any good."

My dentist is married, has three children, is in the prime of life and practices a profession that brings gaugeable results. So much that is positive: successful root treatments, the removal of tartar, the correction of faulty articulation, preventive treatment at the preschool age, the repair and rescue of molars that had been given up for lost, the bridging of ugly gaps—and he is able to appease pain. . . . ("Well, do you still feel anything?"—"Nothing. I don't feel a thing.")

I said: "It's easy for you to talk, Doc. You look on man as a vulnerable, faulty construction requiring care and guidance; but someone who wants more, who demands that man should surpass himself, should become aware of the way he is being exploited, someone who expects man to be capable of changing the world and its established conditions, who like my student sees nothing around him but replete dullness—to him the mechanical gobbling of cake becomes the mechanism of capitalist society as such. . . ."

He sighed, wishing no doubt to go back to his file cards: "I admit that this consumer society, which gives the impression of being a relatively solid block, might horrify a boy of seventeen because he can't understand it; but you, an experienced pedagogue, ought to be on your guard against regarding your real or supposed enemies, cake-eating ladies or mediocre party bureaucrats, as totally evil. Just as I am not prepared to submerge you in the general category 'teacher,' so I expect you not to write me off as a 'dentist' pure and simple; unless we take the easy way out and maintain categorically that all dentists are sadists; that the teachers of Germany fail from generation to generation; that the German woman voted first for Hitler, then for Adenauer, and eats too much cake."

I answered: "Even if I as a teacher, you as a dentist, and your mother as the occasional frequenter of a café are relatively numerous exceptions—as you know, I hold many of my colleagues in high esteem—it is nevertheless possible that all the generalizations you have cited are correct, just as the crude generalization 'Germans are bad drivers' is correct although thousands of German drivers haven't had an accident in years and to judge by the statistics the Belgians—another generalization—come off a lot worse."

(A dentist and a schoolteacher: maybe the parallel doesn't work. He gives painless treatment; I regard pain as an instrument of knowledge, even though I don't bear up very well under toothache and reach for Arantil at the slightest pang. He could manage without me; I am dependent on him. I say: "My dentist"; he says at the most: "One of my patients . . .") So I did not hang up. I confided to the phone: "Yes, Doc. That's right. Exactly."

My dentist never said: "You're wrong." He said: "You may be right. The statistics at least are on your side. Election returns, traffic accidents, the volume of cake consumption can be interpreted and made to suggest inferences such as: The German woman votes for leader figures, eats too much cake, and, as the announcer tells us in daily commercials, makes the best coffee in the world. But this only demonstrates the relative correctness of said generalizations. Advertising and political propaganda content themselves with such serviceable half-truths and exploit them successfully, catering to the public's need for generalizations; but you and your, as I believe, highly gifted student ought to be more demanding. And mind you, I'm speaking as a dentist. Every day I have to combat injury to teeth caused or exacerbated by excessive cake consumption, by sweets as such. Nevertheless I refuse to demand the abolition of Kirsch Torte and hard candy. I can counsel moderation, repair the damage if it's not too late, and warn against generalizations which give an illusion of great leaps forward but—ultimately—result in immobility."

(Later I noted: The modesty of specialists when they speak of their difficulties and limited achievements is the arrogance of our times. This backslapping: Yes yes, of course, we're all workers in the Lord's vineyard. . . . Their constant insistence that we must differentiate at all times, even in our dreams. Their ability to relativize even the greatest horrors . . .)

"And how do you feel about napalm, Doc?"

"Well, measured against the nuclear weapons

known to us, napalm must be termed relatively harmless."

"And what about the living conditions of the Iranian peasants?"

"In the light of conditions in India we can speak, with all due reserve, of a relatively progressive agrarian structure in Iran, though compared to the Sudan India may well strike us as a reformer's paradise."

"Then you see progress?!"

"Within limits, my friend, within limits . . ."

"A new curative toothpaste, for instance . . ."

"No, I wouldn't say that, but Grundig has put a useful gadget on the market. EN3. Ever heard of it? Had one since yesterday. My talking memorandum book, makes it appreciably easier to keep card files. It was recommended to me at the last Congress of Orthopaedic Dentistry at Saint-Moritz: simple, handy, and foolproof. A nice little toy, incidentally I've recorded our telephone conversation with it. You give a very vivid account of how your student came to vomit in public. Like to hear it . . ."—"Our appointment had not included the dog but Scherbaum brought the dachshund . . ."—"But joking aside: Bring the young man to see me. I'd like to meet him."

Wise guy, believer in progress. Competent idiotic specialist. Amiable technocrat. Humanitarian blinded by his occupation. Enlightened philistine. Greathearted dealer in small potatoes. Reactionary modernist. Solicitous tyrant. Gentle sadist. Tooth-plumber tooth plumber . . .

In the corridor I said offhandedly: "Scherbaum, my dentist would like to meet you. Naturally I'll understand if you don't feel like it."

"Why not? If it amuses you."

"It was his idea. I told him about your plan just in passing, of course without mentioning your name. You know I've stopped advising you against it, but I'm curious to know what advice my plumber will give you. Prophylaxis is his pet word. Sometimes he talks quite a lot of nonsense."

On Hohenzollerndamm—we walked the few steps from Elsterplatz to the dentist's—Scherbaum said, as though wishing once again to go easy on me: "I hope you're not expecting a conversion. I'm only going for kicks."

We arrived toward the end of his office hours and had to go into the waiting room for a few minutes. (Before leaving us alone, his assistant turned off the fountain.) Scherbaum leafed through the illustrated magazines. He pushed an open *Stern* over to me: "Your Reich Youth Leader."

I acted as if I hadn't read installment after installment:

"This reading matter will also find an audience."

"Me, for instance."

"Well? What do you think of it?"

"The man goes to a lot of trouble to swindle honestly—like you."

Immediately I felt pain under my porcelain bridges, though I had taken two Arantil tablets before leaving home.

"That was just a factual observation. I could say

the same to myself if I chickened out. But that's over now. I'm going through with it."

"Careful, Philipp. My dentist is very persuasive."

"I can already hear him. The same old record: Be reasonable. Put your trust in reason. Keep your reason. Listen to reason. And where does reason come in?"

We laughed like accomplices. (His assistant should have let the fountain babble.)

My dentist seemed relaxed as usual, almost gay. He greeted Scherbaum without a look of scrutiny, bade me be seated in his Ritter chair, and said: "Well, that looks a lot better. The inflammation has gone down. But perhaps we'd better prolong our rest period just a little . . ." and sent his assistant to the lab. Casually he came to the point: "I've heard about your project. Even though it would be impossible for me to do such a thing, I try to understand you. If you've got to do it—but only if you've really got to—then do it."

Then he began to explain his Ritter chair to Scherbaum and to me as well, as though I were a novice: The adjustable back rest. The complete automation. The three hundred fifty thousand rotations of the Airmatic. The accessory table on the left. The root elevator. The molar forceps. The movable cuspidor with fountain. And a collection of not yet installed porcelain bridges: "You see, there are always people who lack the necessary teeth."

In passing he referred to the function of the TV set within the patient's field of vision: "A little experiment which, I believe, has proved successful. How do you feel about it?"

I ground out my answer: "It's a wonderful distraction. Your thoughts are far away. And even the empty screen in stimulating, somehow stimulating. . . ."

Scherbaum took an interest in everything, including the soothing, distracting, and guiding function of television during dental treatment. He wanted to know how it used to be: "I mean with anaesthesia and so on."

I was already afraid I'd have to listen to his Charité anecdotes—four men against one patient—when he launched on a succinct factual survey of the development of dentistry in the last fifty years. He concluded under a coating of irony: "In contrast to politics, modern medicine can point to achievements which show conclusively that progress is possible if we confine ourselves strictly and exclusively to the findings of natural science and the results of empirical research. All speculation that goes beyond the—I must admit—limited possibilities of scientific knowledge, leads—I should say misleads and necessarily so—to ideological mystifications or, as we say, erroneous diagnoses. Only when politics the world over learns to confine itself—as medicine does—to taking care of people . . ."

Scherbaum said: "You're right. Just what I'd been thinking. That's why I'm going to burn my dog publicly."

(So that's how you get him to pause. He didn't even clear his throat or go "hm, hm." In a dentist's office three heads filled no doubt with erratic speculations. Now what will he? How shall I if he? How will he if

I? What should I if both of them? Only the Bunsen burner preserved its imploring tone. Now! Now!)

"Incidentally, it seems to me that your front teeth . . . Say: bittersweet . . . Exactly. Did you bite your lips as a child? Like this, I mean: with your upper front teeth over your lower lip . . . Because you have a distal bite . . . May I?"

Since then I see Scherbaum in the Ritter chair: "Is it expensive?" How winningly my dentist could laugh: "Among proponents of natural science free treatment is sometimes given." Scherbaum bears a certain resemblance to me after all: "But don't hurt me."

And his reply, as though God the Father in high-buttoned smock and tennis shoes had set himself up as a dentist. "Hurting is not my profession."

How he bent over him. How he illumined his oral cavity with his lamp. And how my Philipp obediently made his big Ah. (I should have asked him for televised entertainment. The Berlin Evening Show. Couldn't I just for a second? And then the commercial?)

"You should have come to me with your milk teeth."

"Is it bad?"

"Oh well. We'll make a set of X-rays, entirely without obligation. And then we'll see."

With the help of his assistant, summoned by a ring of the bell, my dentist X-rayed all Scherbaum's teeth. With the handy Ritter appliance he aimed five times buzzing at Scherbaum's lower jaw and, six times buzzing, shot Scherbaum's upper jaw. Each shot was noted. As he had done with me, he felled Scherbaum's four lower incisors with a single on target shot: "Well, did it hurt?"

Leave a wide margin for insertions that will later be deleted. Check mark memories. Once again, this time in a drizzle, transform the Rhine Promenade at Andernach into a calvary: station after station. Or sift material.

". . . von Dörnberg alleges that the defendant illegally commanded him to carry out death sentences not by shooting as stipulated in the Manual for Courts-Martial but by hanging. Defendent is alleged to have pointed out that in the Eighteenth Army and Narva Army Group (Grasser) areas death sentences were already being carried out by hanging. . . ." Maybe say Schörner after all if we mean Schörner. ". . . defendant allegedly demanded that these hangings should take place at transit camps, Army rest homes, and railroad junctions, and that signs saying 'I am a deserter' should be affixed to the executed men. . . ." Or drop the whole business. Or pay Irmgard Seifert a visit and chew over old letters. Or slip Scherbaumkin's picture into the frame and paste on a little sign with Scotch tape: "I am a deserter because I sat down in the dentist's chair. . . ." I left in midsentence.

"Waiter, a light beer!"—and hung myself on the bar, and was no longer alone. When Scherbaum and Vero Lewand came in, the marks on my beer mat already recorded the third light beer.

"We phoned your place a couple of times and then

we thought . . ." (So they know where I am when I'm not home.)

"We've been asked to a party. And we thought maybe you'd like to . . ."

(In such cases it always looks good to allude to the enormous age gap: "Youth seeks youth.")

"Some university people will be there. Instructors and a few profs. They're not the latest vintage either."

(Just a little more ceremony: "I don't like to go uninvited.")

"It's informal. You can come and go and bring anyone you please."

(And anyway, a Stoic's place is at the bar: "Waiter, check please.")

"Great that you're coming."

"But only for a minute."

"We won't stay forever either. Maybe it'll be boring."

The virtually furnitureless apartment in an old building in Schöneberg was jammed with sixty people minus seven who were just leaving plus eleven who were just coming in or trying to. Without Vero we wouldn't have made it. We kept our coats on because the coatroom was presumed to be farther back, someplace that couldn't be reached but only conjectured: there's more back there, something else, but what? Oh, the real thing, *it*. Amid standees, sitters, and pushing searchers, expectation stood, sat, and pushingly searched. (For what?—For *it*. Not only myself, Scherbaum too stood there estranged. It would be unfair to mention the stale air, the noise, the motionless acrid-smelling heat, or externals such as the extravagant uniformity of dress, the hairdos, the frantic efforts to be colorfully different, which canceled each other out and culminated in monotony. One was struck by labored gaiety and by histrionic gestures that seemed to be banking on a hidden camera; altogether, this party seemed familiar to me: a sequence from a night studio take—or from several intermarried films.)

"What's the name of this picture?"

But Vero Lewand, not Philipp, knew the director, the cameraman, the actors: "Politically they're all very left-wing. They're our people. The one with the Castro lid is our leftest underground publisher. He's just come from Milan where he met some people who'd just come from Bolivia where they'd spoken with Che."

Benchmarks. (There was always some Christ, always a different one, looking at me.)

"What are they talking about?"

"Oh well, themselves."

"But what do they want?"

"Oh change. To change the world."

Somebody from the radio ("Church radio station, but very left-wing!") was introduced to me. He let me know that he was in a hurry. Absolutely had to see Olaf, who had news from Stockholm. "The Angola file you know . . .") Vero knew in which eighth of the standing, sitting, shoving sixty the man from the North was to be found: "Back there, behind the coatroom." (He swam away, leaving a wake.)

"But Vero, tell me, whom does this apartment belong to? I mean, who lets them shoot this picture that I've already seen several times?"

She pointed to someone who had worked up a transatlantic laugh and was projecting his happiness in all directions, although his protruding ears, because they were always being bent so in the crush, clamored for an empty apartment.

"He lives here. But actually the apartment belongs to everybody."

(I searched and found passages in Dostoevsky. Underneath Penny Lane and steeped in All you need is love, the nineteenth century refused to end: Yesterday Yesterday . . .)

Scherbaum became so quiet I was afraid he would attract notice. (He can't be going to throw up again.) As though to prove to me that I was really taking up space in the midst of extreme leftists, several leftists in the middle of the room began first to shout Ho Chi Minh and, immediately after invoking his presence, to sing "The International." (Or rather, fragments of the first stanza were repeated compulsively; there must have been a crack in the record. It must have been my fault that I heard Oh, my lovely Westerwald, growing steadily louder, more martial, and more rousing—and besides I didn't care for the girls.) Too old. You're too old. Don't be unfair. You're only jealous because they're so left and lighthearted. Join in. Look, the character from the Church radio and the left-wing publisher, and a few more defoliated specimens in their late thirties. They're joining in, they've locked arms: swaying, wine-inspired Rhinelanders spashing in the fountain of youth: "Arise, ye wretched of the earth . . ." (. . . over your trails the wind blows so cold . . .) Old kill-joy. Upstart reformist. Typical teacher. (Come on, give it a try. Ho—Ho—Ho . . .)

It seemed to me that Philipp at my side was beginning to age wordlessly. But then two girls sang at him: "Izzat him, Vero? Are you the Scherbaum they're all talking about? Man, it's great. Right outside Kempinski's. Pour on gas. Splat! No more dog. You'll tell us, Vero, when he pulls it off. Great, man. Beautiful!"

When sixty people became fifty-seven—Scherbaum pulled Vero, I followed—six or seven passed us coming upstairs.

Still on the stairs, Scherbaum slapped Vero Lewand's face. The stair-climbing guests took it as a promising sign: "Must be something doing up there."

In the courtyard Scherbaum dealt more blows (no more slaps in the face, now he was punching) and I separated them: "That'll do!—Let's have a peaceful glass of beer together."

Vero didn't cry. I gave Scherbaum my handkerchief because her nose was bleeding. As he was cleaning her up, I heard: "Don't send me home now, Flip, please. . . ."

(Superfluous and probably mean of me to whistle "The International" as we walked off.) In some joint on Hauptstrasse we found room at the bar. Philipp and I talked across Vero, who clung to her coke bottle.

"How'd you like my dentist?"

"Not bad. He knows what he wants."

"He's got to in his job."

"Great idea, that TV in his office."

"Yes. It's a distraction. Going to let him treat you?"

"Maybe.—When this thing is over with."

"You're still going through with it, Philipp?"

"They won't stop me. Not them. Or did you think I'd chicken out because a couple of teeny boppers, who call themselves left-wing, say great, beautiful?"

Prepare my exit and order another round. Vero was bawling into her coke. (A nasal bawling, because obstructed by adenoids.) I waited till Scherbaum had thrown his arm over her shoulder and said: "Come on. Stop it. It's all over now." Then I left. ("Make up. A left-wing movement torn by quarrels isn't a pretty sight.")

Still cold. Still dry and biting. Anyone who leaves a bar is a fugitive. Steel myself. Build up habits. (For instance, a match in the knot of my tie: in reserve.) I looked around: all nod to each other before moistening their thumbs. "Waiter, the check!" always refers to the bigger tab. I wish I were paid up, that I could take the early Pan Am plane and think in the direction of flight.

At home my beginnings lay unmoved. I opened the folder, skimmed through the chapter "Schörner on the Arctic Road," crossed out a few adjectives, closed the folder, and drafted an affidavit which the lawyer defending Philipp Scherbaum might call upon when it became necessary.

I even had trouble with the address: To the Criminal Court of Berlin? Or: to the Public Prosecutor? (For the time being no address.)

Around Scherbaum's act I built up a fence of literary comparisons, relating to one another and all together to Scherbaum's act. I cited surrealist and futurist manifestoes, called on Aragon and Marinetti as witnesses. I cited Luther the Augustinian monk and found useful material in *The Hessian Country Postman*. I termed the happening an art form. Skepticism aside, I imputed symbolic significance to fire (the burnt offering). I crossed out the term "black humor," substituted "premature sophomore shenanigans," crossed that out too, and obtained help from classical quarters, letting Scherbaum play the role of Tasso and recommending Antonio's worldly reason to the court: "I venture to hope that the court, adopting the attitude which the powerful, reason-guided, and soberly perspicacious Antonio took toward the poetic extravagances of the emotion-beclouded Tasso, will reconcile the opposites and, in the spirit of Johann Wolfgang Goethe, come to the magnanimous conclusion: 'Thus in the end the boatman clings/Fast to the rock that was to be his doom.' "

Though speaking as a character witness I could not avoid condemning Scherbaum's act, which I termed a lapse conditioned by spirit of sacrifice, I managed to conclude on a liberal note: "A state which looks upon the activated confusion of so highly gifted and hypersensitive a student as Scherbaum as a public danger demonstrates its insecurity and attempts to replace the benefits of democratic indulgence by authoritarian harshness."

(In the belief that I had done something I went to bed.)

In my class book I found an anonymous scrap of paper: "Will you stop demoralizing Flip!"—and in the faculty room there was a note signed I.S. in my pigeonhole: "I've seen so little of you lately. How come?"—Two handwritings, both hurried, anticipating threat or wish. During class I ignored my girl student. (That pompous antiquated method: For my money, you don't exist.—So what?) As for my colleague, I surprised her by loquacious eagerness. (Amused, supercilious account of the prerevolutionary party.) Then I tried my hand as a student of motivations: "This may be a clue. During the war Scherbaum's father was an air-raid warden. . . ."

"That proves in any case . . ."

"I'm not thinking of the political aspect of his activity. He put out fires, he was even—as Scherbaum expressly states in his father theme—decorated with the War Merit Cross Second Class. He saved lives. Surely you see what I'm getting at. . . ."

"Yes, but your air-raid warden–burnt-offering motivation doesn't convince me. . . ."

"Still, the air-warden in the theme provides the key. Take this: 'When we go swimming in the Wannsee or at St. Peter as we did two years ago, my father, the air-raid warden, always goes with us, but he never takes his clothes off; he sits there fully dressed and watches us.' Well? What do you think of that?"

"I presume you think Scherbaum's father was burned and dislikes to show his scars, possibly covering a large part of his body, in public."

"I came to the exact same conclusion, especially because there's a sentence in Scherbaum's theme that confirms it. 'When I was little, I once saw my father naked. A naked air-raid warden.' "

"In that case you ought to speak with his father."

"I mean to. I very seriously mean to. . . ."

(But I've stopped meaning to. I'm afraid his father's body is covered with burn scars. I fear these inevitabilities. I don't want to dig any deeper. I'm only a teacher. I want this thing to stop. . . .)

Irmgard Seifert's suggestion that we needed "a square meal" gave our conversation a different, but not new, direction. We thought we were up to pig's knuckles. I made it; on her plate there was a lot left over, for she kept having to dig up those old letters out of her mother's fiber suitcase and reel them off sentence by sentence. ("There's no end to it. That's guilt, Eberhard. There can never be an end to it. . . .") Before we paid up and left (it was her treat) I apologized for two three minutes. . . .

"How were the X-rays, Doc?"

My dentist said friendly words about Scherbaum, it must be a real pleasure to teach and guide such a youngster. "Believe me. A regular Lucilius, though to be sure he hasn't found his Seneca yet. As for the X-rays, only trifles. But you know what trifles can lead to. And his distal bite. We'll have to do a little work on that.—As a matter of fact he's already phoned."

"Can that mean that Scherbaum is interested in the state of his teeth?"

"Who isn't?"

"I mean: does he think further? Beyond that point. You know."

"Your student asked whether he should apply to the school health service . . ."

"How sensible."

"I said: Obviously that course is open to you. But I can equally well give you an appointment at any time."

"Did he agree?"

"I didn't want to press him."

"And not a word about the dog?"

"He didn't mention him directly. But he thanked me for reinforcing his resolution, as he put it.—Your student ought to have more encouragement. We ought to encourage him. Do you understand? Encourage him constantly."

(While I helped Irmgard Seifert into her coat and thanked her for the pig's knuckles: He's trying his hand at pedagogy. Should I switch to dentistry? Ridiculous, this jealousy of mine. Either way, I'll lose Scherbaum. . . .)

Just imagine: A dentist and a schoolteacher rule the world. The age of prophylaxis has dawned. Preventive measures are taken against all evils. Since everyone teaches, everyone also learns. Since all are exposed to caries, all are united in the fight against caries. Care and prevention bring peace to the nations. The question of being is no longer answered by religions or ideologies but by hygiene and enlightenment. No more bungling and no halitosis. Just imagine . . .

Our Teachers' Congress convened for two days at the Schöneberg Vicarage. When during an intermission I phoned my dentist and (in markedly critical terms) gave an account of the ceremony: Introductory address, welcoming of the delegates, messages of greeting from the delegates to the Teachers' Congress, treasurer's report, six papers on the integrated pluridisciplinary school, a few Hessian accents, several central preoccupations, followed by resolutions concerning the tenth year of compulsory education, reorganization of the school curriculum, the first phase of the work-as-you-study program, and the status of substitute teachers (including an appeal to Parliament)—when I had finally, more chatting than reporting, communicated the long-windedness of our dynamic school policy, I mockingly quoted my colleague Enderwitz whose opinion I actually share: "The integrated pluridisciplinary school is the best possible means of facing up to the present sociopolitical situation"—when I had concluded my situation report, my dentist proceeded to repay me in kind: he gave me an exhaustive account of the Congress of Orthopaedic Dentistry in Saint-Moritz, mingling quotations from the opening lecture on mandibular malformations with descriptions of the landscape and detailed information about walks through the larch woods and across the Alpine meadows: "The deep blue of the lakes made a lasting impression on me. A magnificent spot!"

In a word, we spared each other nothing on the telephone; over the same line we spoke at cross-purposes. What I really wanted to know—"What about Scherbaum? Has Scherbaum?"—was lost in the duet of shop talk. We hung up. "Call again."

(Just imagine: A dentist and a schoolteacher rule the world. The one listens to the other, the other to the one. Their formula of greeting—"Prevention's the cure!"—becomes, in every conceivable language, the greeting for each and all. Perpetual consultations.—How did he put it? "Call me any time. . . .")

When I went back to Irmgard Seifert in the banquet hall of the Vicarage, the general discussion had begun. True, little was said against the integrated pluridisciplinary school, but interminable speeches expressed esteem for the traditional school and called it to mind in evocative cascades of words. "Though we wholeheartedly welcome certain efforts toward innovation, we must never forget . . ."

Irmgard Seifert and I put on a show of "slight restlessness in the hall." (It was recorded in the minutes.) We leaned back in ostentatious disgust. Scraping of feet, clearing of throats, sneezes that could always be counted on for a laugh: schoolboy methods. We drew little men on our blotters and entertained ourselves with a game we had developed on our walks around the Grunewaldsee as teachers in training.

She: "Rules concerning promotion. A—general provisions, Article Four?"

I: "Work marked 'unsatisfactory' is more prejudicial to promotion than work marked 'inadequate.' "

She marked down a plus for me and I was permitted to ask the next question: "Second state test for teaching positions, Article Five, Paragraph One?"

She: "The test begins with admission."

A plus for Irmgard Seifert. Her turn to question: "School regulations. Punishments. Article One, Paragraph One?"

I: "In the schools and other educational institutions of Greater Berlin corporal punishment is prohibited.—In other words I'm not allowed to thrash my student Scherbaum; but only yesterday I was seriously wondering whether it might not be a good idea to provoke a good fight in the course of which I would break his left arm: hospital, plaster cast, forced leisure. The ultimate outcome: no dog burned in public. I smilingly submit to disciplinary action. What do you think of that?"

But Irmgard Seifert had discovered Scherbaum for herself. (Or had she discovered herself in him?) At the Vicarage, in any case, while up front supplementary motions were being read, she started singing his praises in an undertone; and when we slipped out before the end, she was still shaping him in her image, busily hewing him into a regular man of sorrows. He was to achieve what she at the age of seventeen had not been able to.

"You can't mean that!"

"Yes, Eberhard, I believe in the boy."

She spoke of her "increasing understanding of Scherbaum." She literally confirmed my dentist's strategic guidelines: "If I could only encourage the boy. I should like to be a source of constant encouragement to him. . . ."

That nimble tongue, always at her service. She has no qualms about speaking of an "inner mission." Could it be her association with ornamental fish? I know that in preparing her lessons she speaks across the aquarium. Her fantails and goldfish must have given her that idea. Who else? In a word, Irmgard Seifert is lonely.

What about me, Doc? What about me?—The little Lewand girl has left me another note: "If you don't leave Flip alone, your counterrevolutionary behavior will have consequences." An unvarnished threat, Doc. And nobody helps me. Throw up the whole business and retire: I'm fed up. Fed up! And plunge lovingly into something meaningless: organize snail races, for instance. . . .

During the ten o'clock intermission she wedged Scherbaum between herself and the back wall of the bicycle shed and began to encourage him: "You're right, Philipp. How could you possibly accept our compromise solutions, the daily capitulations characteristic of adults?"

Of me she made an object lesson: "We—you'll back me up on this, Herr Starusch—haven't been capable of a spontaneous action for years."

(All I could think of was that slap in the face. "*I* have. *I* have." That's what I should have said. But I said nothing and my tongue went looking for my porcelain bridges.)

"How often I've wanted to stand up in front of the class and bear witness: That's what I was like when I was seventeen. That's what I did when I was seventeen.—Help me, Philipp. Set an example. Lead me, lead us, lest our failure become universal."

Scherbaum's face fluctuated between sunshine and showers.

"I shall be with you when you embark on your hard errand."

He tried, blinking and with the help of whirring sparrows, to evade her glittering eyes. But there was no hole in the wire mesh.

"Look at me, Philipp. I know you're too modest to recognize the greatness of your deed."

He took refuge in a grin without dimples. Before I could put an end to the embarrassing situation by remarking that intermission was over, Scherbaum said: "I don't even know what you're talking about. I'm not interested in what you did when you were seventeen. Naturally you did something or omitted to do something when you were seventeen. Everybody did something when he was seventeen."

And like Irmgard Seifert, Scherbaum made an object lesson of me: "Herr Starusch, for instance. When I tell him what's going on in Vietnam, he talks about his teen-age gang and lectures me about the Early Anarchism of the seventeen-year-old. But I'm not interested in having a teen-age gang. And I'm not an anarchist, not at all. I want to be a doctor or some such thing. . . ."

Scherbaum walked away from us. Irmgard Seifert and I spent our free period strolling in the yard. What he hadn't wanted to hear, I had to swallow word for word: "The boy hasn't an inkling of his innate greatness. All he has eyes for is his project, his act, and not for the shadow it will cast: its redemptive quality." (A voice without dross.) The yard was empty enough to hold her whispered "redemptive quality . . ." in suspense—a finely rounded balloon.

"Really, Eberhard, since young Scherbaum came into the picture, I've begun to hope again. He has the strength and purity—yes, I'm not afraid to say it—to redeem us. We ought to encourage him."

The sober January cold preserved her words. (Pace back and forth in the frost, open your mouth and say "Strength purity courage.") I asked Irmgard Seifert to be realistic. "Scherbaum's agitation is understandable. Don't make it any worse. It's not fair to inflict our private burdens on the boy. Besides, you're not being honest when you decorate that old story of yours like a Christmas tree. That's phony candlelight, my dear. After all Scherbaum isn't a messiah. Redemption— that's perfectly ridiculous. He's simply a thin-skinned kid who feels the wrongs of the world, not only when they're close to him but also when they're far away. To us Vietnam is at most the product of a mistaken policy or the inevitable consequence of a corrupt social system; but he's not interested in explanations, he sees human beings burning and he's made up his mind to do something about it."

"That's exactly what I, if you don't mind, call the redemptive quality of his act."

"Which won't come off."

"Why not? The time is ripe. . . ."

"Pull yourself together. It's our duty as teachers to make the consequences of his act clear to him."

But Irmgard Seifert was well pleased with herself and her ecstasy. It wasn't only the cold that brought color to her face. She laughed and flooded the yard with the joy that is imputed to the Early Christian martyrs: "If I still had religion, Eberhard, I should say that the boy has been filled with the Holy Ghost. A light emanates from him."

(And stands slender in her coat with a shy, effaced gesture. Hysteria rejuvenates her. If I wait a little longer, if I give her time, a high-strung girl will weep and whimper in the frost: "But there must be . . . We have no right . . . Just a faint shimmer . . . This is happiness, Eberhard, happiness . . ."—What is this talk about happiness! I'm happy when a tree is missing; but the bare chestnut trees are all there in neat rows.)

When I told my dentist about this soul washing and school-yard charlatanism, his diagnosis was brief and to the point: "Your colleague's enthusiasm will suggest to your student what kind of supporters his action is likely to attract. The more she raves the harder it will be for him to light a match.—Keep me posted. Nothing irritates a hero so much as applause before the deed. Heroes are like that."

No. He's not like that. Not a hero. Not interested in leading or in gaining supporters. He can't put on that fanatical look. He's not even impolite. Not brusque not rude not strong. He has never been first. (His themes don't count.) He's never thrust himself forward. (And several times when offered the editorship-in-chief of the school paper, he has declined: "It's not my line.") But he's not timid or inhibited or lazy. He has never fallen behind the class norm. He's never been outstandingly brave or conspicuously daring; there's no reason to believe that heights don't make him dizzy. His mockery is never insulting. His affection is unobtrusive. (He has never been a nuisance to me.) He never lies. (Except in his themes, but they don't count.) It's impossible not to like him. He does little to please. His looks aren't striking. His ears don't stick out. He doesn't talk through his nose like his girl-friend. His voice doesn't proclaim. He's not a messiah. He brings no message. He's entirely different.

They called me Störtebeker. I could catch rats with my bare hands. When I was seventeen, I was drafted into the Labor Service. The Dusters and I were already up for trial. I had been questioned. A lieutenant read my sentence at morning roll call: Combat rehabilitation assimilated to punitive battalion. I cleared mines. I had to clear mines within view of the enemy. (Störtebeker lived through it, Moorkähne was killed.) Now Störtebeker is a schoolteacher full of old stories.

Since all I can do is tell stories and Scherbaum is a good listener, I kept telling him stories. I happen to believe in stories. Between Scherbaum and his act I erected stone by stone, precisely dated, scientifically documented, hence unassailably historical stories. I asked him to take a little walk with me. Starting at the Eichkamp housing development, we headed first for Teufels-Fenn, then for Rubble Mountain (Mont Klamott). We watched the sledding on the artificial hill, skirted the American radar station, enumerated what the view had to offer (Siemens City, the Europe Center with its Mercedes star, and the still growing radio tower in the East Sector). We said: "Pretty big place, Berlin." But I stuck to the point: "You see, Philipp, the basic question that comes up time and time again is: Can experience be transmitted? We've been devoting ourselves for some time now to the French Revolution and its consequences. We've spoken of Pestalozzi's resignation and Georg Forster's tragic failure in Mainz. The waves of the Revolution even struck my placid native city; for the people of Danzig, always fearful of falling into dependency—either on the Polish, the Swedish, or the Russian crown—were at that time in Prussian dependency. Not only the common people, but also the very self-assertive bourgeoisie followed the events in France with interest. But they wanted absolutely no part in the violence, the barricades, the Committee of Public Safety, the guillotine, in other words, in the whole painful business of revolution. When Bartholdy, a seventeen-year-old high-school student, decided, with the support of a few fellow students and dock workers, chiefly of Polish origin—they lived in Hakelwerk—to proclaim the republic of Danzig, he came to grief before he ever got started. On April 13, 1797, the conspirators met in Beutlergasse—where Bartholdy's parents, well-to-do merchants, lived. The neighbors were alerted by the suspicious gathering, as they called it. Beadles were called in. Arrests were made. Bartholdy was condemned to death and only an act of pardon by Queen Louise, whose visit to the city the following year with Frederick William III was greeted with rejoicing, commuted his death sentence to imprisonment. He is said to have spent twenty years in Torgau Fortress. Not even the defeat of Prussia and the resulting transformation of Danzig into a republic altered his fate. As a boy I looked for his home in Beutlergasse. It was marked by no memorial inscription. In the annals of the city his story is mentioned more as a curiosity than as a historical fact. We know nothing of Bartholdy."

We were walking down the hill. The crows over Rubble Mountain provided an eloquent reminder of the origins of this mound which had meanwhile been forested. (I suggested a hot drink at the Schildhorn Lodge.)

"You're no doubt wondering, Philipp: what's he getting at with this story? You probably think it's one more attempt to talk you out of your project, you think I'm trying—as your friend Vero has been insinuating lately in her threatening notes—to demoralize you. No. That's all over. Do it, go right ahead. But surely I'm entitled to measure your project against a historical example. Does the story interest you?"

"Of course. I'll ask you more about it another time. Later."

"My opinion is that Bartholdy's attempt to proclaim the revolution and with it the republic was basically stupid and irresponsible, disastrous not only for him but also for the Polish dock workers. (Only his fellow students, it seems, were acquitted.) Bartholdy wasn't hardheaded enough to be a revolutionary. Of course he had no way of knowing what even a Marx was relatively late in recognizing, that a revolution can be won only with the help of a class that has nothing to lose but everything to gain; but you, Philipp, knowing this and forewarned, ought to realize that your project, the public burning of a dog, can be effective only if broad sections of society—I purposely avoid the word 'class'—are prepared to take your demonstration as a signal for action. That's out of the question. You've seen that to Vero's girl-friends your project is just a matter of thrills. You've seen how determined my esteemed colleague Fräulein Seifert is to misunderstand you."

"What was your Bartholdy's first name?"

"History has even forgotten his first name."

(We were already sitting in the Schildhorn Lodge, warming ourselves with hot punch.) Scherbaum asked questions about the city's economic situation. I spoke of the recession in the lumber trade and of the public debt (two million Prussian talers) which, it is true, was alleviated in 1794 by state subsidies. He wanted details about the strength of the Danzig garrison. The permanent presence of six thousand troops, including artillery, engineers, and hussars impressed him; because facing his occupation force there were only thirty-six thousand civilians, and the Civil Guard, formerly a powerful instrument of the artisans' guilds, had been forced to disarm. When I opened my briefcase, showed him my material on the "Bartholdy

Case," and quoted from the account of a foreign visitor to the city:—"The French system has many supporters here. But I do not believe they will ever think of being disloyal to the Prussian government so long as it rules them with leniency and moderation"—Scherbaum saw the point of the story: "Things haven't changed much since then."

"And so, Philipp, I believe that the Bartholdy case must not be allowed to repeat itself."

(But even over punch, experience cannot be transmitted.) "In the first place a revolution is not what I'm after. And in the second place I've figured this thing out logically. I don't know whether you have an inkling of mathematical theory. . . ."

"I'm familiar with your bad marks in that subject."

"That's only the applied stuff. Anyway my formula is sound. It didn't come out at first because I took Saturday as my invariable. Even the Sunday papers didn't react. And Monday just wasn't feasible. Now I'm operating with Wednesday afternoon. And all of a sudden it works. The Berlin Assembly meets on Thursday. On Friday I'll be in good enough shape to be questioned; I'll give a press conference in the hospital and make a statement. There will be demonstrations of solidarity. Not only here, in West Germany too. Dogs will be burned publicly in several big cities. The movement will spread to foreign countries. Ritualized provocation, Vero calls it. Oh well, you've got to call it something. I'll show you the formula, but not until afterwards, when it's all over."

"But what if it doesn't work, Philipp? What if they kill you?"

"In that case the formula was wrong," said my dentist. "You and your stories. The Bartholdy incident demands to be repeated."

"You think he'll do it . . ."

"If the clear frosty weather holds until next Wednesday, I shall have no opportunity to treat and—perhaps—correct his distal bite."

"Would you care to exchange worries?"

"Tell me, my friend, apart from the inspired examples which you as a teacher hold out to him, has your student a model?—You know, we always orient ourselves by models. I rather tend to think that Bartholdy must for quite some time have been the mainstay of your superego. Right?"

We channelized memories. (In search of the lost model.) I was back in short pants, standing outside the gabled houses on Beutlergasse. He insisted that he had seen his model in Nurmi, the miraculous runner. (We agreed that the need for models must be countered by a supply of prophylactic models: "Prevention's the cure!") When via the—father in the pilot office, son nicknamed Störtebeker—detour, I dished up my theory—the father fought fires as an air-raid warden, the son is prepared to sacrifice by fire—my dentist conceded: "Superficially as your motives are linked, I do not exclude the possibility that the father's presumptive burns may provide a clue. You ought to visit the young man's room. . . ."

She lives with stuffed dogs and reads the words of Chairman Mao. In her room, which is said to be smaller than his room, amid quantities of artsy-craftsy knicknacks, it is the revolutionary Ernesto Che Guevara, in the form of an outsized coarse-grained photograph, who first catches the eye. I found that out from Scherbaum who calls her room a kindergarten and her collection of stuffed animals a zoo. He judges with condescending good nature: "Oh well, it's a matter of taste." She still refuses to part with her collection of sawed-off Mercedes stars, even though he says: "We've graduated from that." She clings to her last year's booty: "Those were happy days—picking star flowers." He says: "Sometimes of course it's more than I can take: she reads Mao like my mother reads Rilke." He speaks of the somber Che as "Vero's pin-up." A memory rises up in him as from the gray dawn of history: "Bob Dylan used to hang there. A present from me. 'He's so damn real,' I wrote on it. Oh well, that was long ago."

Philipp Scherbaum also had a photograph pinned up between the windows of his room: a page out of a small-format newspaper, three narrow columns wide. The middle was broken up by a picture the size of a large passport photo showing a young man of about seventeen: a firm round face, hair combed back energetically after moistening, part on the left. Under the photo smile I recognized a clean-cut, serious-looking Hitler youth; I recognized my own generation: "Who's that?"

(When I asked Scherbaum: "May I come and see you one of these days, Philipp?" he had been polite as usual. "Of course. I've been to your place, haven't I? Except that I can't make tea." And when I did call on him—I even brought flowers for Philipp's mother, of which I unburdened myself in the vestibule—I received an answer, there was no need to ask twice.)

"Him? That's Helmuth Hübener. Belonged to a sect. The Church of Latter-Day Saints, they call themselves. Came from Hamburg, but they had their stuff printed in Kiel. They were a group of four, apprentices and clerks. They held out quite a long time. On October 27, 1942, he was executed here in Plötzensee, after being tortured of course."

Scherbaum allowed me to take the article from the wall, so I could read the reverse page and see the photostat of the official announcement of his execution. (An article among articles. To the right, on the reverse page, the "News in Brief" section followed with a story about a contest for young scientists.) Next to the page number I read *Deutsche Post*.—"Since when do you read the trade-union press?"

"Our postman promotes the rag. Pretty boring but free of charge. And, you know, I'd never heard of Hübener." I remembered vaguely having read something about the seventeen-year-old apprentice clerk and his resistance group in an article—"Witnesses to the Resistance"—that Irmgard Seifert had lent me. (Why hadn't I mentioned him in class? Why always that belated business about the belated general? Why the muddled nonsense about my Duster days?)

Scherbaum didn't leave me much time to rummage in my upper story. Because I didn't say anything, he struck the first blow: "That was the real stuff. Compared to that your teen-age gang was nothing. For more than a year they printed leaflets and distributed them. At different addresses. First to dock workers.

Then to French prisoners of war, in translation of course. And thirdly to soldiers. He started in when he was only sixteen. He didn't waste his time vandalizing churches and that kind of thing. No Early Anarchism either. And he wasn't an incompetent like your Bartholdy. He could take shorthand and even knew Morse code."

(And I like a fool had hoped and feared that I with my gang-leader's past might be his model; or his father the air-raid warden with his hypothetical burns.) To be sure, I kept looking in his room for proofs of the motivation I had constructed, for photographs of ruins, or pictures showing his father on duty. And I reminded him that at the age of seventeen I had been thrown into a punitive battalion—"Have you any idea what it's like clearing mines without covering fire?"—but Scherbaum couldn't be dislodged from his apprenticeship to Hübener the apprentice clerk: "He took down the BBC news report in shorthand. Incidentally, I'm taking a course in stenography. When I've got the thing with Max over with, I'm going to take up telegraphy and radio communications."

(I don't know either, though in the fall of '43 they tried to teach me telegraphy in a premilitary training camp near Neustadt, West Prussia. Maybe I actually did know the Morse code when I was seventeen. Seventeen-year-olds often know things that they can hardly—take Irmgard Seifert—remember when they're forty. Scherbaum is musical: Morse code would come easy to him.)

After I had pinned the page from the trade-union

paper back on the wall, we fell silent. Philipp played with his dachshund. A friendly room, cleaned up with a light hand. Scherbaum's playful order. ("Young People's Voice" the column was called. I made a note of the journalist's name, it was Sander, thought I'd write him.) Philipp's left hand sparred with the long-haired dachshund. I took notes. After the sentence was announced, Hübener was said to have bequeathed words to the judges of the People's Court: "Wait, your turn will come!"

Later the housekeeper brought us tea and pastry. Between two sips Scherbaum counted on his fingers: "How old was Silvertongue when Helmuth Hübener was executed?"

"He joined the party in '33, he was twenty-nine at the time."

"And now he's Chancellor."

"They say he's come to realize . . ."

"And now they let him . . ."

"They saw no objection . . ."

"Him of all people . . ."

Slowly Scherbaum began to explode. At first he was seated, then he jumped up, but his voice did not rise: "I don't want him. He stinks. When I see him on TV, I could throw up like outside Kempinski's. He, he and nobody else, killed Hübener, even if the man who killed him had a different name. I'm going to do it. I've got the gas already. And a storm lighter. Hear that, Max? We've got to . . ."

Philipp took hold of the long hair. It almost looked as if they were playing again.

Even if he doesn't do anything, he has stirred up our filth. I'll have to give up teaching. And similar resolutions. As if a man who had been a decimal for years could start all over again from zero. True, the desire to change the setting keeps business moving, but what is motion? Her ornamental fish also move, always within the same inadequate space. Heavy traffic going nowhere.

I didn't call up. He dialed my number: "I'm in a fix. . . ."

(Has his Airmatic gone on strike? Has a patient bitten his finger? Is his assistant threatening to give notice?)

"Your student is asking something of me for which as a physician I can't take the responsibility. . . ."

(If I could only laugh out loud: "What, Doc? That kid can wear you out, can't he, Doc?")

"It's hard for me to believe that your student hit on that by himself. Was it your idea?"

(Be angelically unsuspecting. "As you must have noticed, Scherbaum hasn't taken me into his confidence in a long time.")

"Or did some passing remark of yours call his attention to this possibility—a purely theoretical possibility, mind you."

("What's wrong, Doc? What's wrong?!" What has caused this deep-seated perplexity? What has undermined this pragmatist's happy self-assurance? "What's the matter, Doc? If there's anything I can do to help . . .")

My student—or mightn't it be better to say: my dentist's almost patient?—has asked him to anaesthetize or partially anaesthetize his long-haired dachshund Max. He is reported to have said: "You've got injections to ward off pain. There must be some that would work on a dog. I mean, so he won't feel anything. You must know a vet. Or maybe you can get the stuff just like that at the drugstore."

"I presume that in spite of certain misgivings you didn't refuse the boy that slight assistance. You wanted to encourage him, didn't you, to give him constant encouragement."

"Weird ideas you've got!"

"It's hardly worth mentioning. A bit of local anaesthetic."

"That's what you think!"

"Well, out with it! Are you going to help him or aren't you?"

"Naturally I had to say no. . . ."

"Naturally. . . ."

"The boy seems desperate.—He has a slight lisp."

"So much disappointed trust. . . ."

"His understanding is all the more to be lauded. 'I understand,' he said. 'As a doctor, you've got to act like a doctor, regardless of the circumstances.' The boy's really amazing. A model and exemplar."

My Scherbaumkins has bitten into cotton. (So unyielding are the resistances.) Maybe I should arrange for the injections? But I don't feel like it any more. I just want to let the curtains down. And crawl backward till I run into pumice trass cement. There,

there! There she stands. Amid the closely piled cored bricks. . . .

Or buy a turtle and contemplate it. How does it manage: the withdrawn life? How much self-pity must become flesh in order that armor may grow: to ward off all hurt?—That was how air-raid shelter concrete came into being. The safe, massive covering. Not to mention the so-called concrete egg, the one-man miniature air-raid shelter developed in 1941 from the sketches of a French prisoner of war, and put into mass production. . . .

Or rewrite my beginning: On January 28, 1955, he was deported from the Soviet-occupied zone to the Federal Republic. Two years later he was tried before the criminal division of the First Provincial Court in Munich. (Shooting and hanging soldiers without court-martial proceedings.) The prosecuting attorney demanded eight years at hard labor. The verdict was: four and a half years of imprisonment. After his appeal was dismissed, Schörner served this sentence in the prison of Landsberg am Lech. Today, aged seventy, he is living in Munich.—So much for the facts. (Or what people call facts.)

Scherbaum came up to me: "I only want to warn you. Vero is planning something. And she'll do it."

"Thank you, Philipp. And otherwise?"

"Just a few little difficulties—But I'm telling you. This thing she's planning—she'll do it."

"You ought to relax. Why not play sick for a week and take it easy. . . ."

"Anyway, now you know. I'm opposed to her doing it."

(He looks tired. No more laugh-dimples. What about me? Does anyone ask about me and how I look? The little burn on my lower lip has healed, so my tongue says.)

I found the third threat in the form of a bookmark in my second volume of the *Letters to Lucilius*. More and more terse: "We demand: Stop tranquilizing him!" She had found the eighty-second letter, "Against the Fear of Death," worth reading: "I have stopped worrying about you . . ."—If only the frost would relax its bite a little, if snow would fall again on every section of the city, if there were a protective cloak, cut wide enough for everything and everybody, if at last snow, the soundless tranquilizer, would muffle every threat.

Unannounced she entered, no, occupied my apartment: "I've absolutely got to speak to you."

"When?"

"Right away."

"That unfortunately is impossible. . . ."

"I won't leave until you . . ."

So I broke off work on my beginning, no, I hastily covered my manuscript; for when my student's girlfriend wants to speak to me—absolutely!—I must transform myself into a great pedagogical ear: "All right, Veronica, what's up? By the way, thanks for your succinct and so delightfully straightforward communications."

"Why are you standing in Flip's way? Can't you see that he's absolutely got to do it? Do you have to wreck it all with your perpetual on-the-one-hand and on-the-other-hand?"

"I've seen that put a lot better. I'm a tranquilizer."

"Reactionary maneuvers! They stink!"

She sat down. Patient but uncertain, I once again set forth my arguments which—I had no choice—on the one hand opposed Scherbaum's project and on the other hand supported it with reservations. This was how our conversation shaped up: when she said "absolute," I rode the word "relative"; to her the answer was plain, I lined up several mutually contradictory opinions, my list didn't suffer from shortages.

"Why, it's as plain as day that this system of capitalist exploitation has to be abolished."

"It all depends on the point of view and on the more or less justified interests of a wide range of groups and organizations. We're living in a democracy after all. . . ."

"You and your pluralistic society!"

"Students also have their special interests, which they should formulate more clearly. Through the school paper, for instance . . ."

"Kid stuff!"

"Didn't you suggest Philipp for editor-in-chief?"

"I used to think you were left . . ."

"And even make a speech?"

". . . but since you've been trying to demoralize

Flip I realize you're a dyed-in-the-wool reactionary, the kind that doesn't even know it."

She sat there in her duffel coat. ("Won't you take your coat off, Veronica?") She didn't sit closed-up as girls sit, but in absinthe-green tights wide open like a boy. Since she spoke through her nose, she whined, even though she had come to tell me off in a big way. (Please classify in relation to leftness: If I'm to the left of my dentist—"You'll admit that much, won't you, Doc?"—Scherbaum is to the left of me, but lately, unless he actually does it, he's been to the right of Irmgard Seifert, who however is not to the left of Vero Lewand, but where then?) Even if Vero was sitting alone, her group was standing behind her: "We demand that you leave Flip alone, as of now."

I spoke into the rubber treads of her thrust-out shoe soles. "Be reasonable. They'll kill him. The Berliners will kill him."

"In certain situations sacrifices are inevitable."

"But Philipp isn't a martyr."

"We demand that you stop demoralizing him. This minute."

"But it's perfectly possible that you want to regard him as a martyr."

"Get this straight. I'm in love with Flip."

(And I hate confessions, I hate sacrifices. I hate articles of faith and eternal truths. I hate the unequivocal.)

"But my dear Veronica, if you really love your Philipp as you have just said with such laudable frankness, then you're the one to stop him."

"Flip doesn't belong to me alone."

"You remember the passage in *Galileo* where Brecht speaks of the pitiful people who need heroes and heroic deeds?"

"Sure. I know all the passages. Flip's mouthing the same stuff as you. Sometimes I think he doesn't want to any more. Here another Wednesday has passed, and still nothing. Now he wants to give the dog injections. But that'll kill half the effect. You've turned him inside out. The kid's through. Starting to doubt. Maybe he'll just burst into tears."

I offered Philipp's girl-friend a cigarette. Nothing could induce her to remove her duffel coat. So I started to pace the floor and tell stories, once upon a time. Naturally I spoke about myself. "I used to say the same thing: The Great Refusal will put an end to authority." I spoke of shipwreck, of the hell known as a punitive battalion, of clearing mines without covering fire. "Even though I survived them, those times made me what I am. I adapted myself. I developed compromise into a way of life. I clutched at reason. And so a radical gang leader became a moderate schoolteacher who in spite of everything regards himself as progressive."

I spoke well because she listened well. (Possibly her breathing through the mouth heightened the impression that she was paying attention, hanging on my words.) The atmosphere that arose in my study-living-bedroom was a sultry mixture of well-measured self-pity and manly melancholy. (The tired-hero jazz.) I was going to trot out a few quotations from Danton, to fill a balloon or two with my need for tender understanding, I was going to yield up my loneliness for demolition. But when Vero Lewand in her duffel coat sank from her chair onto my Berber rug, I stood stiff as a ramrod. (We were ten feet apart, too great a distance no doubt.)

She wriggled on the rug, looking funny and new to it, and said comical things: "C'mon in, Old Hardy, the water's fine. You scared? Say, this rug is great. . . ."

I had only the usual comment: "What is this nonsense? Won't you be reasonable, Vero?"

(And I took off my glasses, intending to wipe them as long as gymnastics were being performed on my rug. Ah, this embarrassed fiddling with the breathing on glasses, how often I had observed it in my colleagues: probably schoolteachers lack inner strength and that is why they reach for their specs.)

Veronica Lewand laughed. (The growths in her nose gave her laughter a tinny tinkling sound.) She was in stitches: "C'mon, Old Hardy! Or can't you make it?"

Before she left, she plucked a few wisps of my shedding Berber from her duffel coat.

Give up, drop out, quit. Withdraw into myself. Wash my hands. Live for pure contemplation. Deep in thought. And never revolt. There isn't even a current worth swimming against; only a number of stagnant, stinking pools which for all I know may be full of fish, and canals with regulated traffic. I've lost my grasp of the situation; I grasp it too well. Meanwhile I've learned why the water falls in one place when it rises in another. So blow up the locks. (That'll make them say they were meaning to switch to rail transportation anyway, that the traffic can be diverted. "We request that in your projected excesses—viz. revolution—you accord priority to the destruction of those institutions and industrial complexes the elimination of which is in any event provided for in our long-term plan. Plenty of hard work ahead of you. Have a good time.") Or break Scherbaum before he goes to pieces. The great prophylaxis: Stop Scherbaum now!

"Listen to me, Philipp. It couldn't be helped. I made love to your girl on my Berber rug. That's the kind of swine I am. I take what's offered. Yes, the offer came from her. Word of honor. You ought to be more attentive to the girl. All you do is talk about your dachshund that's supposed to be doused in gasoline and burned someday. That's not enough for Vero. You'll have to make up your mind: either the dog or the girl."

(But what would I get out of Scherbaum's rebuff: "What do I care what you do on your rug? Stenography is more interesting"?)

In the yard I spoke with Scherbaum about the increasing Vietnam demonstrations: "There's going to be one tomorrow. On Wittenberg-Platz."

"Sure. And then they all go home."

"Five thousand are expected. . .."

"Just the usual blowing off steam."

"We could go together. I was going anyway. . . ."

"I can't. Got steno tomorrow."

"Then I guess I'll have to go alone."

"Sure. Why not? Can't do any harm."

Scherbaum too is becoming a stagnant pool. Since the world pains him, we try to give him local anaesthesia. (Ultimately the P.T.A. will agree to a precisely delimited smokers' corner behind the bicycle shed.) My decision stands: give up, drop out, quit—or read Seneca to Lucilius, talk on the phone with a dentist: Stoic to Stoic.

"Listen to this, Doc. The old beaver says: 'Moreover, the philosopher is not outside the state even if he lives in retirement.'—I feel very much like retiring."

My dentist termed my attempts at withdrawal "sophistical hairsplitting." He linked allusions to his crowded waiting room with Seneca's invocation of fleeting time. The number of his waiting patients proved to him the usefulness of his activity. He called my melancholy (which actually behaved as though induced by an ill-humored coitus) old-fashioned foolishness. ("You ought to resume your walks around the Grunewaldsee, or play pingpong at least. . . .") His telephone lesson was: "You must be aware that the Stoa saw the world as the greater state; to abjure state offices always meant to make oneself free for the world as the greater obligation."

To my tireless grumbling: "But it's all so meaningless. What do we accomplish: changes in the daily schedule"—he opposed a maxim from the seventy-first letter: "And so let us persevere in our plan and carry it out resolutely."

I reminded him that on the Murmansk Front Fight-to-the-Finish Schörner had fed his half-frozen soldiers on Seneca's maxims: "There is no Arctic!"

He let his patients wait: "No philosopher is immune

to false applause. That doesn't trouble a wise man. On the day when Cato was voted out of the praetorship, he played ball on the Campus Martius. And Seneca says . . ."

"No. No more quotations. Your Seneca spent most of his life conducting business of state for the blood-thirsty Nero and writing flowery speeches for him. It was only as an old man, grown incapable of desire, that he became wise. With shriveled penis it may not be so hard to choose a voluntary death and to let your watered virtue bleed into water. Practice inaction and look on at the misery of the world without batting an eyelash. No, Doc! I won't let my student be beaten to a pulp. To hell, Doc, with all your Stoic serenity!"

My dentist laughed over the wire: "That's the way to talk. Incidentally, the youngster dropped in only two hours ago. Not a word about injections for the dog. At my suggestion he's been reading the letters to Lucilius. What do you think the kid has got out of them? Well? Guess what. Your student finds that Seneca and Marcuse agree in their judgment of the late-Roman and late-capitalist consumer society. Remember? In the forty-fifth letter Seneca writes: 'Things are held to be necessary that are largely superfluous.'—I've advised the boy to go on looking for his Marcuse in the Old Stoic's writings. . . ."

After hanging up I was left alone with the question: Has he already given up? And noted slight dismay: A lot of stage thunder. That's what we get excited, talk, plead, and knock ourselves out about. Am I disappointed? If he really—as I can't believe—turns his coat; if he—which is after all possible, though unlikely—just gives in, backs down—I hope not, but I'd understand—I shall try my best not to be disappointed: "Admirable, Philipp. Through reason to abandon a courageous act; I call that showing the higher courage, making the greater sacrifice."

Scherbaum stopped me after school: "Vero has been to see you. I warned you."

"Not worth mentioning, Philipp. As she put it, she absolutely had to see me."

"You've been wasting enough time on me with my shilly-shallying."

"We're all of us trying to reach the best decision. It was only fitting that your girl-friend should have a chance to listen to my advice."

"Well? Did she pull off her big number?"

"She was crude, but I'm used to that."

Scherbaum took irregular steps beside me. I speculated between tree and tree: Has she shot off her mouth? Some kind of teeny-bopper nonsense? Stuck it between my legs . . . Absolutely wanted to show me how big . . . First he gave me a mixture of schnapps and Coca-Cola, then he took down my . . . I envisaged academic consequences: statutory rape. I was already writing headlines for the *Bild-Zeitung*: "Education on Berber Rug!"—"Senior Schoolteacher Likes Absinthe-Green Tights!"—"Whenever She Talked Through Her Nose!"—already improvising an explanation to my embarrassed principal, when Scherbaum stopped still. (He looked ravaged. Uncontrolled gestures. He, who never felt the cold, was shivering.

And that lisp which my dentist had already mentioned.)

"Vero wants to sink you. She'll go to bed with you to make you stop trying to talk me out of it. I wouldn't put it past her."

(Did I say something? Probably I reached for my glasses again. That preposterous reflex, as though simple sentences could cloud lenses.)

"Naturally I tried to talk her out of it. Because in the first place Vero certainly isn't your type, and in the second place you'd be scared shitless of getting mixed up with a minor. Or wouldn't you?"

(He smirked. My Scherbaumkins, who normally had a wholesome grin, smirked obnoxiously.) I took refuge in amused superiority, leaving the question open as to whether Vero Lewand might appeal to me in certain situations, spoke, still jokingly, of the dangers that sometimes hang over a teacher—"It's not always easy, Philipp, to sit in a virtuously lighted glass house"—and finally, propping myself on the usual pedagogic earnestness, asked Scherbaum directly: "But as long as we're discussing these things so frankly, do you have sexual relations with your girlfriend?"

Scherbaum said: "We don't get around to it any more. The thing with Max takes our minds off it. And anyway, that's never been the main thing for us."

Then he stood still and looked into the bare chestnut trees: "I don't really get it. Probably women need to have it fairly regularly or they go nuts."

"Well anyway, Philipp, you needn't worry about

your girl-friend, even if she 'absolutely' has to speak to me again. I'll be cold as ice."

But Scherbaum's worries had a different name: "That's not it. If you've absolutely got to do it with her, okay. It's none of my business. Only I wouldn't want this damn foolishness to have any connection with Max. They're two entirely different things. They can't be mixed."

Admittedly I was waiting. Exaggerated effort over my manuscript masked my watchfulness. (Meditations, based on Schlottau's electromechanical refinements about the recapture of Rzhev, cornerpost of the European front, and the Buffalo Movement.) In between I practiced little sentences: Won't you take your coat off, Vero?—I'm so glad you've broken in on my loneliness.—I must admit that much as I desire you, I am still determined to resist your bewildering directness, though I should not be disinclined, but it can may must not be.—Together we must try to deny ourselves.—May I read you something?—Here, some letters written by Georg Forster, an outstanding figure whose career was a tragic failure, to his wife who by then—he was lying sick in Paris—had already written him off; she was sharing her bed with another.—You don't want me to read? Talk instead? Because my voice is so pleasant? About the war? How all alone and cut off in a clump of woods behind the Russian lines? Not about the war? About my engagement?—You know, you remind me more and more of my former. True, she didn't breathe through her mouth, but she might have. So purposive narrow-eyed direct. For instance, she'd taken up with the plant electrician because while servicing him standing up amid cored cement blocks, she found out what her father, who during the war had commanded the armies on the Murmansk Front, then later in the Southern Ukraine and finally in Kurland . . . Oh yes, we weren't going to talk about the war.—Cigarette? And that plant electrician had built a system of electromechanical switches for a sandbox installation.—You oughtn't to sit on the rug, Vero. It sheds.—With every possible refinement. Do you know anything about interlocking circuits, command switches, and indicator lights?—But that's between ourselves, Vero. See? And won't you admit I have to be careful?

Irmgard Seifert dropped in toward evening. She too "absolutely" had to speak to me. She too declined to take her coat off. Standing in her coat, she said: "A girl student—presumably there's no need to mention names—has come to me with insinuations which I refused to listen to. Nevertheless I must ask you, Eberhard, to explain how such ambiguities . . ."

What was the source of my calm? "My dear Irmgard. I assume this student who babbles insinuations to be Fräulein Lewand. What has she got to insinuate? Why don't you sit down?"

Irmgard Seifert eyed my Berber: "The silly little fool waylaid me after school. With that whining drawl of hers: 'Tell me, what do you think of the rug Herr Starusch has beside his desk?'—When I said your rug was a Berber rug and moreover a fine one, she said: 'But it sheds.'—To convince me she plucked some wool from her coat, which might perfectly well have come from your rug. What have you got to say for yourself?"

(She's taken you in. She's led you on like a lecherous old man—and dropped you. "Yum yum!—Splat splat!")

I started with a laugh because it was funny to think of that taking-off, breathing-on, and wiping of glasses: "The girl goes to amazing lengths. Perhaps her family circumstances, her environment-conditioned independence favor such impressively fanatical decisions. So that's why she wriggled on the rug!"——Head-shaking.——"She came here. Day before yesterday. Unannounced. 'Absolutely' had to speak to me. Wouldn't take no for an answer. Sat where you, in her coat.—— Won't you take your coat off. Irmgard, and sit down? —And started raking me over the coals, gave me hell in fact. Telling me to leave her Flip alone. Calling me a reactionary tranquilizer. Just think of it, Irmgard, tranquilizer, that's what she said . . ."——Laughter and several repetitions of the student coinage.——"And so forth and so on. In the end she flung herself on the rug. I looked on serenely. Offered her a cigarette. Smoked one myself. Because, as the psychologists say, smoking together can appease the aggressive drive. There was nothing more to be said. And when she left I unsuspectingly called her attention to the fact that under her onslaught my Berber had molted a few feathers, as her duffel coat bore witness.—— That's the whole story."

Irmgard Seifert decided to believe me. She took off her coat but was still unwilling to sit down. "Just imagine, Eberhard, the silly fool asked me if I had ever lain down on your shedding Berber."

A little later we were sitting on the couch, smoking. Against a background of recorded music (Telemann, Tartini, Bach), the evening culminated in a long-winded evocation of the past, which, however, was unable to turn us into seventeen-year-olds. For all the hand holding and kneading of palms the distance between us became greater and greater, raising questions as to the dimensions of the couch.

I lined up episodes from my Duster days, she wrote her denunciation of the peasant in the Harz over and over in Sütterlin script; I lost myself in details of the demolition of an altar in the transept of a Catholic church and tried to explain to her the iron armature inside a neo-Gothic plaster Madonna, she insisted that she had sent her second denunciation—or reminder, because the first had brought no reaction—in a registered letter to Clausthal-Zellerfeld; I recalled my personal difficulties as leader of a teen-age gang and proved that the presence of a girl member had led to the subsequent betrayal, she outlined the instructions for operating bazookas and couldn't and wouldn't understand how she could have trained fourteen-year-old boys in the use of that close-combat weapon; and when I tried to drop the wreath of evergreen memories by speaking rather rashly of Vero Lewand and my shedding Berber rug, Irmgard Seifert, after disposing of Vero's early rug experiences as mythomania, picked up the wreath again: "Believe me, Eberhard. I'll have to stand up in front of the class and unmask myself. How can I go on teaching with this existential lie behind my forehead? I still need a push. I admit I'm weak. But as soon as young Scherbaum has set the example, I'll follow, I'll definitely follow him. This can't go on."

I poured more moselle and put on a record. When after a certain amount of pacing, in the course of which I avoided the Berber rug, I tried directly and wordlessly to overcome the distance created by our talk—I sat down abruptly beside la Seifert, leapt to the attack, and tried with my right knee to open her closed lap—she sawed off my half-intention right above the root: "Please, Eberhard. I know you're able to. You don't have to prove it."

And a little later, from out of soft laughter, no, from out of girlish cooing, I heard: "If I were younger and if as a teacher I didn't have to recognize this barrier, if I were free and considerably younger, believe me, Eberhard, I'd take Philipp, I'd hold him in my arms to give him courage, I'd love him, love him passionately!—Oh, if I had his unperverted faith, how loudly and nakedly I should publish the truth."

(They suck themselves fast. They've occupied the walls of her aquarium. They live on others and spread. The evergreen mistletoe with its vitreous berries which, when squeezed, vomit vitreous slime, the friendly mistletoe that is hung over the doors of pious homes, is also a parasite.)

She stayed until shortly after midnight. In the end I had to take Arantil. Irmgard Seifert didn't wish to talk about my dental treatment, past and impending. She kissed me in the doorway: "And don't be angry with me about before."

("Not worth mentioning. I still have a little work to do.") . . . When he came up for trial, two out of sixty-six counts of the indictment were retained: the so-called Neisse Fortress incident, i.e. his unsuccessful attempt at incitement to murder Colonel Sparre and Major Jüngling, and the shooting of Corporal Arndt, whom Schörner had found asleep in a truck. The defendant invoked the so-called Catastrophe Order, Führer Decree No. 7 of February 24, 1943: "Those who take vigorous action will not be subject to punishment even if they exceed the proper measure. . . ." On his return from Soviet captivity Schörner, on the advice of the police, left the Hof-Munich express in Freising, where his daughter Anneliese was waiting for him. At the Munich Central Station crowds of war veterans . . .

I can't go on. Foretaste overlaps with aftertaste. Simultaneous tastes contradict one another. I know what's in my pockets. Words interlock and open pigeonholes in which lie words waiting to interlock and open pigeonholes. I understand everything. Before the predicate enters and pompously occupies the stage, I nod: Yes yes.—Now I'll go to sleep. This lousy bed.

Wake up and find a pencil: Insensibility accompanied by pedantic understanding of every kind of pain and offshoot of pain. Epicurus accuses the Greek Stoics, especially Stilpo, of apatheia, whereas Seneca, an admirer of Epicurus (and probably a secret Epicurean), admits he is sensitive to misfortune, though it is wisdom and not impatientia, the Cynic's incapacity for suffering, that enables him to transcend all misfortune; whereas I at the slightest toothache reach for Arantil: Misfortune equals toothache! Is it conceivable that Nero, consistent with himself as Seneca's disciple, set fire to Rome because a toothache drove him to it?

All right, I won't sleep in bed but on the beastly rug. Look for sleep as for a tangible object: See here, Vero. You can't just lie down on my Berber.—Why not?—Because it smells of ram.—Doesn't bother me. I've got adenoids.—And suppose I lie down on the wool?—It'll stink twice as bad.—But I warn you.—About what?—About me on the rug.—But you can't do that.—Says who?—I'm a minor dependent. My parents are separated. I'm always shuttling back and forth. Besides I'll scream and tell the archangel. You can't do that! You can't do that!

(On my rug I can do what I please. Even lie alone, looking for sleep and finding a dismantled fiancée who has disintegrated into greasy dust balls and got stuck in the ram's skin. Come on come!)

Only I should never have let you keep your coat on, because my Berber is too new not to shed. Now everybody knows and Fräulein Seifert says: Will you kindly explain yourself, Herr Starusch. Don't oblige me to make another report; because when I was only seventeen, shortly before the end of the war, a peasant tried to take liberties with me and I found myself obliged to report him to the competent authorities. . . . Tell me, Vero, why do you wear absinthe-green tights always and everywhere?—The better to hear you with.

Also looking for mines in open terrain. And wandering around among basalt blocks on Mayener Feld. Also pink casting plaster and on the TV screen myself with my mouth full of casting plaster. Also a funeral at Zehlendorf Forest Cemetery. Scherbaum's father and I, sustaining Scherbaum's mother between us, are following the coffin. And behind us a whispering: That's his teacher up front, used to be his teacher. . . . In the end I found sleep on my Berber. Sleep is something.

In the morning while shaving: What the hell, let him do it. I'll just look on and keep cool.

In the morning, along with the growth of my beard I was scraping away my night's growth of good resolutions when my dentist phoned: "This is it. Your student has given up."

(A rotten oyster: spit it out. And cry jubilantly into the phone: "Well, thank God! Frankly it's just what I expected, they all back down.")

"He's given up at your expense. Don't let it bother you. He says he wouldn't want to be like you, peddling the feats of a seventeen-year-old when he's forty, because, so he says, that's what you do."

(I confined myself to Seneca, received quotations in return, and judged in conclusion: "Now he's an adult and that means broken.")

"No, not at all! He's chock-full of plans. Plans which, I gladly admit, my circumspect advice enabled to thrive. He's going to take over the school paper. Informative articles! Black-humored comments! Maybe manifestoes!"

("Actually an excellent decision. That rag is no better than a barbershop gazette.")

"What a task, no, what a mission!"

("Hasn't taken any initiative for months except to raise the question of whether and where students should be allowed to smoke during breaks.")

"Your student wants to make wise use of his time and enlarge his awareness."

("What did little Nero's tutor say: 'Excellent, Lucilius! Devote yourself to yourself, husband time, be stingy with it!' ")

"Incidentally I'll have to give the boy an expansion plate. The treatment starts tomorrow. Late treatment of distal bite is never assured of success. It requires discipline on the patient's part. That's what I told him: We shall succeed only if you make friends, so to speak, with the foreign bodies in your oral cavity. He promised me to stick it out. He promised me several times to stick it out."

("He'll give up, Doc. No staying power. He's just proved it. The school paper too. He won't hold up. After three issues—want to bet, Doc?—they'll be reduced to the smokers' corner again.")

My dentist said: "We'll see," and reminded me of the biting position of my upper teeth: "We'll be starting in very soon ourselves. The brief interval has surely done you good. It's amusing, incidentally, to observe the radical contrast between the student's distal bite and the teacher's congenital and therefore authentic prognathism."

He's all right. His standards never fail him. His prognoses don't have to be correct. His mistakes call themselves partial successes. Relatively speaking, he knows what's what. He skis, plays chess, and likes boiled brisket of beef. His poorly attended lectures at the people's universities of Steglitz, Tempelhof, and Neukölln are carefully prepared. A man who is not shaken by defeats. Affable and assured of steady demand, he says: "Next, please."

After the teachers' meeting—tediously devoted to the procurement of school supplies—I told Irmgard Seifert: "By the way, Scherbaum has given up. He's taking over the school paper."

"In other words, so-called reason has triumphed again. Bravo!"

"Whom would you have liked to triumph?"

"I said bravo, didn't I? Hurrah for the school paper!"

"Did you by any chance expect Scherbaum to show the courage you and I lack, yes, you too?"

"And I'd already decided to make a fresh start."

"From scratch?"

"I was going to stand up in front of my class and read those dreadful letters, sentence by sentence.—But now it's no use. I give up too."

"Why so despairing? Donate the letters to Editor-in-Chief Scherbaum. He'll publish them in the school paper. They'll be a big hit."

"You wanted to hurt me, didn't you?—You've hurt me."

She suffers too willingly, too easily, too loudly. Must I apologize now: "A thoughtless word, let's forget it. . . ." Recently we were listening to Gregorian chants at her place. After the Halleluia, she said: "It's like the flashing of the Grail. The profound Paschal mystery is made manifest. Ah, Eberhard, this is how our redemption might have flowered from the blood of the Lamb. . . ."

She was surprised and hurt when I took the long-playing record off the turntable and scratched it with my bottle opener: "Tell that to your ornamental fish before they pass on."—"Yes," she said, "I'll have to change the water."

Scherbaum called his first editorial conference. They decided to dispense with ads in order to preserve their independence. The name of the school paper was to be changed.

"Well, Philipp. What is the new name to be?"

"I proposed *Dots and Dashes.*"

"I see."

"My first article will be about Helmuth Hübener's resistance group. I'm going to compare the activities of Hübener and Kiesinger in 1942."

"And how's Max?"

"Better. He must have eaten something that didn't agree with him. But now he's eating again."

"And your distal bite?"

"I'm getting a built-in brace. Pretty complicated. But I'll see it through. Definitely."

"Of course you will, Philipp.—I'm going back myself tomorrow. He's going to grind down six of my tusks. Second round."

"Well, have a good time."

(We tried to laugh together. We succeeded.)

What's concrete doing here? Build an impregnable system out of books echeloned in depth. Get my beginnings going or resume my Forster studies. (Between Nassenhuben and Mainz . . .) Books and suchlike mousetraps.

Why didn't I buy those two volumes in Friedenau? Why did I ride into town in the wet cold to try on Kurfüstendamm? (Only one book was available, the other had to be ordered.) I'd have found both at Wolff's.

After my purchase I moved against inhibitions in the direction of Kempinski's. After a long period of dry frost it was drizzling. Not much traffic on the sidewalk outside the café and anyone crossing it was in a hurry. Under a compulsion which I recognized to be sentimental but could not dismiss, I assumed a waiting stance on the spot which Philipp's calculations had designated as the scene of the crime. (A man in a tweed coat.) Collar turned up, I glanced at my wrist watch pretending—to whom?—to have an appointment. The rising temperature and sleety rain had reduced perforated blackened the piles of snow on the edge of the sidewalk. The pavement gave no sign. Wetness that crept through the soles of my shoes. Had I expected to find traces: On this spot Philipp Scherbaum, seven-

teen, high-school student, vomited in January 1967 at
the sight of cake-eating ladies?

The terrace was moderately occupied. Nothing was
right: only a few elderly ladies, two or three solitary
gentlemen, in the background a small group of trained
nurses, and up front, the center of attraction, an In-
dian with wife in exotic silk. Both drank tea and ate
no cake. But Vero Lewand was eating cake.

She was sitting in her duffel coat, stretching out absinthe-green legs and eating walnut layer cake at a
quick steady pace, spoonful after spoonful. We saw
each other: I saw her eating—she saw that I saw her
eating. She didn't stop spooning because I was
watching her spooning. Nor did she spoon more
quickly or less regularly. I did not remove my glasses,
breathe on them, and wipe them. She was eating in
protest. I saw that she was eating walnut layer cake in
protest. The elderly ladies at the next table drank
coffee and ate no cake. None of the ladies had a dog.

"Taste good, Veronica?"

"Natch. It's expensive."

"But that can't taste good."

"Would you like a piece?"

"If I must."

"Be my guest."

I decided in favor of Schwarzwald Kirsch Torte.
Vero Lewand treated herself to a second order: meringue with whipped cream. After that we were silent
in different directions. When cake and meringue
came, we spooned in silence. It couldn't be denied:
the cake was delicious. Her duffel coat no longer revealed anything. The Indians paid and left. Behind us,

after irregular pauses but always in unison, the nurses laughed. Groups of West German tourists under transparent raincoats hesitated on the sidewalk, went their way, and saved their money. The infrared tubes under the terrace roof were still adjusted to freezing weather. Three tables to the left of us a Negro in a camel's-hair coat sat down under the crushing top heat. His German was adequate: "Schwarzwälder Kirschtorte."

"How about it, Vero? Should I order some more?"

"This'll do."

"Wouldn't you like something light? Some shortcake?"

Again there was nothing for it but to offer Vero a cigarette. She smoked past me. Pauses cast spacious balloons offering room for dialogues on the windy Rhine Promenade in Andernach. (I suppose my former fiancée is entitled to participate in everything; if only I knew how often I sit at her table unbidden.)

"Tell me, Vero. Were you ever in Andernach on the Rhine?"

"Were you ever in Haparanda, Herr Starusch?"

(Her voice is not dependent on the weather; it's not a cold.)

"Tell me, Vero, why don't you have your adenoids removed?"

"Why don't you grow some?"

(Now she's playing with her silver spoon; in a minute it will be missing.)

"By the way, Fräulein Seifert has called my attention to the fact that my rug sheds."

"Didn't you know that before?"

(Later, much later, she made me a present of the spoon.)

"Perhaps you'll let me pay. All right?"

A leaflet was left on the table. "Fire! Fire!"

We walked away with cold feet and a sweet after-taste.

Part Three

Afterward the fish was gone and the bones remained. Airy spaces easy to populate. Afterward souvenirs were sold. Something was supposed to happen and to a certain extent happened later, though somewhere else. Afterward bills poured in. No one admits he did it. Afterward the prophylaxis was continued. Afterward begins beforehand.

The work on my upper teeth proceeded in very much the same way as the work on my lower teeth. Even now that everything had died away and been paid for, my dentist gives me answers; and yesterday when I asked him whether I shouldn't admit that for all his affability he was rather abrupt, not to say terse, he answered prolixly: "It's relatively unimportant whether we actually spoke or not. Why worry? I didn't say what you wanted to hear, but allowed you to make me say what I held to be true and almost said. Even your subsequent corrections—you do like to make changes—are my ideas, misunderstood. Go ahead, laugh!"

I bade him consider that his numerous patients, all answerable to him, might have confused him and blurred his memory.

"You forget my card file. Your card is right here: After an ample rest period—and after your difficulties with your student seemed to have been straightened out—when, to be precise, between February 7 and 13 we modified your upper teeth and attenuated, without entirely eliminating, your prognathism, at a time when I had already begun to treat your student Scherbaum's distal bite, I said while grinding your first molar: My dear Herr Starusch. Now that you've been rather shaken by your student's thank the Lord abandoned project—the youngster managed to put even me in a thoughtful mood—you ought to relinquish your fuzzy fictions: Your Krings—or whatever he may have been called—is a typical frustrated colonel who, like many soldiers without real professional training, tried to get a foothold in industry. Comparable cases are known to us. Kringsing is going on all over. Your Krings wasn't satisfied with economic success, so he amused himself on the family tabletop winning battles that his superiors had lost. (My barber, a former captain, delivers himself of similar victorious fantasies into the mirror.) This swagger of his led to occasional altercations between the Colonel and his daughter, whom you are trying to re-create as a monster; whereas I prefer to see your fiancée as a level-headed but not unloving young girl who grew more and more displeased at her fiancé's hectically frequent escapades. . . ."

(He ground down six teeth conically into bridge abutments. On the TV, when my dentist's representations didn't happen to be occupying the screen, an entertainment program of the Free Berlin station was on: "Rendezvous with Rudolf Schock." I saw the Kammersänger sing, but I heard him whisper.)

"If you will recall: At that time you drove a Mercedes convertible much admired in the Lower Eifel, year of manufacture 1932. You were a perfect snob, who liked to park his spiffed-up bus in the sun and his prognathous profile beside it. Who could have blamed the giddy Frau Schlottau for falling for the convertible and its driver with his deerskin gloves and Mussolini chin. (In those days you had a certain something.)

"So it happened that one bright April morning you drove through the village of Kretz and parked your sun chariot outside the Schlottaus' still unstuccoed one-family house. Abrupt braking made puddles splash and chickens flutter. (No cloud marred the simonized splendor.) Husband Schlottau, an honest truck driver, who drove cement mix to a large building site in Niedermendig for an Andernach construction firm affiliated with the nearby cement works, was on the road when you dropped in on Lotte Schlottau; and if the truck driver hadn't left his driver's license at home that April morning, you would have succeeded once again in certifying your ego. A little way past Kruft, Schlottau missed his papers, turned around, reached the village of Kretz, saw the parked sun chariot in the midst of his chickens and in front of his unstuccoed cottage, braked (though less abruptly), did not admire the Mercedes minutely and expertly but went quickly into the house, found his marriage bed occupied, did not become a homicide, did not hurl anything fragile, did not emit death rattles, bellow like bull, or go out of his mind, about-faced instantly and without a word relinquished the stud-muddled bed to the happy couple, leapt chicken-dispersing into his heavily loaded truck, set the powerful engine in motion, drove a short way forward and sharp right, shifted gears, backed up, seeking and finding a position that enabled him in full confidence to dump one and one-half tons of concrete mix into the open Mercedes, into the silver-black Sunmobile, into the swift proud beauty famous between Mayen and Andernach, into Industrial Engineer Eberhard Starusch's gas buggy.

"While the hydraulic tipping device gave the truck platform the necessary slant, Schlottau climbed down from the cab and looked on as the slowly slipping concrete filed, overfilled the cabriolet and, gray and obedient, embedded the radiator plus Mercedes star, the gracefully curved mudguards, the convertible top, and the luggage compartment with the spare tire strapped to it. The four swift wheels also acquired a concrete overcoat. There was even enough left for the space between the gas tank and Schlottau's lot. The chickens tilted their heads. Schlottau's only reaction was a distal biting of the lower lip.

"What a lump of concrete! Newspaper wags demanded that the strange fossil be placed on exhibition at the Ethnological Museum in Mayen, that the boulder be installed in the courtyard of the Genofevaburg amid Roman and Early Christian basalt fragments, to be admired by the numerous visitors. School classes visited the monument to your defeat until it was processed with pneumatic hammers and finally towed away (at your expense). (Schlottau's concrete had even put your deerskin gloves in the glove compartment under seal.)

"And the payoff—though of this no one can be absolutely sure—it seems you didn't even complete your studies. That's what they're saying in the Lower Eifel. An unverifiable rumor. Granted. But this much is a fact: You were fired. Your engagement was broken off. And only because you had the gall to take your case to Labor Court, your firm, fearing for its reputation, granted you, though the cement works would have won the case, an indemnity to which your fiancée's father contributed: they wanted to get rid of you, quickly and as far as possible quietly. The expense be damned. That's how one gets to be a schoolteacher. But now, please rinse. . . ."

Who can laugh when, with aspirator dangling from open mouth and dental substance dwindling away, something funny enters his field of vision? (Let him rave.)

I countenanced my dentist's notions but corrected a few details: "Good story. But I didn't drive a Mercedes convertible, Krings did. (They left me the Borgward.) And it wasn't my car but Krings' that was turned into a lump of concrete. Not because of any studding feats (though I wouldn't have put that past the old boy) but for revenge, some war veterans diverted concrete mix from its normal function. Schlottau, I still believe, had nothing to do with it. (He ate out of the old man's hand.) It happened on a construction site in Koblenz. (One of those glassed-in cigar boxes they were putting up in the middle fifties.)

Anyway there was a roof-raising. We were invited because our firm had supplied the cement and building materials. Even Aunt Mathilde had put on her black silk. Linde and her girl-friend in striped summer dresses. Though it was already September. Even Schlottau, who had driven the old man's Mercedes, gave the appearance of a guest in his dark-blue single-breasted suit. There was a breeze on the flat roof above the twelfth story. The ceremonial wreath had to be tied down. Bottled beer was handed around. The girls shivered in their summer dresses. For a time I stood to one side with Schlottau. The head mason's speech, snippeted by the wind, went on and on. And that swinish stud said to me: 'Your fiancée, my compliments, she's okay. No kidding, Herr Starusch. Class. Got to hand it to you.'—And once I managed to stand right next to Linde who was leaning over the parapet. (Down below lay our pumice-concrete construction units, our steel-reinforced floor slabs and coffer slabs.) But I only confined myself to thinking and did nothing. No witnesses, because everybody was listening to Krings to whom the sweeping view from the new building had dictated a speech. I heard him carry off a victory over the wind blowing from the direction of Ehrenbreitstein. He spoke of treason at Kursk. Of the nonexistent Arctic. Of the Red flood that could only be stemmed by a Stoic bulwark. And at the end the word 'Stalingrad' fell. With a quotation from Seneca grafted onto it, it sounded well-behaved and gave promise of victory. 'This battle is not yet decided!' Because no one applauded, I heard Linde: 'I'll turn you into Paulus, into Paulus!'

"Down below, beside our standard cored blocks we found the Mercedes under quickly setting concrete. (Look, Doc: Krings is laughing.) Nothing gets him down: 'Splendid! Splendid! Well, Schlottau? Your production, eh? A bit of revenge in the forenoon. But now we're quits, aren't we?' (And look, Doc, look!) Not only Schlottau, who may have been the instigator of Operation Concrete after all, but also his accomplices, the war-veteran masons in their work clothes, form one big unanimous mouth: 'Sure thing, Herr Field Marshal General!'

"So much for the Mercedes in concrete. But perhaps, while I take the liberty of rinsing, a third possibility will occur to you. What do you think of it: Linde is sitting at the wheel of the Mercedes which is obliged to wait behind a truck full of concrete mix because ahead of my truck and her Mercedes the gate is down at a grade crossing. . . ."

The first day of treatment passed off indecisively. From tooth to tooth and between teeth dentist and patient lined up their mutually contradictory stories and theories. Occasionally general considerations of pedagogy and preventive dental medicine at the preschool age provided a breather. The Scherbaum case was also discussed: "Imagine, Doc, he's been speaking in the plural lately: 'We have decided unanimously . . .' And the draft of his first article, 'What was King Silvertongue doing when . . . ?' begins something like this: 'We are high-school students. We are doing all right at school. In us hopes can be put. Sometimes we try to overshoot the mark. That is understandable. In high-school students that is still permissible. Sometimes we want to drop everything, because it stinks. That too is understandable because it really does stink and because we are high-school students: high-school students are entitled to want to drop everything just because it stinks. Once upon a time there was a king. The high-school students called him King Silvertongue. . . .' "

But my dentist wanted to speak only of Scherbaum's distal bite. When I tried to get him interested in the case of Vero Lewand he rebuffed me: "That's something for an ear, nose, and throat man. . . ." Kammersänger Rudolf Schock sang: "Love drives me on to look for love. . . ."

A passage in Scherbaum's first article (which was not published): "We are a good class. They say we'll get somewhere. Sometimes we don't want to get anywhere. That's understandable: Students who don't want to get anywhere are sure to get somewhere. King Silvertongue didn't want to get anywhere and then he did get somewhere. . . ."

Today it is hard for me to speak consecutively of the inauguration of the Air-Raid Shelter Church. Too many deterrents. (Not only Kammersänger Rudolf Schock and my dentist.) Scherbaum uses me as a cloakroom for his defeats. Irmgard Seifert goes in and out of my apartment. A girl student wriggles on my Berber rug, forcing me to take off, breathe on, and wipe my glasses.

While I now say: "Frau Mathilde Krings, sister of the Field Marshal General and aunt of my former fiancée Sieglinde Krings, funded the remodeling of the Air-Raid Shelter Church in Koblenz . . ." I say at the same time: "When my student Philipp Scherbaum took over the editorship of the school paper *Dots and Dashes,* he was not able to publish his first article comparing the activity of the National Socialist Georg Kiesinger with the activity of the resistance fighter Helmuth Hübener in the year 1942 without cuts, although he had taken the precaution of introducing Kiesinger under a nickname. . . ."

And when I now say: "While the windows were pierced in the large concrete structure (and the Kammersänger sang something from the operetta *Fledermaus*), Mathilde Krings who with us and members of the high clergy was visiting the building site said: 'What do you think of the acoustics, Ferdinand?' " I hear at the same time Vero Lewand's words: "Aw, come on, Old Hardy! You probably can't . . ." and the confession of my colleague Irmgard Seifert: "I love you, Eberhard . . ." and there's even room for her following sentence: "Now please don't say that you love me too. . . ."

Inauguration and auto-censorship, attempted seduction and declaration of love do not contradict one another. Loudly as Vero Lewand calls her former boy-friend a "manipulated fence-sitter," urgently as Scherbaum tries to explain to me why he had to give in to the representations of his fellow students, selflessly as Irmgard Seifert's love clamors for self-expression all around the Grunewaldsee, finding words like "to serve through painful renunciation," I let

Krings test the acoustics of the Air-Raid Shelter Church after the Kammersänger has tested them.

Krings quoted his Seneca: "Let us train our minds to desire what the situation demands."

Then he spoke his "There is no Arctic!" into the room encased in five hundred cubic feet of reinforced concrete which had once provided protection against those who controlled the air over the territory of the Reich.

What Krings uttered in medium volume the hall amplified into victorious reports on the situation at Stalingrad immediately after Krings had replaced Paulus and taken over the supreme command: "We have regained the initiative!"

Today it would be easy for me to put my student Scherbaum into the sacral reinforced concrete edifice and make his confession public: "I had to delete Silvertongue. They said it was too controversial for the first issue. If we attack Kiesinger, we've got to attack Brandt. The story is that he even wore a Norwegian uniform at that time. So I said: Shit on your Kiesinger. But the part about Hübener stands or I resign. . . ."

(To Linde I said while we were visiting the building site: "If we get married someday, it's got to be here. . . .")

While copper-band impressions were being made of all six ground-down teeth, while all six stumps were being painted with a nonirritating protective varnish and safe-guarded against outside influences with

aluminum shells, I concentrated on the infinitely en-
joyable rendezvous with Schock, a hundred-and-
eighty-five-thousand-mark production, as I later
figured out. Herr Schock received roughly ten thousand, the director, Eisbrenner his name was, three
thousand. Make-up spent four thousand three hundred
on hair, wigs, and cosmetics. A chief electrician and
ten assistant electricians made five thousand six
hundred and eighty-nine marks in six shooting days. I
counted it up. Expenses for props and scenery, for fan
palms, costumes bought, rented second-hand, rented
new, made to order, and backdrops (a fireman was
obtained free of charge). All this throws little light on
my condition while six aluminum shells were being
put on. For actually, as long as the telecast was on
and becoming steadily more expensive, I was preoccu-
pied by the word "dwindle."

Wanting to dwindle away. No longer to offer a target. To make myself smaller than visible. Like certain
people who disappear for a moment around the corner
(for a smoke) and then you can't lay hands on them
because they've spontaneously dwindled away (but
where to?). To dwindle away is more than to vanish.
Take an eraser, which cheerfully wears itself out on
error; just as I on the school front am wearing myself
down to insignificance, to the point where I shall be
recognizable only in particles: That, no that, no this
crumb is typical Starusch. He has worn himself down
with his student. (Now Scherbaum holds me responsible for his failure.) A schoolteacher who throws himself wholly into his work and tries to do everything at

once. But it's pointless now. ("I'm disappointed, Philipp, dismayed and disappointed. . . .")

As the treatment proceeded, as three days later he removed the aluminum shells, as he tried on the unfinished bridges, and as the pink plaster was laid on with a spatula, I tried to hate my dentist.

(A feature picture was being shown on TV: "Malcolm X, a political murder.")

As the plaster began to set in my oral cavity, he said: "Your inhibitions toward your colleague can be accounted for: Schlottau undermined your self-confidence."

Layer by layer I began to expose him: He who allegedly wants to pacify the world with the help of worldwide Sickcare, he who sees himself in constant struggle against the advance of caries, who at the top of his lungs preaches periodic dental examinations at the preschool age, he—he and none other—slips away several times in the course of a consultation and vanishes into the toilet. There I showed him, quickly, avidly, with no more inhibitions than a baby, ingurgitating enormous quantities of sticky sweets. Erect in the tiny cubicle, he indulges loudly, hastily, with glazed eyes. And sometimes between patient and patient he sits down and nevertheless goes on swallowing. "You," I said, "you try to talk me into inhibitions, maybe to make me doubt my potency, and there you sit—There!—in the can, sucking caramels with glittering eye, lecherously munching chocolate creams, slobbering syrups, beside yourself when the bag is empty. And right after the orgy—There!—you reach

for your Water Pik that you've taken with you to remove the traces of your cloying goo with pulsating jets
of water—and you claim to be a doctor?"

When my dentist tried to justify his excesses in the
toilet as a scientific testing of the Water Pik, even his
assistant giggled. Then he spoke of certain compul-
sions which in the course of protracted treatment are
transmitted from patient to physician. "It's a case of
psychic infection. What did you do a week ago when
your relationship with your student was exposed to
painful tensile tests? Well, how did you face up to the
pain?"

I admitted that unhappy as I had been, abandoned
in my misery and frankly desperate, I had eaten two
bars of milk chocolate within five minutes.

"You see," he said, "your misery is contagious,"
and aided by his assistant broke the pink casting plaster out of my oral cavity.

Today I associate with my dentist as though nothing had happened, over the phone: "And how's Scherbaum getting along?"

He reports matter-of-factly on the length and difficulty of a late treatment of distal bite and praises my
student's perserverance: "Especially for a young man
of eighteen this kind of orthodontic appliance with its
ugly labial bar is an annoying foreign body, and in
time becomes a psychological burden which not everyone can bear."

I reported to him on Scherbaum's activity as editor-in-chief: "After all his compromises he can at least
lay claim to a slight success. He, he of all people, has

put through the smokers' corner: 'All right, now you can puff!' Even Irmgard Seifert voted in favor. And guess what! Scherbaum doesn't smoke, he's a fanatical nonsmoker."

Occasionally a letter with newspaper clippings. Passages marked in red. Two three phone calls a week. Once we went to an art exhibit together in the Hansa Quarter. Once we met by chance on Kurfürstendamm and went to the Bristol for tea. Twice he came to my place to look at my Celtic shards and Roman basalt fragments. But he never invites me to his house.

We treat each other with kid gloves. Our comments on the political unrest in the city, the mayor's resignation, and police excesses are reserved: "It was bound to happen." At the most I hear discreet allusions: "I hear we can expect a breakdown of certain inhibitions in the streets pretty soon."

We referred only with ironic circumstances to the days of treatment when we laid each other bare and came far too close to one another.

"I admit, Doc, that after two hours of strenuous effort that first attempt to include sex in relations with Irmgard Seifert proved a failure. And yet, when we were smoking again, she said: 'It won't prevent me from loving you. We must be patient with one another.'—And so we have been. The frequent intercuts are to blame. She's always cutting herself in, you know, she, forcing me with her strategicotactical details to deliver a lecture on trass cement and its utility for underwater construction. Even the bleak, though cinematically interesting ugliness of the Lower Eifel scene, the eroded pumice-mining region and the two active stacks of the Krings Works, is too much for our relationship; especially as for some time now I've been running into not only my former fiancée in the abandoned basalt pits, but my girl student Veronica Lewand as well. Linde and Vero are cooking up something together: plots against me . . . There, Doc, do you see?"

My dentist spoke in passing about the Malcolm X picture—"Violence seems to have a future"—and then added: "Let's for the moment set aside your perfectly normal sexual disturbances and talk about cement. I've been gathering information. There aren't any Krings Works. In Kruft we have the Tubag Trass, Cement, and Stone Works, Inc., a fully owned subsidiary of Dyckerhoff. Today this Dyckerhoff family enterprise, producers of stone and bricks since 1922, boasts a many-sided production program, yet by comparison with the sister plant in Neuwied, Tubag's cement production is relatively small. But this only in passing, to clear up the question of ownership. An inquiry at the Andernach Labor Office has further disclosed that during the mid-term vacation of 1954–1955 you were carried on the Tubag payroll as a summer-job student; no question of any industrial engineer."

My dentist, preparing the aluminum shells on the accessory table, waited to see if I would venture any objections. I could only joke helplessly: "You ought to be a dick. Honest to God, you ought to be a dick."

He smiled. (Maybe he does work for the police.) "It was relatively easy to get hold of these documents.

I simply had them Xeroxed. We dentists work hand in glove. And a colleague in Andernach—Dr. Lindrath—informed me that one of his daughters, now married and a practicing pediatrician in Koblenz, remembers a student by your name, though only vaguely. But that may be accidental. Besides, her first name is Monica. Well? Does that ring a bell? Monica Lindrath? Here in profile? Here full face? Here with girl-friends on the Rhine Promenade in Andernach? No?—Pretty girl."

When I remained impassive, he abandoned his interrogation and picked up the first aluminum shell in his tweezers: "Never mind. I'm willing to believe a Sieglinde existed, if not in Andernach perhaps in Mayen. After all, we've all of us been engaged. Far be it from me to restrict your gift of invention. While I'm putting on the protective caps didn't you want to tell me about Daughter Krings' big Stalingrad game against Papa Krings?"

Ah, how is the gold become dim.—I ought to have my junior class write a theme about these words from Lamentations, or perhaps just about the little words "oh" and "ah." About oh yes, oh really, oh no. About ah me, ah as a cry of lamentation. About the astonished, angry, scarcely breathed oh. About the ah in Kleist and the ironical oh in Mann. About the child's oh and the frail old man's ah. How does the oh brought on by a particularly successful sunset differ from an oh in the presence of the ocean? The ah in song: "Ah, I have lost her. . . ." And the ah in politics: "Ah, my dear colleague, Barzel . . ." Of

course the oh in advertising: "Oh, you rinse with
Pril. . . ." And the oh of women, the oh-oh-ohoh, already known to Scherbaum. (And the oh before first
names: "Oh, Irmgard, we ought to . . ."—"Oh, Vero,
I'd like to . . ."—"Oh, Lindelindelindelinde . . .")

While he put on the aluminum shells, I put on a
dress rehearsal of the battle of Stalingrad and showed
my action outside the Hotel Kempinski. In Cement
Shack D Krings was victorious in the sandbox. On the
corner of Kurfürstendamm and Fasanenstrasse afternoon crowds. Linde reacted listlessly. I held the white
spitz short on the leash. She allowed "Winter Storm"
to take its course—the café terrace was fully occupied—although the absence of fuel in the Stalingrad
pocket would have precluded an offensive movement.
The spitz held still when I emptied the bottle of gasoline over his coat. Schlottau's electromechanical
switch system worked smoothly, providing a certain
visual effect. Since I had prepared the spitz with
Valium, he kept calm. When, for instance, both sides
counterattacked at once. (An onlooker said: "Is that
for fleas?") After winning the dress rehearsal, Krings
read the invitation aloud; and into the reading of the
list of guests as into the reading of my leaflet "Fire
fire" I faded the arrival of the first guests and the
lighting of my storm lighter. High government officials
came from Mainz, Bundeswehr officers, a pensioned
school principal, newspapermen, the usual corporation heads. The jet flame burned the palm of my left
hand, singed my tweed coat, and sent a ball of fire
leaping on the leash. In the cement shack a free-and-

easy cocktail party began. (Blow on my palm.) The snippets of conversation gave little inkling of the impending sandbox game and the passers-by outside Kempinski's were equally slow on the uptake. (I should have brought some ointment as a precaution.) The guests talked shop: economic forecasts, personnel questions, jokes about the defense ministry, and vacation reminiscences predominated. Even some laughter at first: "Guess it's a happening." In the cement shack civilized merriment set the tone. I had to let go the leash: my hand. (Someone did a parody of the President.) The spitz writhed, and leapt at the tables, heaped with cakes. One table was overturned. Linde in her beige cocktail dress and Aunt Mathilde in her black silk were the only ladies. Live sounds: "Him over there. I saw him. Him with the glasses . . ." Drinks were served with the help of a hired waiter. Someone threw a tablecloth over the glowing, still quivering spitz. Linde filled the glasses too full. I was jostled and (when I started handing out the leaflets) beaten. Schlottau tested the light signals. I lost my glasses. Like the dress rehearsal, the première of the Krings Offensive went off victoriously according to plan. They struck with umbrellas fists briefcases. Joining forces with Hooth, he established bases for the advance on Astrakhan. (The rising blister on the palm of my hand.) Shortly before midnight the last guests left. I shouted: "Read my leaflets first. . . ." Aunt Mathilde also retired. On Kurfürstendamm I bled (a cut in my right eyebrow) and in Cement Shack D Schlottau and I were witnesses as Linde defeated her father in the sandbox. "That's gasoline, not napalm!"

I shouted. Linde proved to Krings that he intended to mount an offensive spearhead with units that had been decimated in "Operation Thunderclap." "Do you capitulate?" When I tried to break through to Fasanenstrasse, I was knocked down. "Never!" (I was frightened.) Krings repeated the word "Never!" On the pavement (I was still shouting) I found my glasses. They were unbroken. Sieglinde laid a German Army revolver (zero eight) on the edge of the sandbox: "Then you know what you have to do." On the sidewalk outside the café terrace of the Hotel Kempinski I was glad when I heard a police siren. (Because they'd have.) In Cement Shack D Schlottau and I stood like two pillars. The cops came in with their night sticks. (I made no attempt to defend myself.) The transformers of the electromechanical sandbox installation hummed. Someone shouted: "That guy ought to be killed. . . ." Krings picked up the zero eight and said: "I wish to be alone. . . ." I clutched my glasses. Linde left at once. Before they dragged me away, I shouted a little more. Schlottau wanted to argue. They laughed: "We know all about it." Krings waved him away. In the paddy wagon I kept on shouting: "Napalm!" He couldn't even dig up a Seneca quotation. Then everything grew black. (My embarrassment.) I was very gay. Outside the shack Schlottau and I smoked two cigarettes. I only came to at the police station. (I had matches.) My hands. No shot rang out. When, asked what my profession was, I said "schoolteacher" a policeman knocked my glasses off my face. We left. (Only then did my glasses expire.) Schlottau wished me a good night.

"But," I said to my dentist, "that isn't the end."

(On the screen a commercial was on; we had missed the murder of Malcolm X.) But the six aluminum shells were in place.

"Only a few details to fill in: Scherbaum comes to see me in the hospital, brings me chocolate and newspapers, and Krings, I'm told, as defeat creeps closer, fights his mounting depression by escalating his consumption of chocolate creams."

My dentist understood: "Ah yes, pain!—But *we'll* stick to Arantil. Take two now to see you home. . . ."

And this and that. (And I and I.) And the feeling of lightness afterward and the gasping for air afterward. And about the weather and what became of the spitz. And someone shouted: "Why doesn't he burn himself?" And a government official from Mainz asked: "Do you mean the Volga bridges are intact?" And overlappings and changes of locale. Schlottau hauls off and I find my glasses in among Hooth's armored prongs. (And here and here.) The Kempinski terrace and jet flames from the transformers, all in the sandbox. And applause and approval. That's how it should have been, at last somebody who's got some courage. In May and in January. The stars were gone from the sky and it was sunny, frosty, and clear. . . .

"Tell me, Scherbaum, aren't you glad it didn't come off?"—"I don't know."—"But if you had to ask yourself today: Should I?"—"I don't know."—"But suppose something else somewhere else?"—"No idea how I'd."—"And suppose I did something, maybe not this but something else?"—"You'll never do anything."

Three weeks after my dental treatment, three weeks after, my bite corrected, I tried to ascertain certain other changes in myself—I managed for the first time to have intercourse with Irmgard Seifert in a manner that seemed relatively satisfactory to both of us— three weeks after the dentist's intervention and a few days after I had stopped taking Arantil—it was hard for me to break the habit and my teaching suffered— early in March, on the fourth to be precise, I proposed to Irmgard Seifert.

Since I relied on our jaunt once around the Grunewaldsee to start me off, the decisive word fell on the wooden bridge across the now ice-free passage leading to the Hundekehlesee. "I am very much tempted, my dear Irmgard, to go to the jeweler's and buy two different-sized rings. . . ."

Irmgard Seifert asked for a cigarette. "Since some weeks ago you slapped my face on this very spot, I can only assume that you mean it seriously."

I was grateful for the bantering tone: "My dear Irmgard, the slap was the introduction to our engagement, but if you say no I'll slap with both hands, forgo an engagement, and punish you by marrying you right away."

She took a drag at her just-lighted cigarette and threw it away: "Then to limit the damage, I shall say yes in an undertone and without ceremony."

We dispensed with a party, although for a few days I had been itching to give a party; I even wanted to invite my dentist. We sent out cards. He offered congratulations and gave us a first edition of Schmekel's book on *The Middle Stoa*.

I announced it to my junior class with an "Incidentally . . ." Next day Vero Lewand (wordlessly) thrust a silver cake spoon at me, engraved with the name of its former owner. (That's how you come by souvenirs.)

In the April issue of the school paper *Dots and Dashes* I found a squib by Scherbaum: "What engagement has the engaged couple undertaken?" With his succinct sentences he harried the word "engagement" over absurd ground: "An engagement has been contracted. A dissolved engagement presupposes an engagement that has been contracted. If one wishes to reactivate a dissolved engagement, one must first dissolve the dissolution of the engagement. Dissolved engagements are more costly than contracted ones. . . ."

Irmgard Seifert termed the squib "in pretty bad taste." She asked me to call a teachers' meeting to consider the confiscation of the April issue. I asked Scherbaum to apologize to her: "You surely understand that Fräulein Seifert can't react like a young girl to your sometimes offensive playing with words." As editor-in-chief Scherbaum continued to go easy on me. "Of course. Sure thing. I certainly had no intention of getting you into trouble with her."

We are still not disengaged. In the May issue of the school paper, the "Flash" column carried a note on the average daily cigarette consumption in the "legal" smokers' corner, then the announcement of an official visit. "The Shah of Persia is coming to Berlin. We didn't invite him"—and just before an ad for the Antoine Dancing School, under "Announcement," the not incorrect sentence: "Fräulein Seifert and Herr Starusch are still engaged."

Irmgard tried to laugh too: "I suppose it's not Scherbaum, but the little Lewand girl, who is responsible for this chicanery. What do you think, Eberhard?"

(So she was, and she's still at it. She's the coming man. In the students' committee of the Students' Cooperation Organization she has the majority behind her. She has introduced a motion of no-confidence in Scherbaum. She's determined to give him the ax. Immediately after the Shah's visit, she started her counterpaper: "We have resolved not to put up with any more compromises. . . ." She's right up front. And several times I've seen her in the paper, locking arms, double-timing, right up front. . . .)

The idea of becoming engaged to Irmgard Seifert came to me on the last day of treatment. For the last time he gave me his signals—"Now comes the nasty little pinprick"—"Now rinse please"—and for the last time an internal dialogue threw balloons on the television screen. My dentist and I encircled the globe. Our models of an all-embracing order—his medical, my pedagogical principle of care—outdid each other and canceled each other out. We were daringly radical and absolutely sincere. We irrigated the Sahara. We drained the swamps of tradition. He lulled the aggressive drive to sleep: "Within the scope of worldwide Sickcare, violence, that is, its receptors, will be tranquilized or, in technical terms, locally anaes-thetized. . . ." I pacified by pedagogy: "With the help of the mass media, and within the framework of a worldwide educational system, the student status will be extended to old age. . . ." But conscientiously as we vied with one another in pole vaulting, a vestige of earthly gravity beguiled us time and again into measuring our strength in knuckle pulling.

On the First Program a film for skiers and would-be skiers was on: "From telemark to wedel."

Because he treated me like an onion which, skin minus skin, became steadily smaller and more vitre-ous, I supplanted powder snow and downhill runs with a documentary on a spiritist séance in which my dentist and his assistant (as medium) participated: the usual table lifting.

No sooner had he administered my four injections than the room monitor showed more than our well-re-hearsed trio: congestion prevailed in the office. Now fluid, now compact manifestations: sensitive astral bodies, disappointingly similar to the bed-sheet ghosts of folk conception, gave each other a telepathic ren-dezvous.

My ma was there too. I asked her if it was wise to enter into another engagement and obtained the moth-erly advice that the air should be cleared first. After several exchanges transmitted by the medium I found out that my ma knew all about Irmgard Seifert: "Just don't do anything dumb. Those stupid letters gotta go first. 'Cause there won't be any peace if she keeps on talking about those days and the things that happened. . . ."

Three weeks later, just after we decided to become engaged, I took my mother's advice and asked for the packet of letters.

She said: "You want to destroy them, don't you?"

Though actually I'd only been going to lock them up, I said: "Yes, I want to set you free of them."

On our next walk around the Grunewaldsee she gave me the packet. I piled up the letters in a hollow on the sandy east shore. They burned away quickly.

On the way home Irmgard Seifert called my attention to a relevant "prohibited" sign: "We were lucky a ranger didn't catch us. . . ."

In my dentist's telekinetically enlarged office my ma, even before the aluminum shells were removed, gave me further advice, while on the screen, conditioned perhaps by the underlying skiing picture, there were milky spooky goings-on. (The astral bodies were wedeling.)

My ma admonished me to drink less beer and to find a different laundry; she wasn't at all pleased with the state of my shirts. "Take a look at the corners. They just don't know how to iron a collar nowadays."

Then she asked me to keep a special eye on one of my students, because he might be in danger that summer in connection with an impending "highly placed visitor." "You know, son, he's the same like you were. Always up front, harum-scarum and devil-may-care. The worries I had . . ."

I asked my ma's forgiveness and promised to keep an eye on Scherbaum. (And nothing happened to him outside the opera house, but Vero Lewand was able to display contusions and a bloody nose.)

My dentist removed my aluminum shells. I attempted further conversations with the departed: "But they're all still alive, Doc. Because though Krings picked up the Army revolver his daughter had put down on the edge of the sandbox, he preferred, like Paulus, not to shoot himself. The following morning he summoned the family, including Schlottau and myself, to his study, admitted his defeat, and acquainted us, after mentioning the voluntary death of the philosopher Seneca and the nullity of death, with his decisions: 'I have decided to usher in a victorious new era in another field; I'm going into politics.'

"After that I arrived at a decision: I broke off my engagement to his daughter. He accepted, giving it to be understood that my decision met with his approval. And Schlottau, unasked, said: 'That makes sense.'

"And so our family war game broke up; but if you don't mind, Doc . . ."

My dentist was opposed to variants and wouldn't stand for a last confrontation with Linde: "That's all, my friend. End, curtain, and no afterthoughts. As a dentist, I listen daily to these triangle stories that put on historical or up-to-the-minute costumes. Disguises borrowed from the wardrobe of economic theory, religion, criminology, and sometimes even of tax law are expected to warm the selfsame pathetic triangle. Before you try to make us witness the Linde-Schlottau wedding, let's take a look at the skiers: they're alive, they wedel, they send up powder, make tracks, laugh, and in the end drink their Ovaltine. In short: Have you finally buried your former fiancée?"

"I have done what long ago in my native city the painter Anton Möller did to the burgomaster's daughter, his promised bride. . . ."

"So there's another story after all?"

"Restructuring" Vero Lewand calls the procedure. As long as he was busy preparing the special cement, drying the prepared teeth with hot air, and setting the two bridges in place, I animated the screen with the parable of Painter Möller.

But I did not merely unfold the classical triangle story (which my dentist would gladly have sacrificed to progress), I also took the liberty of alluding to his own triangular situation; for to whom is it a secret that between his wife—the mother of his children—and his assistant, my dentist plays the role of a typical old-fashioned triangle man?

"And such was the case of my compatriot, the gifted Anton Möller, who in 1692 was commissioned to paint a Last Judgment for the Danzig City Council: a commission for which the painter, who up until then had wallowed in manneristic allegories, was indebted to his father-in-law to be, the city's burgomaster. The patrician's daughter was to be married as soon as the Hanseatically generous fee for the Last Judgment should fall due and be paid.

"Möller had quickly completed the paradisiacally

tedious part of the panel in accordance with the prevailing fashion—to get it over with. He was looking
forward to Purgatory and the descent into Hell, to
which, as the scion of a seaport town, he was planning
to give a nautical twist. The sinners were to float
downstream in freight barges, sloops, and graceful
skiffs on a river, for which the Mottlau, a tributary of
the Vistula, was obliged to sit. And in one of the
downward-bound skiffs he wanted a naked woman—
sin incarnate; he couldn't help it, allegory was second
nature to him.

"But even sin couldn't and can't be portrayed without a model. A raftsman's daughter—a voluptuous
child of the riverfront—stood still on supporting leg
and unweighted leg lending him her dimensions, and,
when the painter's betrothed inspected the well-ad-
vanced descent into Hell, was taken immediately for
the objectionable member of a triangular relationship
which you, my dear Doc, though yourself involved in
a triangle, affect to regard as obsolete and outmoded;
yet it showed Painter Möller the way to art.

"His betrothed raised the roof. The young girl, who
was pretty but not voluptuous enough to represent sin,
stirred up her father, and the council and aldermen as
well. Möller was asked to be false to his art. He was
given the choice either of making the raftsman's
daugher, who was known to the whole town, unrecog-
nizable—or of forgoing his fee and the burgomaster's
daughter.

"The outcome was the first artistic compromise, the
one I had in mind while attempting to speak of Ferdinand Krings; because, you see, the original makes no

bones about likewise bearing the name of Ferdinand. Möller gave the raftsman's daughter a new face which resembled that of his betrothed; how else was he to make sin peer out of his picture after he had been forbidden the laughing face of the suburban whore—the raftsman lived near St. Barbara's in the Lower City.

"The outcry over the public and sinful representation of a burgomaster's daughter is even recorded in the city chronicles: the guilds and corporations, siding with Möller, laughed uproariously and sang satirical songs. Already political strife was in the air. (Something about brewing rights and fishery leases.) At this point the aldermen forgot their threats and, led by the burgomaster, took to pleading.

"The outcome was that second artistic compromise which guided me too when I put Papa Krings and Daughter Krings in a setting of cement, pumice, trass, and tuff; not around the body of the raftsman's daughter, but around the silly-pretty face of his betrothed, Möller placed a reflecting bell jar, which to this day asks a riddle: What is this delicate little face, rather goatlike in its narrowness and mystically blurred behind glass, doing on all that lusciously rounded flesh? (Just look at the reflections that bell jar can give off; it mirrors everything, everything—the world and its contradictions. . . .)

"And in that same skiff that was to carry sin to Hell, Möller, while he was at it, painted all the aldermen and the burgomaster as well: embarrassing likenesses and not under glass.

"The outcome was the third artistic compromise to which I too shall incline; for just as I shrink back from calling you and your assistant by name—what would your wife say?—so Painter Möller was not prepared to let the alderman, along with burgomaster and daughter, go to Hell: he painted himself into the Mottlau transfigured as Hades. With powerful arms he holds back the skiff, and as he does so looks at us: If it weren't for me, things would rapidly go downhill.

"The artist as savior. He helps sin to safety. He does not abandon the triangle. Just as you are secretly attached to the trigon. Right, Doc? Tell the truth. Right?"

The bridges were in place and my dentist turned off the TV. His assistant held the mirror to my face. "What do you say now?"

(Now I can show myself. It snaps shut. With a bite that closes a man has a new start. He can laugh more lustily. It makes him hungrier, it wants to bite into apples. With this I can get engaged. Yes. Say yes. Yes. Say yes. So many teeth—and they all stand for me. With this I'll go out into the streets. . . .)

My dentist—and not his assistant—helped me on with my coat: "As soon as the anaesthetic wears off, your tongue will look for the old gaps. But not for long."

And when I was already in the doorway, he gave me the slip of paper: "I've prescribed the family size as a precaution. That ought to do it.—You've been a pleasant patient. . . ."

The Hohenzollerndamm was really outside. On my

way to Elsterplatz I ran into Scherbaum: "Well, Philipp? I've been redeemed, my bite's complete."

By way of explanation I showed him my attenuated prognathism; Scherbaum showed me his belatedly treated distal bite: "This is the labial bar. Kind of a nuisance."

My speech was still palatal: "Have a good time!"

Scherbaum said: "I'll stick it out."

We laughed about nothing. Then he went off, then I went off and bit into the air ahead of me. . . .

Lindelindelindelinde . . . (Stored-up murder plots.) I took the train after she had taken the train. January 1965: Frau Schlottau is spending the winter holidays on the island of Sylt with her husband and children, doctor's advice. Daily walks across the wind-polished dunes. With closed mouth against the pore-widening wind over the lonely downs. Breathing iodine around the Elbow or around Point Hörnum, where bay and ocean mingle to form whirlpools. Every day Father maps out an itinerary. Behold the family: the boys in rubber boots in the lead, Mother in parka occupies the middle ground, Father armed with binoculars brings up the rear. Thus they may be seen looking for sea shells and health up beach and down.

And I, lurking in wait, my tongue propped against a fresh growth of tartar, flat in the whistling beach grass, snickering because the boys find nothing but light bulbs generously cast up by the sea. With shivery flaky foam the wind chases them across the beach at low tide, unmarred as though they might still. "Take 'em home! Daddy, take 'em home!"

(Yesterday comes again, bringing the electric bill.)

An instructor at the Cologne Sports Academy, I had hired out for the mid-term holidays as a bathmaster. I operated the wave machine at the celebrated Seawater Swimming Pool with Artificial Waves. In tennis shoes I shuffled over the tepid tiles. I cast muffled glances in the direction of the Wave Pool Restaurant above the shower and locker rooms. Behind its glass front elderly vacationers and local nonswimmers were working up an appetite: one or two families, but no Schlottaus.

When will she come, her family in her wake? Wider at the hips but still the wiry mountain goat, snappy and unmanageable in and about the barn and charming only on hillsides. When will she come with miscellaneous orders in her heart: "Ulli, you're not to go swimming until I say now we're going swimming."— "Daddy, don't stare at people like that!"—"No diving, Wolfi, do you hear me? There will be no diving."

The clan is hiking in rubber boots, visiting Kampen, Keitum, Morsum. They want—doctor's advice—to get acclimated first. They're still gaping at the thatched Frisian houses. They're still pointing out ships on the horizon to each other. "Look at the lighthouse! Look at the jet! Look at the gulls on that battered pillbox. . . ."

They eat what the sea has to offer: halibut and turbot, plaice and flounder. Daddy wants eel—Mummy changes the order to cod. He has a craving for mussel chowder—she decrees: no soup today. The children

get half portions, mostly red perch fillets to avoid
bones. They alternate between succulent and expensive at Kiefer's and insipid at the pension: veal stew in
flour sauce. And for dessert: semolina pudding with
raspberry syrup.

The family has quickly got used to the strange sur-
roundings. Recreation without movies. (Daddy and
Mummy write postcards with gulls and seals on them
to Grampa and Aunt Mathilde.) A successful marriage. At night before they go to bed, she reads—but
what does she read? (Serialized novels in beat-up illustrated magazines and no more Clausewitz,
Schramm, Liddell Hart.)

In his galley, beside the controls of the wave
machine, the fake bathmaster reads his Marxengels in
a pocket edition and inhales Nietzsche's posthumous
works page by page.

Now the children are clamoring: "Mummy, when
are we going in the wave pool?"—"Daddy, you
promised. When are we going in the wave pool, wave
pool . . ." Inert only a moment ago, the bathmaster's
tongue rubs against the new, steadily accumulating
tartar. (Aw come on, come on!) Restlessly it roves,
sending messages of fuzzy enamel and windy gaps between his exposed, cold-and-heat-fearing tooth necks.
When the master of the house wants his tongue to go
lazily to bed, it gets up and roams around, more and
more determined to undermine this one canine, rendered vulnerable by receding gums, with coaxing
thrusts, with gentle jostling.

Now, entering through the gentlemen's and ladies'

door, preshowered (with soap) and slightly irritated by the many bath regulations, they are in his hands.

So simple, a wave machine: two pistons alternately exerting pressure on sea water warmed to 72 degrees. (Twenty minutes of calm are followed by ten minutes of storm.) The naïve principle of surf, mechanized. (Excessive undertow is avoided by divergencies in the rhythm of the rising and falling pistons.) Possibly the inventor watched children teaching a pond to make waves by throwing stones into it. Now the easily serviced machine is functioning. It suffices to press a button: Wave pool! Wave pool!

Jubilation within the tiled walls. Body-minded elderly gentlemen, overflowing ladies, a dozen Bundeswehr recruits from Hörnumer Ecke (admitted as per prearrangement on a low-priced group ticket)—and the youth of Westerland who now in January are permitted to bathe at reduced prices on presentation of identity cards. And in their midst: she she she. Around the pelvis a mother hen, higher up a girl. She with her brood that will soon inherit. She with her already obese fucker.

Now they step, mother hen in the lead, into the water. Let them take their time getting wet, let them shout for joy.

"Hey, Mummy, these waves are great!"

And take your tongue off the tartar to give it a start.

"No diving, Wolfi. Ulli, stay with Daddy!"

First speed: moderate breakers emerge from their grating, maintaining an orderly interval.

"Stay here in front with Mummy or you'll have to get out and you'll never again . . ."

Only now does the instructor from Cologne shift with his little finger from first to second speed; for his wave machine has three speeds.

(Leaf back and find that all purposive action can be reduced to the purpose of acquiring more power.)

Therefore quickly, before the bathing mood can shift into fear and flight to the tiles surmounting the pool, shift into third, running both pistons at the same rhythm so the undertow can come into its own. Rough weather ahead. Because this preshowered company with their brass numbers on their wrists, the ladies fat and the gentlemen graying, the Bundeswehr recruits, the Westerland youngsters and she with her clan: all will be sorely tried.

The very first wave, commanded by the second speed, flings her—it hurts—against the tile steps. The undertow pulls her back. The trusty third speed picks her up, carries her over the steps and dashes her against the front wall of the recently opened wave bath. No, it's not glazed brick that's cracking, it's ribs.

(He had just looked for and found relevant passages in Nietzsche's posthumous works of the eighties, and now the bathmaster's eyes leap from his book to the glass front of the Wave Pool Restaurant: there noses are pressed flat.)

For already the backwash wants to take back and smooth over what the breaker has done; but it has a loud-mouthed brother: nothing is taken back! A broken engagement is a broken engagement! (Tartar: petrified hatred.)

After the fourth breaker has broken against the front wall the children drift around boneless. Once again her strident voice: "Wolfi, Ulli, OhmyGod!"—no inquiry about Daddy. After that no peep nor plaint attempts to halt the tempest and invoke the heavenly mercy that calms the waves.

Even in the Wave Pool Restaurant there is an atmosphere of religious awe behind the glass front: looks bad in the aquarium, very bad. The waiters let the punch grow cold. A few diners take pictures. The bathmaster puts a bookmark in his book and contemplates reality. He props his tongue against the one, already wobbly canine: how elastically it gives way. He wants to drive them out of the temple. Already the half-brick wall trembles. For when this building was approved, neither the architect nor the town building commission had reckoned with such a storm. Now cheap construction exacts its price: mortar gives way, gives up. Already the last breaker wells broad-shouldered from the bent grating. It leaps over the undertow, picks up the silent drifting company in its arms in passing, and, bursting through the wall, hurls them out into the January afternoon. At one stroke it dashes them, laved in brine, on the flags of the forecourt behind the beach promenade. The light children are carried to the edge of the aquarium, where the cunning seals are dreaming of herring and more herring. ("Mummy, when are we going to feed the seals, feed the seals . . .") Already, borne on the wind, the gulls are coming. Later on, the photographers. Three four times more the gaping front wall spews out water. Then the pool is empty. Prompted by curiosity, the locker-room attendants venture from the men's and women's sections into the drafty vestibule. In the restaurant, behind the breath-clouded glass front, checks are paid. Running empty, still hungry, the pistons of the wave machine clamor. The fake bathmaster turns them off. Tired, partly satisfied, he packs up his books, goes to his room, tries to be sad.

Somewhat disappointed because it had all gone so quickly, I soon—before the police stepped in and cordoned off the scene of the crime—left the summer and winter resort: the Hamburg-Altona express took me with it over the Hindenburg Causeway.

On my desk I found my beginning: the gesture of fighting to the finish—or the Schörner case.—Two years later Vero Lewand left school (shortly before her final exams) and married a Canadian linguist. Scherbaum is studying medicine. Irmgard Seifert is still engaged. As for me, an abscess has formed on the lower left. The porcelain bridge was sawed through. The abscess was scraped out. My dentist showed me a small sac adhering to the root tip: tissue suffused with pus and water. Nothing lasts. There will always be pain.

Isaac Bashevis Singer

Winner of the 1978 Nobel Prize for Literature

James A. Michener

Winner of the Pulitzer Prize in Fiction

The Bridge at Andau	23863-6	$1.95
The Bridges at Toko-Ri	23856-3	$1.95
Caravans	23832-6	$2.25
Centennial	23494-0	$2.95
The Drifters	23862-8	$2.75
The Fires of Spring	23860-1	$2.25
Hawaii	23761-3	$2.95
Iberia	23804-0	$2.95
Kent State: What Happened and Why	23869-5	$2.50
A Michener Miscellany	C2526	$1.95
Rascals in Paradise	24022-3	$2.50
Return to Paradise	23831-8	$2.25
Sayonara	23857-1	$1.95
The Source	23859-8	$2.95
Sports in America	23204-2	$2.50
Tales of the South Pacific	23852-0	$2.25